COLLECTION 2

D0432837

COLLECTION 2

The Curse of the Mummy's Tomb
Let's Get Invisible!
Night of the Living Dummy

R.L. Stine

Hippo

Scholastic Children's Books,
Commonwealth House, 1-19 New Oxford Street, London WC1A 1NU, UK
a division of Scholastic Ltd
London ~ New York ~ Toronto ~ Sydney ~ Auckland

The Curse of the Mummy's Tomb
Let's Get Invisible!
Night of the Living Dummy
First published in the USA by Scholastic Inc., 1993
First published in the UK by Scholastic Ltd, 1994

ISBN 0 590 13540 6

Typeset by Contour Typesetters, Southall, London
Printed by Cox & Wyman Ltd, Reading, Berks

10 9 8 7 6 5 4 3 2 1

CONTENTS

The Curse of the Mummy's Tomb

I saw the Great Pyramid and got thirsty.

Maybe it was all that sand. So dry and yellow, it seemed to stretch on forever. It even made the sky look dry.

I poked my mum in her side. "Mum, I'm really thirsty."

"Not now," she said. She had one hand up on her forehead, shielding her eyes from the bright sun as she stared up at the enormous pyramid.

Not now?

What does "not now" mean? I was thirsty. *Now*!

Someone bumped me from behind and apologized in a foreign language. I never dreamed when I saw the Great Pyramid there'd be so many other tourists. I suppose half the people in the world decided to spend their Christmas holidays in Egypt this year.

"But, Mum—" I said. I didn't mean to whine. It was just that my throat was so dry. "I'm really thirsty."

"We can't get you a drink now," she answered, staring at the pyramid. "Stop acting as if you were four years old. You're twelve, remember?"

"Twelve-year-olds get thirsty, too," I muttered. "All this sand in the air, it's making me choke."

"Look at the pyramid," she said, sounding a little irritated. "That's why we came here. We didn't come here to get a drink."

"But I'm *choking*!" I cried, gasping and holding my throat.

Okay, so I wasn't choking. I exaggerated a little, just trying to get her attention. But she pulled the brim of her straw hat down and continued to stare up at the pyramid, which shimmered in the heat.

I decided to try my dad. As usual, he was studying the handful of guidebooks he always carried everywhere. I don't think he'd even looked at the pyramid yet. He always misses everything because he always has his nose buried in a guidebook.

"Dad, I'm really thirsty," I said, whispering as if my throat were strained to get my message across.

"Wow. Do you know how wide the pyramid is?" he asked, staring at a picture of the pyramid in his book.

"I'm thirsty, Dad."

"It's thirteen acres wide, Gabe," he said, really

4

excited. "Do you know what it's made of?"

I wanted to say Plasticine.

He's always testing me. Whenever we go on a trip, he always asks me a million questions like that. I don't think I've ever answered one right.

"Some kind of stone?" I answered.

"That's right." He smiled at me, then turned back to his book. "It's made of limestone. Limestone blocks. It says here that some of the blocks weigh up to a thousand tonnes."

"Whoa," I said. "That's more than you and Mum put together!"

He turned his eyes from the book and frowned at me. "Not funny, Gabe."

"Just kidding," I said. Dad's pretty sensitive about his weight, so I try to tease him about it as often as I can.

"How do you think the ancient Egyptians moved stones that weighed a thousand tonnes?" he asked.

Quiz time wasn't over.

I took a guess. "In lorries?"

He laughed. "Lorries? They hadn't invented the *wheel*."

I shielded my eyes and stared up at the pyramid. It was really huge, much bigger than it looks in pictures. And much dryer.

I couldn't imagine how they pulled those big stones across the sand without wheels. "I don't know," I confessed. "I'm really thirsty."

"No one knows how they did it," Dad said.

So it was a trick question.

"Dad, I really need a drink."

"Not now," he said. He squinted at the pyramid. "Gives you a funny feeling, doesn't it?"

"It gives me a thirsty feeling," I said, trying to get my point across.

"No. I mean, it gives me a funny feeling to think that our ancestors—yours and mine, Gabe—may have walked around these pyramids, or even helped to build them. It gives me kind of a chill. How about you?"

"I suppose so," I told him. He was right. It *was* kind of exciting.

We're Egyptian, you see. I mean, both sets of my grandparents came from Egypt. They moved to the United States around 1930. My mum and dad were both born in Michigan. We were all very excited to see the country our ancestors came from.

"I wonder if your uncle Ben is down inside that pyramid right now," Dad said, shielding his eyes from the sun with one hand.

Uncle Ben Hassad. I had nearly forgotten about my uncle, the famous archaeologist. Uncle Ben was another one of the reasons we had decided to come to Egypt over the holidays. That and the fact that my mum and dad had some business to do in Cairo and Alexandria and some other places.

Mum and Dad have their own business. They sell refrigeration equipment. It usually isn't very exciting. But sometimes they travel to cool places, like Egypt, and I get to go with them.

I turned my eyes to the pyramids and thought about my uncle.

Uncle Ben and his workers were digging around in the Great Pyramid, exploring and discovering new mummies, I suppose. He had always been fascinated by our ancestors' homeland. He had lived in Egypt for many years. Uncle Ben was an expert on pyramids and mummies. I even saw his picture once in *National Geographic*.

"When are we going to see Uncle Ben?" I asked, tugging Dad's arm. I accidentally tugged too hard, and the guidebooks fell out of his hands.

I helped him pick them up.

"Not today," Dad said, making a face. He didn't like to bend over to pick things up. His stomach got in the way. "Ben's going to meet us in Cairo in a few days."

"Why don't we go up to the pyramid and see if he's there now?" I asked impatiently.

"We're not allowed," Dad replied.

"Look—camels!" Mum poked me on the shoulder and pointed.

Sure enough, some people had arrived on camels. One of the camels seemed to be having a coughing fit. I suppose he was thirsty, too. The people riding the camels were tourists and they looked very uncomfortable. They didn't seem to know what to do next.

"Do you know how to get down from a camel?" I asked my dad.

He was squinting at the pyramid, studying the top of it. "No. How?"

"You don't get down from a camel," I said. "You get down from a duck."

I know. I know. It's a very old joke. But my dad and I never get tired of it.

"Do you see the camels?" Mum asked.

"I'm not blind," I replied. Being thirsty always puts me in a bad mood. Besides, what was so exciting about camels? They were really gross-looking, and they smelled like my gym socks after a basketball game.

"What's your problem?" Mum asked, fiddling with her straw hat.

"I *told* you," I said, not meaning to sound so angry. "I'm thirsty."

"Gabe, really." She glanced at Dad, then went back to staring at the pyramid.

"Dad, do you think Uncle Ben can take us inside the pyramid?" I asked enthusiastically. "That would really be outstanding."

"No, I don't think so," he said. He tucked his guidebooks under his arm so he could raise his binoculars to his eyes. "I really don't think so, Gabe. I don't think it's allowed."

I couldn't hide my disappointment. I had all these fantasies about going down into the pyramid with my uncle, discovering mummies and ancient treasures. Fighting off ancient Egyptians who had come back to life to defend their sacred tomb, and escaping after a wild chase, just like Indiana Jones.

"I'm afraid you'll just have to appreciate the pyramid from the outside," Dad said, peering over the yellow sand, trying to focus the binoculars.

"I've already appreciated it," I told him glumly. "Can we go and get a drink now?"

Little did I know that in a few days, Mum and Dad would be gone, and I would be deep inside the pyramid we were staring at. Not just inside it, but *trapped* inside it, *sealed* inside it— probably forever.

We drove from al-Jizah back to Cairo in the funny little rented car Dad had picked up at the airport. It wasn't a long drive, but it seemed long to me. The car was just a little bit bigger than some of my old remote-control cars, and my head hit the ceiling with every bump.

I'd brought my Game Boy with me, but Mum made me put it away so that I could watch the Nile as the road followed along its bank. It was very wide and very brown.

"No one else in your class is seeing the Nile this Christmas," Mum said, the hot wind blowing her brown hair through the open car window.

"Can I play with my Game Boy now?" I asked.

I mean, when you get right down to it, a river is a river.

An hour or so later, we were back in Cairo with its narrow, crowded streets. Dad took a wrong turning and drove us into a kind of market.

We were trapped in a little alley behind a herd of goats for nearly half an hour.

I didn't get a drink till we got back to the hotel, and by that time, my tongue was the size of a salami and hanging down to the floor just like Elvis's. He's our cocker spaniel back home.

I'll say one nice thing about Egypt. The Coke tastes just as good as the Coke back home. It's the Classic Coke, too, not the other kind. And they give you plenty of ice, which I like to crunch with my teeth.

We had a suite at the hotel, two bedrooms and a sort of living room. If you looked out of the window, you could see a tall, glass skyscraper across the street, just like you'd see in any city.

There was a TV in the living room, but everyone spoke Arabic on it. The shows didn't look too interesting, anyway. Mainly a lot of news. The only channel in English was CNN. But that was news, too.

We had just started to talk about where to go for dinner when the phone rang. Dad went into the bedroom to answer it. A few minutes later he called Mum in, and I could hear the two of them discussing something.

They were talking very quietly, so I thought it must have something to do with me and they didn't want me to hear it.

As usual, I was right.

They both came out of the bedroom a few

minutes later, looking pretty worried. My first thought was that my grandmother had phoned to say that something bad had happened to Elvis back home.

"What's wrong?" I asked. "Who called?"

"Your dad and I have to go to Alexandria. Straight away," Mum said, sitting down beside me on the sofa.

"Huh? Alexandria?" We weren't supposed to go there until the end of the week.

"Business," Dad said. "An important customer wants to meet us first thing tomorrow morning."

"We have to take a plane that leaves in an hour," Mum said.

"But I don't *want* to," I told them, jumping up from the sofa. "I want to stay in Cairo and see Uncle Ben. I want to go to the pyramids with him. You promised!"

We argued about it for a short while. They tried to convince me there were a lot of great things to see in Alexandria, but I held my ground.

Finally, Mum had an idea. She went into the bedroom, and I heard her making a phone call to someone. A few minutes later, she came back with a smile on her face. "I talked to Uncle Ben," she announced.

"Wow! Do they have phones in the pyramid?" I asked.

"No. I talked to him at the small lodge he's staying at in al-Jizah," she replied. "He said he'd come and keep an eye on you, if you want. While your dad and I are in Alexandria."

"Yeah?" This was starting to sound outstanding. Uncle Ben is one of the coolest guys I've ever known. Sometimes I couldn't believe he was Mum's brother.

"It's your choice, Gabe," she said, glancing at my dad. "You can come with us, or you can stay with Ben till we get back."

Some choice.

I didn't have to think about it for more than one-eighteenth of a second. "I'll stay with Uncle Ben!" I declared.

"One other thing," Mum said, grinning for some reason. "You might want to think about this."

"I don't care *what* it is," I insisted. "I choose Uncle Ben."

"Sari is also on her Christmas holidays," Mum said. "And she's staying with him, too."

"Drat!" I cried, and I flung myself down on the sofa and began pounding the cushions with both fists.

Sari is Uncle Ben's stuck-up daughter. My only cousin. She's the same age as me—twelve—and she thinks she's so great. She goes to boarding school in the United States while her dad works in Egypt.

13

She's really pretty, and she knows it. And she's brainy. And the last time I saw her, she was a couple of centimetres taller than me.

That was last Christmas, I suppose. She thought she was really hot stuff because she could get to the last level of *Super Mario Land*. But it wasn't fair because I don't have Super Nintendo, only standard Nintendo. So I never get to practise.

I think that's what she liked about me best, that she could beat me at games and things. Sari is the most competitive person I know. She has to be first and best at everything. If everyone around is catching the flu, she has to be the *first* one to catch it!

"Stop pounding the sofa like that," Mum said. She grabbed my arm and pulled me to my feet.

"Does that mean you've changed your mind? You're coming with us?" Dad asked.

I thought about it. "No. I'll stay here with Uncle Ben," I decided.

"And you won't argue with Sari?" Mum asked.

"*She* argues with me," I said.

"Your mum and I have got to hurry," Dad said.

They disappeared into the bedroom to pack. I turned on the TV and watched some kind of game show in Arabic. The contestants kept laughing a lot. I couldn't work out why. I hardly know a word of Arabic.

14

After a while, Mum and Dad came out again, dragging suitcases. "We'll never get to the airport in time," Dad said.

"I've talked to Ben," Mum told me, brushing her hair with her hand. "He'll be here in an hour, hour and a half. Gabe, you don't mind staying alone here for just an hour, do you?"

"Huh?"

Not much of an answer, I'll admit. But her question took me by surprise.

I mean, it never occurred to me that my own parents would leave me all alone in a big hotel in a strange city where I didn't even know the language. I mean, how could they do that to me?

"No problem," I said. "I'll be fine. I'll just watch TV till he comes."

"Ben's on his way already," Mum said. "He and Sari will be here in no time. And I phoned down to the hotel manager. He said he'd have someone look in on you from time to time."

"Where's the bell boy?" Dad asked, nervously pacing to the door and back. "I called down there ten minutes ago."

"Just stay here and wait for Ben, okay?" Mum said to me, walking up behind the sofa, leaning over, and squeezing my ears. For some reason, she thinks I like that. "Don't go out or anything. Just wait right here for him." She bent down and kissed me on the forehead.

"I won't move," I promised. "I'll stay right

here on the sofa. I won't go to the toilet or anything."

"Can't you ever be serious?" Mum asked, shaking her head.

There was a loud knock on the door. The bellboy, a bent-over old man who didn't look as if he could pick up a feather pillow, had arrived to take the bags.

Mum and Dad, looking very worried, gave me hugs and more final instructions, and told me once again to stay in the room. The door closed behind them, and it was suddenly very quiet.

Very quiet.

I turned up the TV just to make it a little noisier. The game show had gone off, and now a man in a white suit was reading the news in Arabic.

"I'm not scared," I said aloud. But I had kind of a tight feeling in my throat.

I walked to the window and looked out. The sun was nearly down. The shadow of the skyscraper slanted over the street and onto the hotel.

I picked up my Coke glass and took a sip. It was watery and flat. My stomach growled. I suddenly realized that I was hungry.

Room service, I thought.

Then I decided I'd better not. What if I called and they only spoke Arabic?

16

I glanced at the clock. Seven-twenty. I wished Uncle Ben would arrive.

I wasn't scared. I just wished he'd arrive.

Okay. Maybe I was a little nervous.

I paced back and forth for a bit. I tried playing *Tetris* on the Game Boy, but I couldn't concentrate, and the light wasn't very good.

Sari is probably a champ at *Tetris*, I thought bitterly. Where *were* they? What was taking so long?

I began to have horrible, frightening thoughts: What if they can't find the hotel? What if they get mixed up and go to the wrong hotel?

What if they're in a terrible car crash and die? And I'm all by myself in Cairo for days and days?

I know. They were stupid thoughts. But they're the kind of thoughts you have when you're alone in a strange place, waiting for someone to come.

I glanced down and realized I had taken the mummy hand out of my jeans pocket.

It was small, the size of a child's hand. A little hand wrapped in papery brown gauze. I had bought it at a garage sale a few years ago, and I always carried it around as a good luck charm.

The kid who'd sold it to me called it a "Summoner." He said it was used to summon evil spirits, or something. I didn't care about that. I just thought it was an outstanding bargain for two dollars. I mean, what a great thing to find at a garage sale! And maybe it was even real.

I tossed it from hand to hand as I paced the length of the living room. The TV was starting to make me nervous, so I turned it off.

But now the quiet was making me nervous.

I slapped the mummy hand against my palm and kept pacing.

Where were they? They should've been here by now.

I was beginning to think that I'd made the wrong choice. Maybe I should've gone to Alexandria with Mum and Dad.

Then I heard a noise at the door. Footsteps.

Was it them?

I stopped in the middle of the living room and listened, staring past the narrow front hallway to the door.

The light was dim in the hallway, but I saw the doorknob turn.

That's strange, I thought. Uncle Ben would knock first—wouldn't he?

The doorknob turned. The door started to creak open.

"Hey—" I called out, but the word choked in my throat.

Uncle Ben would knock. He wouldn't just barge in.

Slowly, slowly, the door squeaked open as I

stared, frozen in the middle of the room, unable to call out.

Standing in the doorway was a tall, shadowy figure.

I gasped as the figure lurched into the room, and I saw it clearly. Even in the dim light, I could see what it was.

A mummy.

Glaring at me with round, dark eyes through holes in its ancient, thick bandages.

A mummy.

Pushing itself off the wall and staggering stiffly towards me into the living room, its arms outstretched as if to grab me.

I opened my mouth to scream, but no sound came out.

I took a step back, and then another. Without realizing it, I'd raised my little mummy hand in the air, as if trying to fend off the intruder with it.

As the mummy staggered into the light, I stared into its deep, dark eyes.

And recognized them.

"Uncle Ben!" I screamed.

Angrily, I heaved the mummy hand at him. It hit his bandaged chest and bounced off.

He collapsed backwards against the wall, laughing that booming laugh of his.

And then I saw Sari poking her head in the doorway. She was laughing, too.

They both thought it was hilarious. But my heart was pounding so hard, I thought it was going to pop out of my chest.

"That wasn't funny!" I shouted angrily, clenching my hands into fists at my sides. I took a deep breath, then another, trying to get my breathing to return to normal.

"I told you he'd be scared," Sari said, walking into the room, a big, superior grin on her face.

Uncle Ben was laughing so hard, he had tears running down his bandaged face. He was a big man, tall and broad, and his laughter shook the room. "You weren't *that* scared—were you, Gabe?"

"I knew it was you," I said, my heart still pounding as if it were a wind-up toy someone had wound up too tight. "I recognized you straight away."

"You certainly *looked* scared," Sari insisted.

"I didn't want to spoil the joke," I replied, wondering if they could see how terrified I really was.

"You should've seen the look on your face!" Uncle Ben cried, and started laughing all over again.

"I told Daddy he shouldn't do it," Sari said, dropping down onto the sofa. "I'm amazed the hotel people let him come up dressed like that."

Uncle Ben bent down and picked up the mummy hand I had tossed at him. "You're used to me and my practical jokes, right, Gabe?"

"Yeah," I said, avoiding his eyes.

Secretly, I scolded myself for falling for his stupid costume. I was always falling for his jokes. Always. And, now, there was Sari grinning at me from the sofa, knowing I was so scared that I'd practically had kittens.

Uncle Ben pulled some of the bandages away from his face. He stepped over and handed the little mummy hand back to me. "Where'd you get that?" he asked.

"Garage sale," I told him.

I started to ask him if it was real, but he surrounded me in a big bear hug. The gauze felt rough against my cheek. "Good to see you, Gabe," he said softly. "You've grown taller."

"Almost as tall as me," Sari chimed in.

Uncle Ben motioned to her. "Get up and help me pull this stuff off."

"I quite like the way you look in it," Sari said.

"Get over here," Uncle Ben insisted.

Sari got up with a sigh, tossing her straight black hair behind her shoulders. She walked over to her dad and started unravelling the bandages.

"I got a little carried away with this mummy thing, Gabe," Uncle Ben admitted, resting his arm on my shoulder as Sari continued working. "But it's just because I'm so excited about what's going on at the pyramid."

"What's going on?" I asked eagerly.

"Daddy's discovered a whole new burial chamber," Sari broke in before her dad had a chance to tell me himself. "He's exploring parts of the pyramid that have been undiscovered for thousands of years."

"Really?" I cried. "That's outstanding!"

Uncle Ben chuckled. "Wait till you see it."

"See it?" I wasn't sure what he meant. "You mean you're going to take me into the pyramid?"

My voice was so high that only dogs could hear it. But I didn't care. I couldn't believe my good luck. I was actually going inside the Great Pyramid, into a section that hadn't been discovered until now.

"I have no choice," Uncle Ben said dryly. "What else am I going to do with you two?"

"Are there mummies in there?" I asked. "Will we see actual mummies?"

"Do you miss your mummy?" Sari said, her stupid idea of a joke.

I ignored her. "Is there treasure down there, Uncle Ben? Egyptian relics? Are there wall paintings?"

"Let's talk about it at dinner," he said, tugging off the last of the bandages. He was wearing a plaid sportshirt and baggy canvas trousers under all the gauze. "Come on. I'm starving."

"Race you downstairs," Sari said, and shoved me out of the way to give herself a good head start out of the room.

We ate downstairs in the hotel restaurant. There were palm trees painted on the walls, and miniature palm trees planted in big pots all around

23

the restaurant. Large wooden ceiling fans whirled slowly overhead.

The three of us sat in a large booth, Sari and I opposite Uncle Ben. We studied the long menus. They were printed in Arabic and English.

"Listen to this, Gabe," Sari said, a smug smile on her face. She began to read the Arabic words aloud.

What a show-off.

The white-suited waiter brought a basket of flat pitta bread and a bowl of green stuff to dip the bread in. I ordered a club sandwich and chips. Sari ordered a hamburger.

Later, as we ate our dinner, Uncle Ben explained a little more about what he had discovered at the pyramid. "As you probably know," he started, tearing off a chunk of the flat bread, "the pyramid was built some time around 2500 B.C., during the reign of the Pharaoh Khufu."

"*Gesundheit*," Sari said. Another stupid joke.

Her father chuckled. I made a face at her.

"It was the biggest structure of its time," Uncle Ben said. "Do you know how wide the base of the pyramid is?"

Sari shook her head. "No. How wide?" she asked with a mouthful of hamburger.

"I know," I said, grinning. "It's thirteen acres wide."

24

"Hey—that's right!" Uncle Ben exclaimed, obviously impressed.

Sari flashed me a surprised look.

That's one for me! I thought happily, sticking my tongue out at her.

And one for my dad's guidebooks.

"The pyramid was built as a royal burial ground," Uncle Ben continued, his expression turning serious. "The Pharaoh made it really enormous so that the burial chamber could be hidden. The Egyptians worried about tomb robbers. They knew that people would try to break in and take all of the valuable jewels and treasures that were buried alongside their owners. So they built dozens of tunnels and chambers inside, a confusing maze to keep robbers from finding the real burial room."

"Pass the ketchup, please," Sari interrupted. I passed her the ketchup.

"Sari's heard all this before," Uncle Ben said, dipping the pitta bread into the dark gravy on his plate. "Anyway, we archaeologists thought we'd uncovered all of the tunnels and rooms inside this pyramid. But a few days ago, my workers and I discovered a tunnel that isn't on any of the charts. An unexplored, undiscovered tunnel. And we think this tunnel may lead us to the actual burial chamber of Khufu himself!"

"Outstanding!" I exclaimed. "And Sari and I will be there when you discover it?"

Uncle Ben chuckled. "I don't know about that, Gabe. It may take us years of careful exploration. But I'll take you down into the tunnel tomorrow. Then you can tell your friends you were actually inside the ancient pyramid of Khufu."

"I've already been in it," Sari bragged. She turned her eyes to me. "It's very dark. You might get scared."

"No, I won't," I insisted. "No way."

The three of us spent the night in my parents' hotel room. It took me hours to get to sleep. I suppose I was excited about going into the pyramid. I kept imagining that we found mummies and big chests of ancient jewels and treasure.

Uncle Ben woke us up early the next morning, and we drove out to the pyramid outside al-Jizah. The air was already hot and sticky. The sun seemed to hang low over the desert like an orange balloon.

"There it is!" Sari declared, pointing out of the window. And I saw the Great Pyramid rising up from the yellow sand like some kind of mirage.

Uncle Ben showed a special permit to the blue-uniformed guard, and we followed a narrow, private road that curved through the sand behind the pyramid. We parked beside several other cars and vans in the blue-grey shadow of the pyramid.

As I stepped out of the car, my chest was thudding with excitement. I stared up at the enormous, worn stones of the Great Pyramid.

It's over four thousand years old, I thought. I'm about to go inside something that was built four thousand years ago!

"Your trainer's untied," Sari said, pointing.

She certainly knew how to bring a person back down to earth.

I bent in the sand to tie my trainer laces. For some reason, the left one was always coming untied, even when I double-knotted it.

"My workers are already inside," Uncle Ben told us. "Now, stick close together, okay? Don't wander off. The tunnels really are like a maze. It's very easy to get lost."

"No problem," I said, my trembling voice revealing how nervous and excited I was.

"Don't worry. I'll keep an eye on Gabe, Dad," Sari said.

She was only two months older than me. Why did she have to act as if she was my babysitter or something?

Uncle Ben handed us both torches. "Clip them onto your jeans as we go in," he instructed. He gazed at me. "You don't believe in curses, do you? You know—the ancient Egyptian kind."

I didn't know how to reply, so I shook my head.

27

"Good," Uncle Ben replied, grinning. "Because one of my workers claims we've violated an ancient decree by entering this new tunnel, and that we've activated some curse."

"We're not scared," Sari said, giving him a playful shove towards the entrance. "Get going, Dad."

And seconds later, we were stepping into the small, square opening cut into the stone. Stooping low, I followed them through a narrow tunnel that seemed to slope gradually down.

Uncle Ben led the way, lighting the ground with a bright halogen torch. The pyramid floor was soft and sandy. The air was cool and damp.

"The walls are granite," Uncle Ben said, stopping to rub a hand along the low ceiling. "All of the tunnels were made of limestone."

The temperature dropped suddenly. The air felt even wetter. I suddenly realized why Uncle Ben had made us wear our sweatshirts.

"If you're scared, we can go back," Sari said.

"I'm fine," I replied quickly.

The tunnel ended abruptly. A pale yellow wall rose up in front of us. Ben's torch darted over a small, dark hole in the floor.

"Down we go," Ben said, groaning as he dropped to his knees. He turned back to me. "Afraid there are no stairs down to the new tunnel. My workers installed a rope ladder. Just take your time on it, take it slowly, one rung at a time, and you'll be fine."

"No problem," I said. But my voice cracked.

"Don't look down," Sari advised. "It might make you dizzy, and you'll fall."

"Thanks for the encouragement," I told her. I pushed my way past her. "I'll go down first," I said. I was already tired of her acting so superior. I decided to show her who was brave and who wasn't.

"No. Let me go first," Uncle Ben said, raising a hand to stop me. "Then I'll shine the light up at the ladder and help you down."

With another groan, he manoeuvred himself into the hole. He was so big, he nearly didn't fit.

Slowly, he began to lower himself down the rope ladder.

Sari and I leaned over the hole and peered down, watching him descend. The rope ladder wasn't very steady. It swung back and forth under his weight as he slowly, carefully, made his way down.

"It's a long way down," I said softly.

Sari didn't reply. In the shadowy light, I could see her worried expression. She was chewing on her lower lip as her dad reached the tunnel floor.

She was nervous, too.

That cheered me up a lot.

"Okay, I'm down. You're next, Gabe," Uncle Ben called up to me.

I turned and swung my feet onto the rope ladder. I grinned at Sari. "See ya."

I lowered my hands to the sides of the rope ladder—and as I slid them down, I cried out.

"Ow!"

The rope wasn't smooth. It was coarse. It cut my hands.

The sharp stab of pain made me lift my hands.

And before I even realized what was happening, I started to fall. . . .

Two hands reached down for mine. They shot through the air and grabbed my wrists.

"Hold on!" Sari cried.

She had slowed my fall just enough to allow me to grab back onto the sides of the rope ladder.

"Oh, wow!" I managed to utter. That was the best I could do. I gripped the rope for dear life, waiting for my heart to stop pounding. I closed my eyes and didn't move. I squeezed the ropes so hard, my hands ached.

"Saved your life," Sari called down to me, leaning into the opening, her face centimetres from mine.

I opened my eyes and stared up at her. "Thanks," I said gratefully.

"No problem," she replied and burst out laughing, laughing from relief, I suppose.

Why couldn't I save *her* life? I asked myself angrily. Why can't *I* ever be the big hero?

"What happened, Gabe?" Uncle Ben called from the tunnel floor below. His booming voice echoed loudly through the chamber. The wide circle of light from his torch danced across the granite wall.

"The rope cut my hands," I explained. "I wasn't expecting—"

"Just take your time," he said patiently. "One rung at a time, remember?"

"Lower your hands. Don't slide them," Sari advised, her face poking through the hole above me.

"Okay, okay," I said, starting to breathe normally.

I took a deep breath and held it. Then, slowly, carefully, I made my way down the long rope ladder.

A short while later, all three of us were standing on the tunnel floor, holding our lighted torches, our eyes following the circles of light. "This way," Uncle Ben said quietly, and he headed off to the right, walking slowly, stooping because of the low ceiling.

Our trainers crunched on the sandy floor. I saw another tunnel leading off to the right, then another tunnel on the left.

"We're breathing air that is four thousand years old," Ben said, keeping his light aimed on the floor ahead of him.

"Smells like it," I whispered to Sari. She laughed.

The air really did smell old. Sort of heavy and musty. Like someone's attic.

The tunnel widened a little as it curved to the right.

"We're going deeper into the earth," Ben said. "Does it feel like you're going downhill?"

Sari and I both muttered that it did.

"Dad and I explored one of the side tunnels yesterday," Sari told me. "We found a mummy case inside a tiny room. A beautiful one in perfect condition."

"Was there a mummy inside it?" I asked eagerly. I was dying to see a mummy. The museum back home had only one. I'd stared at it and studied it all my life.

"No. It was empty," Sari replied.

"Why didn't the mummy have any hobbies?" Uncle Ben asked, stopping suddenly.

"I don't know," I answered.

"He was too wrapped up in his work!" Uncle Ben exclaimed. He laughed at his own joke. Sari and I could only muster weak smiles.

"Don't encourage him," Sari told me, loud enough for her dad to hear. "He knows a million mummy jokes, and they're all just as bad."

"Wait. Just a sec," I said. I bent down to tie my trainer lace, which had come undone again.

The tunnel curved, then divided into two

tunnels. Uncle Ben led us through the one on the left, which was so narrow we had to squeeze through it, making our way sideways, heads bent, until it widened into a large, high-ceilinged chamber.

I stood up straight and stretched. It felt so good not to be squashed up. I stared around the large room.

Several people came into view at the far wall, working with digging tools. Bright spotlights had been hung above them on the wall, attached to a portable generator.

Uncle Ben brought us over to them and introduced us. There were four workers, two men and two women.

Another man stood off to the side, a clipboard in his hand. He was an Egyptian, dressed all in white except for a red bandanna around his neck. He had straight black hair, slicked down and tied in a ponytail behind his head. He stared at Sari and me, but didn't come over. He seemed to be studying us.

"Ahmed, you met my daughter yesterday. This is Gabe, my nephew," Uncle Ben called to him.

Ahmed nodded, but didn't smile or say anything.

"Ahmed is from the university," Uncle Ben explained to me in a low voice. "He requested permission to observe us, and I said okay. He's very quiet. But don't get him started on ancient curses. He's the one who keeps warning me that I'm in deadly danger."

Ahmed nodded, but didn't reply. He stared at me for a long while.

Weird guy, I thought.

I wondered if he'd tell me about the ancient curses. I loved stories about ancient curses.

Uncle Ben turned to his workers. "So? Any progress today?" he asked.

"We think we're getting really close," a young, red-haired man wearing faded jeans and a blue denim work shirt replied. And then he added, "Just a hunch."

Ben frowned. "Thanks, Quasimodo," he said.

The workers all laughed. I suppose *they* liked Uncle Ben's jokes.

"Quasimodo was the Hunchback of Notre Dame," Sari explained to me in her superior tone.

"I know, I know," I replied irritably. "I get it."

"We could be heading in the wrong direction altogether," Uncle Ben told the workers, scratching the bald spot on the back of his head. "The tunnel might be over there." He pointed to the wall on the right.

"No, I think we're getting warm, Ben," a young woman, her face smudged with dust, said. "Come over here. I want to show you something."

She led him over to a large pile of stones and debris. He shone his torch where she was pointing. Then he leaned closer to examine what she was showing him.

"That's very interesting, Christy," Uncle Ben said, rubbing his chin. They fell into a long discussion.

After a while, three other workers entered the chamber, carrying shovels and pick-axes. One of them was carrying some kind of electronic equipment in a flat metal case. It looked a little like a lap-top computer.

I wanted to ask Uncle Ben what it was, but he was still in the corner, involved in his discussion with the worker called Christy.

Sari and I wandered back towards the tunnel entrance. "I think he's forgotten about us," Sari said suddenly.

I agreed, shining my torch up at the high, cracked ceiling.

"Once he gets down here with the workers, he forgets everything but his work," she said, sighing.

"I can't believe we're actually inside a pyramid!" I exclaimed.

Sari laughed. She kicked at the floor with one shoe. "Look—ancient soil," she said.

"Yeah." I kicked up some of the sandy soil, too. "I wonder who walked here last. Maybe an Egyptian priestess. Maybe a pharaoh. They might have stood right here on this spot."

"Let's go exploring," Sari said suddenly.

"Huh?"

Her dark eyes gleamed, and she had a really devilish look on her face. "Let's go, Gabey—let's explore some tunnels or something."

"Don't call me Gabey," I said. "Come on, Sari, you know I hate that."

"Sorry," she apologized, giggling. "You coming?"

"We can't," I insisted, watching Uncle Ben. He was having some kind of argument with the worker carrying the thing that looked like a laptop. "Your dad said we had to stick together. He said—"

"He'll be busy here for hours," she interrupted, glancing back at him. "He won't even notice we've gone. Really."

"But, Sari—" I started.

"Besides," she continued, putting her hands on my shoulders and pushing me backwards towards the chamber door, "he doesn't want us hanging around. We'll only get in the way."

"Sari—"

"I went exploring yesterday," she said, pushing me with both hands. "We won't go far. You can't get lost. All the tunnels lead back to this big room. Really."

"I just don't think we should," I said, my eyes on Uncle Ben. He was down on his hands and knees now, digging against the wall with some kind of a pick.

"Let go of me," I told her. "Really. I—"

And then she said what I knew she'd say. What she *always* says when she wants to get her way.

"Are you chicken?"

"No," I insisted. "You know your dad said—"

"Chicken! Chicken! Chicken!" She began clucking like a chicken. Really obnoxious.

"Stop it, Sari." I tried to sound tough and menacing.

"Are you chicken, *Gabey*?" she repeated, grinning at me as if she'd won some big victory. "Huh, *Gabey*?"

"Stop calling me that!" I insisted.

She just stared at me.

I made a disgusted face. "Okay, okay. Let's go exploring," I told her.

I mean, what else could I say?

"But not far," I added.

"Don't worry," she said, grinning. "We won't get lost. I'll just show you some of the tunnels I looked at yesterday. One of them has a strange animal picture carved on the wall. I think it's some kind of a cat. I'm not sure."

"Really?" I cried, instantly excited. "I've seen pictures of relief carvings, but I've never—"

"It may be a cat," Sari said. "Or maybe a person with an animal head. It's really weird."

"Where is it?" I asked.

"Follow me."

We both gave one last glance back to Uncle Ben, who was down on his hands and knees, picking away at the stone wall.

Then I followed Sari out of the chamber.

We squeezed through the narrow tunnel, then turned and followed a slightly wider tunnel to the right. I hesitated, a few steps behind her. "Are you sure we'll be able to get back?" I asked, keeping my voice low so she couldn't accuse me of sounding frightened.

"No problem," she replied. "Keep your light on the floor. There's a small chamber on the other end of this tunnel that's pretty neat."

We followed the tunnel as it curved to the right. It branched into two low openings, and Sari took the one to the left.

The air grew a little warmer. It smelled stale, as if people had been smoking cigarettes there.

This tunnel was wider than the others. Sari was walking faster now, getting farther ahead of me. "Hey—wait!" I cried.

I looked down to see that my trainer lace had come untied *again*. Uttering a loud, annoyed groan, I bent to retie it.

"Hey, Sari, wait for me!"

She didn't seem to hear me.

I could see her light in the distance, growing fainter in the tunnel.

Then it suddenly disappeared.

Had her torch burned out?

No. The tunnel probably curved, I decided. She's just out of my view.

"Hey, Sari!" I called. "Wait! *Wait!*"

I stared ahead into the dark tunnel.

"Sari?"

Why didn't she answer me?

"Sari!"

My voice echoed through the long, curving tunnel.

No reply.

I called again, and listened to my voice fading as the echo repeated her name again and again.

At first I was angry.

I knew what Sari was doing.

She was deliberately not answering, deliberately trying to frighten me.

She had to prove that she was the brave one, and I was the scaredy cat.

I suddenly remembered another time, a few years before. Sari and Uncle Ben had come to my house for a visit. I think Sari and I were seven or eight.

We went outside to play. It was a grey day, threatening rain. Sari had a skipping rope and was showing off, as usual, showing me how good she was at it. Then, of course, when she let me try it, I tripped and fell, and she laughed like mad.

I'd decided to get back at her by taking her to this deserted old house a few roads away. The kids in the neighbourhood all believed the house was haunted. It was a great place to sneak in and explore, although our parents were always warning us to stay away from it because it was falling apart and dangerous.

So I led Sari to this house and told her it was haunted. And we sneaked in through the broken basement window.

It got even darker outside, and started to rain. It was perfect. I could tell Sari was really scared to be alone in the creepy old house. I, of course, wasn't scared at all because I'd been there before.

Well, we started exploring, with me leading the way. And somehow we got separated. And it started thundering and lightning outside. There was rain pouring in through the broken windows.

I decided maybe we should get home. So I called to Sari. No answer.

I called again. Still no answer.

Then I heard a loud crash.

Calling her name, I started running from room to room. I was scared to death. I was sure something terrible had happened.

I ran through every room in the house, getting

more and more scared. I couldn't find her. I shouted and shouted, but she didn't answer me.

I was so scared, I started to cry. Then I totally panicked, and I ran out of the house and into the pouring rain.

I ran through the thunder and lightning, crying all the way home. By the time I got home, I was soaked through and through.

I ran into the kitchen, sobbing and crying that I'd lost Sari in the haunted house.

And there she was. Sitting at the kitchen table. Comfortable and dry. Eating a big slice of chocolate cake. A smug smile on her face.

And now, peering into the darkness of the pyramid, I knew Sari was doing the same thing to me.

Trying to scare me.

Trying to make me look bad.

Or *was* she?

As I made my way through the low, narrow tunnel, keeping the light aimed straight ahead, I couldn't help it. My anger quickly turned to worry, and troubling questions whirred through my mind.

What if she *wasn't* playing a trick on me?

What if something bad *had* happened to her?

What if she had missed a step and fallen into a hole?

Or had got herself trapped in a hidden tunnel? Or . . . I didn't know what.

43

I wasn't thinking clearly.

My trainers thudded loudly over the sandy floor as I started to half-walk, half-jog through the winding tunnel. "Sari?" I called, frantically now, not caring whether I sounded frightened or not.

Where was she?

She wasn't that far ahead of me. I should at least be able to see the light from her torch, I thought.

"Sari?"

There was no place for her to hide in this narrow space. Was I following the wrong tunnel?

No.

I had been in the same tunnel all along. The same tunnel I had watched her disappear in.

Don't say *disappear*, I scolded myself. Don't even *think* the word.

Suddenly the narrow tunnel ended. A small opening led into a small, square room. I flashed the light quickly from side to side.

"Sari?"

No sign of her.

The walls were bare. The air was warm and stale. I moved the torch rapidly across the floor, looking for Sari's footprints. The floor was harder, less sandy here. There were no footprints.

"Oh!"

I uttered a low cry when my light came to rest on the object against the far wall. My heart pounding, I eagerly took a few steps closer until I was just a few metres from it.

It was a mummy case.

A large, stone mummy case, at least three metres long.

It was rectangular, with curved corners. The lid was covered. I stepped closer and aimed the light.

Yes.

A human face was carved on the lid. The face of a woman. It looked like a death mask, the kind we'd studied at school. It stared wide-eyed up at the ceiling.

"Wow!" I cried aloud. A real mummy case.

The carved face on the lid must have been brightly painted at one time. But the colour had faded over the centuries. Now the face was grey, as pale as death.

Staring at the top of the case, smooth and perfect, I wondered if Uncle Ben had seen it. Or if I had made a discovery of my own.

Why is it all by itself in this small room? I wondered.

And what does it hold inside?

I was working up the courage to run my hand over the smooth stone of the lid when I heard the creaking sound.

And saw the lid start to rise up.

45

"Oh!" a hushed cry escaped my lips.

At first I thought I had imagined it. I didn't move a muscle. I kept the light trained on the lid.

The lid lifted a tiny bit more.

And I heard a hissing sound come from inside the big coffin, like air escaping from a new coffee jar when you first open it.

Uttering another low cry, I took a step back.

The lid rose up another inch.

I took another step back.

And dropped the torch.

I picked it up with a trembling hand and shone it back onto the mummy case.

The lid was now open nearly a metre.

I sucked in a deep breath of air and held it.

I wanted to run, but my fear was freezing me in place.

I wanted to scream, but I knew I wouldn't be able to make a sound.

The lid creaked and opened another couple of centimetres.

Another centimetre.

I lowered the torch to the opening, the light quivering with my hand.

From the dark depths of the ancient coffin, I saw two eyes staring out at me.

I uttered a silent gasp.

I froze.

I felt a cold chill travel down my back.

The lid slowly pushed open another centimetre.

The eyes stared out at me. Cold eyes. Evil eyes. Ancient eyes.

My mouth dropped open. And before I even realized it, I started to scream.

Scream at the top of my voice.

As I screamed, unable to turn away, unable to run, unable to move, the lid slid open all the way.

Slowly, as if in a dream, a dark figure raised itself from the depths of the mummy case and climbed out.

"*Sari!*"

A broad smile widened across her face. Her eyes glowed gleefully.

"Sari—that *wasn't* funny!" I managed to shout in a high-pitched voice that bounced off the stone walls.

But now she was laughing too hard to hear me.

Loud, scornful laughter.

I was so furious, I searched frantically for something to throw at her. But there wasn't anything, not even a pebble on the floor.

Staring at her, my chest still heaving from my fright, I really hated her then. She had made a total fool of me. There I had been, screaming like a baby.

I knew she'd never let me live it down.

Never.

"The look on your face!" she exclaimed when she finally stopped laughing. "I wish I had a camera."

I was too angry to reply. I just growled at her.

I pulled the little mummy hand from my back pocket and began rolling it around in my hand. I always fiddled with that hand when I was upset. It usually helped to calm me.

But now I felt as if I'd *never* calm down.

"I *told* you I'd found an empty mummy case yesterday," she said, brushing the hair back off her face. "Didn't you remember?"

I growled again.

I felt like a total fool.

First I'd fallen for her dad's stupid mummy costume. And now this.

Silently I vowed to myself to pay her back. If it was the last thing I ever did.

She was still chuckling about her big-deal joke. "The look on your face," she said again, shaking her head. Rubbing it in.

"You wouldn't like it if I scared *you*," I muttered angrily.

"You *couldn't* scare me," she replied. "I don't scare so easily."

"Hah!"

That was the best comeback I could think of. Not very clever, I know. But I was too angry to be clever.

I was imagining myself picking Sari up and tossing her back into the mummy case, pulling down the lid, and locking it—when I heard footsteps approaching in the tunnel.

Glancing over at Sari, I saw her expression change. She heard them, too.

A few seconds later, Uncle Ben burst into the small room. I could see immediately, even in the dim light, that he was really angry.

"I thought I could trust you two," he said, talking through gritted teeth.

"Dad—" Sari started.

But he cut her off sharply. "I trusted you not to wander off without telling me. Do you know how easy it is to get lost in this place? Lost forever?"

"Dad," Sari started again. "I was just showing Gabe this room I discovered yesterday. We were going to come straight back. Really."

"There are *hundreds* of tunnels," Uncle Ben said heatedly, ignoring Sari's explanation. "Maybe thousands. Many of them have never been explored. No one has ever been in this section of the pyramid before. We have no idea what dangers there are. You two can't just wander off by yourselves. Do you know how frantic I was when I turned round and you had gone?"

"Sorry," Sari and I both said in unison.

"Let's go," Uncle Ben said, gesturing to the door with his torch. "Your pyramid visit is over for today."

We followed him into the tunnel. I felt really awful. Not only had I fallen for Sari's stupid joke, but I'd made my favourite uncle really angry.

Sari always gets me into trouble, I thought bitterly. Ever since we were little kids.

Now she was walking ahead of me, arm in arm with her dad, telling him something, her face close to his ear. Suddenly they both burst out laughing and turned back to look at me.

I could feel my face getting hot.

I knew what she'd told him.

She'd told him about hiding in the mummy case and making me scream like a scared baby. And now they were both chuckling about what a jerk I was.

"Merry Christmas to you, too!" I called bitterly.

And that made them laugh even harder.

We spent the night back at the hotel in Cairo. I beat Sari in two straight games of Scrabble, but it didn't make me feel any better.

She kept complaining that she had only vowels, and so the games weren't fair. Finally, I put my Scrabble set back in my room, and we sat and stared at the TV.

The next morning, we had breakfast in the room. I ordered pancakes, but they didn't taste like any pancakes I'd ever eaten. They were tough and grainy, as if they were made of cowhide or something.

"What are we doing today?" Sari asked Uncle Ben, who was still yawning and stretching after two cups of black coffee.

"I have an appointment at the Cairo Museum," he told us, glancing at his wristwatch. "It's just a couple of streets away. I thought you two might like to wander around the museum while I have my meeting.

"Ooh, thrills and spills," Sari said sarcastically. She slurped up another spoonful of Frosties.

The little Frosties box had Arabic writing all over it, and Tony the Tiger was saying something in Arabic. I wanted to save it and take it

51

home to show my friends. But I knew Sari would make fun of me if I asked her for it, so I didn't.

"The museum has an interesting mummy collection, Gabe," Uncle Ben said to me. He tried to pour himself a third cup of coffee, but the pot was empty. "You'll like it."

"Unless they climb out of their cases," Sari said.

Pathetic. Really pathetic.

I stuck my tongue out at her. She tossed a soggy Frostie across the table at me.

"When are my mum and dad getting back?" I asked Uncle Ben. I suddenly realized I missed them.

He started to answer, but the phone rang. He walked into the bedroom and picked it up. It was an old-fashioned black telephone with a dial instead of buttons. As he talked, his face filled with concern.

"Change of plans," he said a few seconds later, hanging up the receiver and coming back into the living room.

"What's the matter, Daddy?" Sari asked, shoving her cereal bowl away.

"It's very strange," he replied, scratching the back of his head. "Two of my workers came down with a bug last night. Some kind of mysterious illness." His expression became thoughtful, worried. "They took them to a hospital here in Cairo."

He started to gather up his wallet and some other belongings. "I think I'd better get over there straight away," he said.

"But what about Gabe and me?" Sari asked, glancing at me.

"I'll only be gone an hour or so," her dad replied. "Stay here in the room, okay?"

"In the *room*?" Sari cried, making it sound like a punishment.

"Well, okay. You can go down to the lobby, if you want. But don't leave the hotel."

A few minutes later, he pulled on his safari jacket, checked one last time to make sure he had his wallet and keys, and hurried out of the door.

Sari and I stared at each other glumly. "What do you want to do?" I asked, poking the cold uneaten pancakes on my plate with a fork.

Sari shrugged. "Is it hot in here?"

I nodded. "Yeah. It's about a hundred and twenty degrees."

"We have to get out of here," she said, standing up and stretching.

"You mean go down to the lobby?" I asked, still poking the pancakes, pulling them into pieces with the fork.

"No. I mean get *out* of here," she replied. She walked over to the mirror and began brushing her straight, black hair.

"But Uncle Ben said—" I started.

"We won't go far," she said, and then quickly added, "if you're afraid."

I made a face at her. "Okay," I said. "We could go to the museum. Your dad said it was nearby."

If she wanted to disobey her dad and go out, that was fine with me. From now on, I decided, *I'll* be the macho man. No repeats of yesterday— ever again.

"The museum?" She made a face. "Well . . . okay," she said, turning to look at me. "It's not as if we're babies. We can go out if we want."

"Yes, we can," I said. "I'll leave Uncle Ben a note and tell him where we're going, in case he gets back before we do." I went over to the desk and wrote a note to Uncle Ben.

"If you're afraid, *Gabey*, we can just walk around the block," she said in a teasing voice, staring at me, waiting to see how I'd react.

"No way," I said. "We're going to the museum. Unless *you're* afraid."

"No way," she mimicked.

We took the lift down to the lobby and asked the receptionist where the Cairo Museum was. She said to turn right outside the hotel and walk two blocks.

Sari hesitated as we stepped out into the bright sunshine. "You sure you're up to this?"

"What could go wrong?" I replied.

"Let's go. This way," I said, shielding my eyes from the bright sunlight with my hand.

"It's so hot," Sari complained.

The street was crowded and noisy. I couldn't hear anything over the honking of car horns.

Drivers here lean on their horns the minute they start up their cars, and they don't stop honking till they arrive at their destinations.

Sari and I stayed close together, making our way through the crush of people on the pavement. All kinds of people passed by.

There were men in American-style business suits walking alongside men who appeared to be wearing loose-fitting white pyjamas.

We saw women who would look quite at home on any street in America, wearing colourful leggings and stylish skirts and trousers. Women in jeans. Followed by women dressed in long, flowing black dresses, their faces covered by heavy, black veils.

"This certainly doesn't look like back home!" I exclaimed, shouting over the blare of car horns.

I was so fascinated by all the interesting-looking people crowding the narrow pavement that I forgot to look at the buildings. Before I knew it, we were standing in front of the museum, a tall, stone structure looming above the street behind steeply sloping steps.

We climbed the steps and entered the revolving door of the museum.

"Wow, it's so quiet in here!" I exclaimed, whispering. It was nice to get away from the honking horns, the crowded pavements, and shouting people.

"Why do you think they honk their horns so much?" Sari asked, holding her ears.

"Just a custom, I suppose," I replied.

We stopped and looked around.

We were standing in the centre of an enormous open lobby. Tall marble staircases rose up on the far left and far right. Twin white columns framed a wide doorway that led straight back. An enormous mural across the wall to the right showed an aerial view of the pyramids and the Nile.

We stood in the middle of the floor, admiring the mural for a while. Then we made our way to the back wall and asked a woman at the information desk for the mummy room. She flashed us a nice smile and told us in perfect English to take the stairs to the right.

Our trainers thudded loudly over the shiny marble floor. The staircase seemed to go up forever. "This is like mountain climbing," I complained, halfway up.

"Race you to the top," Sari said, grinning, and took off before I had a chance to reply.

Of course she beat me by about ten steps.

I waited for her to call me "slowcoach" or "snail face" or something. But she had already turned to see what lay ahead of us.

A dark, high-ceilinged room seemed to stretch on forever. A glass case stood centred in the doorway. Inside was a detailed construction of wood and clay.

I went up close to take a good look. The construction showed thousands of workers dragging enormous blocks of limestone across the sand towards a partially built pyramid.

In the room behind the display I could see huge stone statues, large mummy cases, displays of glass and pottery, and case after case of artifacts and relics.

"I think this is the place!" I exclaimed happily, rushing over to the first display case.

"Ooh, what's that? Some kind of giant dog?" Sari asked, pointing to an enormous statue against the wall.

The creature appeared to have a fierce dog's

head and a lion's body. Its eyes stared straight ahead, and it seemed ready to pounce on anyone who came near it.

"They put creatures like that in front of tombs," I told Sari. "You know. To protect the place. Scare away grave robbers."

"Like guard dogs," Sari said, stepping up close to the ancient sculpture.

"Hey—there's a mummy in this case!" I exclaimed, leaning over an ancient stone coffin. "Look!"

Still staring back at the enormous sculpture, Sari walked up beside me. "Yup. It's a mummy, okay," she said, unimpressed. I suppose she's seen a lot more of them than me.

"It's so small," I said, staring at the yellowed linen wrapped so tightly around the skinny head and body.

"Our ancestors were shrimps," Sari replied. "Think it was a man or a woman?"

I glanced at the plaque on the side of the coffin. "It says it's a man."

"Suppose they didn't exercise much in those days," she said and laughed at her own joke.

"They did a great wrapping job," I said, examining the carefully wrapped fingers on the hands, which were crossed over the mummy's chest. "I was a mummy the Hallowe'en before last, and my costume completely unravelled after ten minutes!"

Sari tutted.

"Do you know how they made mummies?" I asked, moving around to view it from the other side. "Do you know the first thing they did? They removed the brain."

"Yuck. Stop," she said, sticking out her tongue and making a disgusted face.

"Don't you *know* about this?" I asked, delighted that I had some truly gruesome information that she didn't.

"Please—enough," she said, holding up one hand as if to fend me off.

"No, this is interesting," I insisted. "The brain had to come out first. They had this special tool. It was like a long, skinny hook. They'd push it up the corpse's nose until it reached the brain and then wiggled it back and forth, back and forth, until the brain became mush."

"*Stop!*" Sari pleaded, covering her ears.

"Then they took a long spoon," I continued gleefully, "and scooped the brain out a bit at a time."

I made a scooping motion with my hand. "Scoop, scoop. They scooped the brain out through the nose. Or sometimes they popped off an eyeball and scooped the brain out through the eyeball socket."

"Gabe—I *mean* it!" Sari cried. She really looked as if she was about to throw up. She was green!

59

I loved it.

I never knew that Sari had a squeamish bone in her body. But I was really making her sick.

Outstanding! I thought.

I would definitely have to remember this technique.

"It's all true," I told her, unable to hold back a wide grin.

"Just shut up," she muttered.

"Of course sometimes they didn't pull the brain out of the nose. Sometimes they just sliced off the head. Then they drained the brains out through the neck and put the head back on the body. They just bandaged it back on, I suppose."

"Gabe—"

I'd been staring at her the whole time, watching for her reaction. She was looking sicker and sicker. She was breathing really heavily. Her chest was sort of heaving. I really thought she was going to lose her breakfast.

If she did, I'd never let her forget it.

"That's really gross," she said. Her voice sounded funny, as if it was coming from underwater or something.

"But it's true," I said. "Didn't your dad ever tell you about how they made mummies?"

She shook her head. "He knows I don't like—"

"And you know what they did with the guts?" I asked, enjoying the startled look on her face. "They put them in jars and—"

I suddenly realized that Sari's startled look wasn't for me.

She was actually staring over my shoulder.

"Huh?" I turned round and saw why she suddenly looked so surprised.

A man had entered the room and was standing just in front of the first display case. It took me a few seconds to recognize him.

It was Ahmed, the strange, silent Egyptian with the black ponytail who had greeted us in such an unfriendly manner down inside the pyramid. He was dressed the same, in loose-fitting white trousers and shirt with a scarlet bandanna around his neck. And his expression was just as unfriendly. Angry, even.

Sari and I both backed away from the mummy case, and Ahmed, his eyes darting from one of us to the other, took a step towards us.

"Gabe, he's coming after us!" Sari whispered.

She grabbed my arm. Her hand was cold as ice.

"Let's get out of here!" she cried.

I hesitated. Shouldn't we stop and say hello to him first?

But something about the stern, determined look on Ahmed's face told me that Sari was right.

We turned and began walking really fast away from him into the vast room, Sari a few steps ahead of me.

I turned and saw that Ahmed was jogging after us.

He shouted something to us, his voice angry, threatening. I couldn't make out the words.

"Run!" Sari cried.

And now we were both running at full speed, our trainers drumming loudly over the polished marble floor.

We scooted round an enormous glass display case containing three upright mummy cases. Then we ran straight down the wide aisle between sculptures and shelves of ancient pottery and pyramid relics.

Behind us, I could hear Ahmed shouting furiously, "Come back! Come back!"

He sounded really angry.

"He's gaining on us!" I called to Sari, who was still a few steps ahead.

"There's got to be a way *out* of here!" she answered breathlessly.

But I saw immediately that there wasn't. We were nearly at the back wall. We passed a gigantic sphinx, then stopped.

There was nowhere to go.

No doorway. No exit.

We both turned and saw Ahmed's eyes grow wide with triumph.

He had us cornered.

Ahmed stopped a few metres in front of us. He was panting like a dog, gasping for air, and holding his side. He glared at us angrily.

Sari glanced at me. She looked pale, really frightened. We both had our backs pressed against the wall.

I swallowed hard. My throat felt tight and dry.

What was he going to do to us?

"Why did you run?" Ahmed finally managed to say, still holding his side as if he had a stitch. "Why?"

We didn't reply. We both stared back at him, waiting to see what he was about to do.

"I came with a message from your father," he told Sari, breathing hard. He raised the red bandanna from his neck and wiped his perspiring forehead with it.

"A message?" Sari stammered.

"Yes," Ahmed said. "You know me. We met

again yesterday. I don't understand why you ran."

"I'm sorry," Sari said quickly, glancing guiltily at me.

"We weren't thinking clearly," I said. "Sari frightened me, and I followed her."

"Gabe was telling me all this frightening stuff," she said, jabbing me hard in the side with her elbow. "It was *his* fault. He scared me with all this mummy stuff. So when I saw you, I wasn't thinking clearly, and . . ."

Both of us were babbling. We both felt so relieved that he wasn't chasing us—and so embarrassed that we had run away from him.

"Your father sent me to get you," Ahmed said, his dark eyes trained on me. "I didn't think I'd have to chase you through the whole museum."

"Sorry," Sari and I said in unison.

I felt like a complete jerk. I'm sure Sari did, too.

"Daddy came back to the hotel and saw Gabe's note?" Sari asked, straightening her hair with her hand as she moved away from the wall.

"Yes." Ahmed nodded.

"He got back from the hospital awfully fast," Sari said, glancing at her wristwatch.

"Yes," Ahmed replied again. "Come. I will take you back to the hotel. He is waiting for you there."

We followed him in silence, Sari and I walking side by side a few steps behind him.

As we made our way down the long staircase, we glanced sheepishly at each other. We were both feeling really foolish for running away like that.

A short while later, we were back on the crowded, noisy pavement, a constant stream of cars honking past, all moving in starts and stops, drivers hanging out of car windows, shouting and shaking their fists.

Ahmed checked to make sure we were with him, then turned right and began leading the way through the crowd. The sun was high over the buildings now. The air was hot and humid.

"Hey, wait—" I called.

Ahmed turned back, but kept walking.

"We're going the wrong way," I called to him, shouting over the cries of a street peddler behind a cart of vegetables. "The hotel is back that way." I pointed.

Ahmed shook his head. "My car is just up there."

"We're driving back to the hotel?" Sari asked, her voice revealing her surprise.

"It's only two blocks," I said to Ahmed. "Sari and I could walk back by ourselves if you want. You really don't have to take us."

"It's no trouble," Ahmed replied, and he placed his hands firmly, one on my shoulder, one on Sari's, and continued to guide us to his car.

We crossed the street and continued walking.

The pavement grew even more crowded. A man swinging a leather briefcase accidentally clipped my shoulder with it. I cried out in pain.

Sari laughed.

"You've got a great sense of humour," I muttered sarcastically.

"I know," she replied.

"If we'd walked, we would have been at the hotel by now," I said.

Ahmed must have overheard, because he said, "The car's in the next street."

We made our way quickly through the crowds. A short while later, Ahmed stopped at a small, four-door estate car. It was covered with dust, and the bumper on the driver's side was dented.

He pulled open the back door, and Sari and I piled in. "Ow," I complained. The leather seats were burning hot.

"The wheel is hot, too," Ahmed said, climbing in and fastening his seat belt. He touched the steering wheel a few times with both hands, trying to get used to the heat. "They should invent a car that stays cool inside when it's parked."

The engine started on the second try, and he pulled away from the kerb and into the line of traffic.

Immediately, he began honking the horn at the car in front of us. We moved slowly, stopping every few seconds, through the narrow street.

"I wonder why Daddy didn't come to get us," Sari said to me, her eyes on the crowds passing by the dusty car window.

"He said he would wait for you at the hotel," Ahmed replied from the front seat.

He made a sudden sharp turn onto a wider avenue and began to pick up speed.

It took me a long while to realize that we were heading in the wrong direction—*away* from our hotel. "Uh...Ahmed...I think the hotel is back that way," I said, pointing towards the back window.

"I believe you are mistaken," he replied softly, staring straight ahead through the windscreen. "We will be there shortly."

"No. Really," I insisted.

One thing about me is I have a really good sense of direction. Mum and Dad always say they don't need a map when I'm around. I almost always know when I'm heading the wrong way.

Sari turned to glance at me, an expression of concern beginning to tighten her features.

"Settle back and enjoy the ride," Ahmed said, staring at me through the rearview mirror. "Have you fastened your seat belts? Better do it right now."

He had a smile on his face, but his voice was cold. His words sounded like a threat.

"Ahmed, we've gone too far," I insisted, starting to feel really afraid.

Outside the window, the buildings were lower, more rundown. We seemed to be heading away from the centre of town.

"Just settle back," he replied with growing impatience. "I know where I'm going."

Sari and I exchanged glances. She looked as worried as I did. We both realized that Ahmed was lying to us. He wasn't taking us to the hotel. He was taking us out of town.

We were being kidnapped.

Seeing Ahmed's eyes on me in the rearview mirror, I fiddled with the seat belt, pretending to fasten it. As I did this, I leaned close to Sari and whispered in her ear, "Next time he stops."

At first she didn't get my meaning. But then I saw that she understood.

We both sat tensely, eyes on the door handles, waiting in silence.

"Your father is a very clever man," Ahmed said, staring at Sari in the mirror.

"I know," Sari replied in a tiny voice.

The traffic slowed, then stopped.

"Now!" I screamed.

We both grabbed for the door handles.

I pushed my door open and flung myself out of the car.

Horns were honking in front of me and behind me. I could hear Ahmed's surprised shout.

Leaving the car door open, I turned to see that Sari had made it to the street, too. She turned to me as she slammed her door shut, her eyes wide with fear.

Without a word, we started to run.

The car horns seemed to grow louder as we headed into a narrow side street. We were running side by side, followed the narrow brick street as it curved between two rows of tall, white stucco buildings.

I feel like a rat in a maze, I thought.

The street grew even narrower. Then it emptied into a wide circle filled with a small market of fruit and vegetable stands.

"Is he following us?" Sari cried, a few steps behind me now.

I turned back and searched for him, my eyes darting through the small crowd gathered in the market.

I saw several people in flowing white robes. Two women entered the market, dressed in black, carrying a basket loaded high with bananas. A boy on a bicycle swerved to keep from running straight into them.

"I can't see him," I called back to Sari.

But we kept running just to make sure.

I'd never been so scared in my life.

Please, *please*, I begged silently, don't let him be following us. Don't let him catch us!

Turning a corner, we found ourselves in a wide, busy avenue. A truck bounced past, pulling a trailer filled with horses. The pavement was

70

crowded with shoppers and business-people.

Sari and I pushed our way through them, trying to lose ourselves in the crowd.

Finally, we came to a stop near the entrance of what appeared to be a large department store. Breathing hard, I rested my hands on my knees, leaned forward, and tried to catch my breath.

"We've lost him," Sari said, staring back in the direction from which we'd come.

"Yeah. We're okay," I said happily. I smiled at her, but she didn't return the smile.

Her face was filled with fear. Her eyes continued to stare into the crowd. One hand tugged nervously at a strand of her hair.

"We're okay," I repeated. "We got away."

"There's only one problem," she said quietly, her eyes still on the crowd bustling towards us on the pavement.

"Huh? Problem?"

"Now we're lost," she replied, finally turning to face me. "We're lost, Gabe. We don't know where we are."

I suddenly had a heavy feeling in the pit of my stomach. I started to utter a frightened cry.

But I forced myself to hold it in.

I forced myself to pretend I wasn't afraid.

Sari had always been the brave one, the winner, the champ. And I was always the wimp. But now I could see that she was really scared. This was my chance to be the cool one, my

71

chance to show her who was really the champ.

"No problem," I told her, gazing up at the tall glass and concrete buildings. "We'll just ask somebody to direct us to the hotel."

"But no one speaks English!" she cried, sounding as if she were about to cry.

"Uh . . . no problem," I said, a little less cheerily. "I'm sure someone . . ."

"We're lost," she repeated miserably, shaking her head. "Totally lost."

And then I saw the answer to our problem parked at the kerb. It was a taxi, an empty taxi.

"Come on," I said, tugging her arm. I pulled her to the taxi. The driver, a thin, young man with a wide black moustache and stringy black hair falling out of a small grey cap, turned round in surprise as Sari and I climbed into the back seat.

"The Cairo Centre Hotel," I said, glancing reassuringly at Sari.

The driver stared back at me blankly, as if he didn't understand.

"Please take us to the Cairo Centre Hotel," I repeated slowly and clearly.

And then he tossed back his head, opened his mouth, and started to laugh.

The driver laughed till tears formed in the corners of his eyes.

Sari grabbed my arm. "He's working for Ahmed," she whispered, squeezing my wrist. "We've walked right into a trap!"

"Huh?" I felt a stab of fear in my chest.

I didn't think she was right.

She *couldn't* be right!

But I didn't know what else to think.

I grabbed the door handle and started to leap out of the taxi. But the driver raised a hand, signalling for me to stop.

"Gabe—*go!*" Shari pushed me hard from behind.

"Cairo Centre Hotel?" the driver asked suddenly, wiping the tears from his eyes with a finger. Then he pointed through the windshield. "Cairo Centre Hotel?"

Sari and I both followed his finger.

There was the hotel. Right across the street.

He started to laugh again, shaking his head.

"Thanks," I shouted, and climbed out.

Sari scrambled out behind me, a wide, relieved smile on her face. "I don't think it's *that* funny," I told her. "That cab driver has a strange sense of humour."

I turned back. The driver was still staring at us, a broad smile on his face.

"Come on," she urged, tugging at my arm. "We have to tell Daddy about Ahmed."

But to our surprise, our hotel room was empty. My note was still on the table where I had left it. Nothing had been moved or touched.

"He hasn't been back here," Sari said, picking up the note and crumpling it into a ball in her hand. "Ahmed lied—about everything."

I flopped down on the sofa with a loud sigh. "I wonder what's going on," I said unhappily. "I just don't get it."

Sari and I both screamed as the door to the room flew open.

"Daddy!" Sari cried, running to hug him.

I was so glad it was Uncle Ben, and not Ahmed.

"Daddy, the strangest thing—" Sari started.

Uncle Ben had his arm around her shoulder. As he led her across the room towards the sofa, I could see that he had a really dazed expression on his face.

"Yes, it's strange," he muttered, shaking his head. "Both of my workers ..."

"Huh? Are they okay?" Sari asked.

"No. Not really," Uncle Ben replied, dropping onto the arm of the armchair, staring hard but not really focusing on me. "They're both ... in a state of shock. I suppose that's how to describe it."

"They had an accident? In the pyramid?" I asked.

Uncle Ben scratched the bald spot at the back of his head. "I don't really know. They can't talk. They're both ... speechless. I think something— or someone—frightened them. Scared them speechless. The doctors are completely confused. They said that—"

"Daddy, Ahmed tried to kidnap us!" Sari interrupted, squeezing his hand.

"What? Ahmed?" He narrowed his eyes, his forehead wrinkling up in confusion. "What do you mean?"

"Ahmed. The man at the pyramid. The one who wears the white suits with the red bandanna and always carries the clipboard," Sari explained.

"He told us you sent him to get us," I said. "He came to the museum—"

"Museum?" Uncle Ben climbed to his feet. "What were you doing at the museum? I thought I told you—"

"We had to get out of here," Sari said, putting a hand on her dad's shoulder, trying to calm him. "Gabe wanted to see mummies, so we went to the museum. But Ahmed came and took us to his car. He said he was taking us to you at the hotel."

"But he was driving the wrong way," I continued the story. "So we jumped out and ran away."

"Ahmed?" Uncle Ben kept repeating the name, as if he just couldn't believe it. "He came to me with excellent credentials and references," he said. "He's a cryptographer. He studies ancient Egyptian. He's mainly interested in the wall writings and symbols we uncover."

"So why did he come for us?" I asked.

"Where was he going to take us?" Sari asked.

"I don't know," Uncle Ben said. "But I certainly intend to find out." He hugged Sari. "What a mystery," he continued. "You're both okay?"

"Yeah. We're okay," I replied.

"I've got to get to the pyramid," he said, letting go of Sari and walking to the window. "I gave my workers the day off. But I've got to get to the bottom of this."

Clouds rolled over the sun. The room suddenly grew darker.

"I'll order up some room service for you," Uncle Ben said, a thoughtful expression on his face. "Will you two be okay here till I get back tonight?"

"No!" Sari cried. "You can't leave us here!"

"Why can't we come with you?" I asked.

"Yes! We're coming with you!" Sari exclaimed, before Uncle Ben had a chance to reply.

He shook his head. "Too dangerous," he said, his eyes narrowing as he glanced first at me, then at Sari. "Until I can find out what happened to my two workers in there—"

"But, Daddy, what if Ahmed comes back?" Sari cried, sounding really frightened. "What if he comes here?"

Uncle Ben scowled. "Ahmed," he muttered. "Ahmed."

"You can't leave us here!" Sari repeated.

Uncle Ben stared out of the window at the darkening sky. "I suppose you're right," he said finally. "I suppose I'll have to take you with me."

"Yes!" Sari and I both cried, relieved.

"But you have to promise to stick close," Uncle Ben said sternly, pointing a finger at Sari. "I mean it. No wandering off. No more practical jokes."

I realized I was seeing a whole new side to my uncle. Even though he was a well-known scientist, he had always been the jolly, practical joker of the family.

But now he was worried.

Seriously worried.

No more jokes until the frightening mystery had been cleared up.

We had sandwiches downstairs in the hotel restaurant, then drove through the desert to the pyramid.

Heavy clouds rolled across the sun as we drove, casting shadows over the sand, colouring the desert darkly in shimmering shades of blue and grey.

Before long, the enormous pyramid loomed on the horizon, appearing to get larger as we approached on the nearly empty motorway.

I remembered the first time I had seen it, just a few days before. Such an amazing sight.

But now, watching it through the car windshield, I felt only dread.

Uncle Ben parked the car near the low entrance he had discovered behind the pyramid. As we walked out, the wind whipped at the ground, tossing the sand up, whirling it around our legs.

Uncle Ben raised a hand to stop us at the tunnel entrance.

"Here," he said. He reached into his supply pack and pulled out equipment for Sari and me. "Clip this on."

He handed each of us a bleeper. "Just push the button, and it will bleep me," he said, helping me clip mine to the belt of my jeans. "It's like a homing device. If you push the button, it sends electronic signals to the unit *I'm* wearing. Then I can track you down by following the sound levels. Of course, I don't expect you to use it because I expect you to stay close to me."

He handed us torches. "Watch your step," he instructed. "Keep the light down at your feet, a few metres ahead of you on the floor."

"We *know*, Daddy," Sari said. "We've done this before, remember?"

"Just follow instructions," he said sharply, and turned into the darkness of the pyramid opening.

I stopped at the entrance and pulled out my little mummy hand, just to make sure I had it.

"What are you doing with that?" Sari asked, making a face.

"My good luck charm," I said, slipping it back into my pocket.

She groaned and gave me a playful shove into the pyramid entrance.

A few minutes later, we were once again making our way carefully down the long rope ladder and into the first narrow tunnel.

Uncle Ben led the way, the wide circle of light from his torch sweeping back and forth across the tunnel ahead of him. Sari was a few steps behind him, and I walked a few steps behind her.

The tunnel seemed narrower and lower this time. I suppose it was just my mood.

Gripping the torch tightly, keeping the light

aimed down, I dipped my head to keep from hitting the low, curved ceiling.

The tunnel bent to the left, then sloped downhill where it split into two paths. We followed the one to the right. The only sound was that of our shoes scraping against the sandy, dry floor.

Uncle Ben coughed.

Sari said something. I couldn't hear what it was.

I had stopped to shine my light on some spiders on the ceiling, and the two of them had walked several metres ahead of me.

Following my light as it moved over the floor, I saw that my trainer lace had come untied once again.

"Oh, man—not again!"

I stooped to tie it, putting the torch on the ground beside me. "Hey—wait!" I called.

But they had started to argue about something, and I don't think they heard me. I could hear their voices echoing loudly down the long, twisting tunnel, but I couldn't make out their words.

I hurriedly double-knotted the shoe lace, grabbed the torch, and climbed to my feet. "Hey, wait!" I shouted anxiously.

Where had they gone?

I realized that I couldn't hear their voices any more.

This *can't* be happening to me again! I thought.

"Hey!" I shouted, cupping my hands over my mouth. My voice echoed down the tunnel.

But no voices called back.

"Wait!"

Typical, I thought.

They were so involved in their argument, they forgot all about me.

I realized that I was more angry than frightened. Uncle Ben had made such a big deal about us sticking close together. And then he'd walked off and left me alone in the tunnel.

"Hey, where *are* you?" I shouted.

No reply.

Beaming the light ahead of me on the floor, I ducked my head and began jogging, following the tunnel as it curved sharply to the right.

The floor began to slope upwards. The air became hot and musty smelling. I found myself gasping for breath.

"Uncle Ben!" I called. "Sari!"

They must be around the next curve in the tunnel, I told myself. It hadn't taken me that long to tie my shoelace. They couldn't have got that far ahead.

Hearing a sound, I stopped.

And listened.

Silence now.

Was I starting to hear things?

I had a sudden flash: Was this another stupid practical joke? Were Sari and Uncle Ben hiding, waiting to see what I'd do?

Was this another pathetic trick of theirs to frighten me?

It could be. Uncle Ben, I knew, could never resist a practical joke. He had laughed like a hyena when Sari told him how she'd hidden in the mummy case and scared about ten years off my life.

Were they both hiding in mummy cases now, just waiting for me to stumble by?

My heart thumped in my chest. Despite the heat of the ancient tunnel, I felt cold all over.

No, I decided. This isn't a practical joke.

Uncle Ben was too serious today, too worried about his stricken workers. Too worried about what we'd told him about Ahmed. He wasn't in any mood for practical jokes.

I began making my way through the tunnel again. As I jogged, my hand brushed against the bleeper at my waist.

Should I push it?

No, I decided.

That would only give Sari a good laugh. She'd be eager to tell everyone how I'd started beeping for help after being in the pyramid for two minutes!

I turned the corner. The tunnel walls seemed to close in on me as the tunnel narrowed.

"Sari? Uncle Ben?"

No echo. Maybe the tunnel was too narrow for an echo.

The floor grew harder, less sandy. In the dim yellow light, I could see that the granite walls were lined with jagged cracks. They looked like dark lightning bolts coming down from the ceiling.

"Hey—where *are* you two?" I shouted.

I stopped when the tunnel branched in two directions.

I suddenly realized how scared I was.

Where had they disappeared to? They *had* to have realized by now that I wasn't with them.

I stared at the two openings, shining my torch first into one tunnel, then the other.

Which one had they gone into?

Which one?

My heart pounding, I ran into the tunnel on the left and shouted their names.

No reply.

I backed out quickly, my light darting wildly over the floor, and stepped into the tunnel to the right.

This tunnel was wider and higher. It curved gently to the right.

A maze of tunnels. That's how Uncle Ben had described the pyramid. Maybe thousands of tunnels, he had told me.

Thousands.

Keep moving, I urged myself.

Keep moving, Gabe.

They're right up ahead. They've *got* to be!

I took a few steps and then called out to them.

I heard something.

Voices?

I stopped. It was so quiet now. So quiet, I could hear my heart pounding in my chest.

The sound again.

I listened hard, holding my breath.

It was a chattering sound. A soft chattering. Not a human voice. An insect, maybe. Or a rat.

"Uncle Ben? Sari?"

Silence.

I took a few more steps into the tunnel. Then a few more.

I decided I'd better forget my pride and bleep them.

So what if Sari teased me about it?

I was too frightened to care.

If I beeped them, they'd be right there to get me in a few seconds.

But as I reached to my waist for the bleeper, I was startled by a loud noise.

The insect chittering became a soft *cracking* sound.

I stopped to listen, the fear rising up to my throat.

The soft cracking grew louder.

It sounded like someone breaking twigs in two.

Only louder. Louder.

Louder.

Right under my feet.

I turned my eyes to the floor.

I shone the light at my shoes.

It took me so long to realize what was happening.

The ancient tunnel floor was cracking apart beneath me.

The cracking grew louder, seemed to come from all directions, to surround me.

By the time I realized what was happening, it was too late.

I felt as if I were being pulled down, sucked down by a powerful force.

The floor crumbled away beneath me, and I was falling.

Falling down, down, down an endless black hole.

I opened my mouth to scream, but no sound came out.

My hands flew up and grabbed—nothing!

I closed my eyes and fell.

Down, down into the swirling blackness.

I heard the torch clang against the floor.

Then I hit. Hard.

I landed on my side. Pain shot through my body, and I saw red. A flash of bright red that grew brighter and brighter until I had to close my eyes. I think the force of the blow knocked me out for a short while.

When I opened my eyes, everything was a grey-yellow blur. My side ached. My right elbow throbbed with pain.

I tried the elbow. It seemed to move okay.

I sat up. The haze slowly began to lift, like a curtain slowly rising.

Where was I?

A sour smell invaded my nostrils. The smell of decay. Of ancient dust. Of death.

The torch had landed beside me on the concrete floor. I followed its beam of light towards the wall.

And gasped.

The light stopped on a hand.

A human hand.

Or was it?

The hand was attached to an arm. The arm hung stiffly from an erect body.

My hand trembling, I grabbed up the torch and tried to steady the light on the figure.

It was a mummy, I realized. Standing on its feet near the far wall.

Eyeless, mouthless, the bandaged face seemed to stare back at me, tense and ready, as if waiting for me to make the first move.

A mummy?

The light darted over its featureless face. I couldn't steady my hand. My whole body was shaking.

Frozen in place, not able to move off the hard floor, I gaped at the frightening figure. I suddenly realized I was panting loudly.

Trying to calm myself, I sucked in a deep breath of the putrid air, and held it.

The mummy stared blindly back at me.

It stood stiffly, its arms hanging at its sides.

Why is it standing there like that? I wondered, taking another deep breath.

The ancient Egyptians didn't leave their mummies standing to attention.

Realizing that it wasn't moving forward to attack me, I began to feel a bit calmer.

"Easy, Gabe. Easy," I said aloud, trying to steady the torch I gripped so tightly in my hand.

I coughed. The air was so foul. So *old*.

Groaning from the pain in my side, I climbed to my feet and began rapidly shining the light back and forth beyond the silent, faceless mummy.

I was in an enormous, high-ceilinged chamber. Much bigger than the chamber Uncle Ben's workers had been digging in.

And much more cluttered.

"Wow." I uttered a low cry as the pale light of the torch revealed an amazing scene. Dark, bandaged figures hovered all around me.

The vast chamber was *crammed* with mummies!

In the unsteady light, their shadows seemed to reach towards me.

Shuddering, I took a step back. I moved the light slowly over the strange, hideous scene.

The light burned through the shadows, revealing bandaged arms, torsos, legs, covered faces.

There were so many of them.

There were mummies leaning against the wall. Mummies lying on stone slabs, arms crossed over their chests. Mummies leaning at odd angles, crouched low or standing tall, their arms straight out in front of them like Frankenstein's monsters.

Against one wall stood a row of mummy cases, their lids propped open. I turned, following the arc of my light. I realized that my fall had dropped me into the centre of the room.

Behind me, I could make out an amazing array of equipment. Strange, prong-like tools I had never seen before. Tall stacks of cloth. Gigantic clay pots and jars.

Easy, Gabe. Easy.

Breathe slowly.

I took a few reluctant steps closer, trying to hold the torch steady.

A few more steps.

I walked up to one of the tall stacks of cloth. Linen, probably. The material used for making mummies.

Gathering my courage, I examined some of the tools. Not touching anything. Just staring at them in the wavering light of the torch.

Mummy-making tools. Ancient mummy-making tools.

I stepped away. Turned back towards the crowd of unmoving figures.

My light travelled across the room and came to rest on a dark square area on the floor. Curious, I moved closer, stepping around twin mummies, lying on their backs, their arms crossed over their chests.

Easy, Gabe.

My trainers scraped noisily along the floor as I made my way hesitantly across the vast chamber.

The dark square on the floor was nearly the

size of a swimming pool. I bent down at its edge to examine it more closely.

The surface was soft and sticky. Like tar.

Was this an ancient tar pit? Was this tar used in the making of the mummies that hovered so menacingly around the room?

I had a sudden chill that froze me to the spot.

How could this tar pit be soft after *four thousand years*?

Why was everything in this chamber—the tools, the mummies, the linen—preserved so well?

And why were these mummies—at least two dozen of them—left out like this, scattered about the room in such strange positions?

I realized that I had made an incredible discovery here. By falling through the floor, I had found a hidden chamber, a chamber where mummies had been made. I had found all of the tools and all of the materials used to make mummies four thousand years ago.

Once again, the sour smell invaded my nose. I held my breath to keep myself from gagging. It was the smell of four-thousand-year-old bodies, I realized. A smell that had been bottled up in this ancient, hidden chamber—until now.

Staring at the twisted, shadowy figures gazing back at me in faceless horror, I reached for the bleeper.

Uncle Ben, you must come quickly, I thought.

I don't want to be alone down here any longer. You must come here *now*!

I pulled the bleeper off my belt and brought it up close to the light.

All I had to do, I realized, was push the button, and Uncle Ben and Sari would come running.

Gripping the small square tightly in my hand, I moved my hand to the button—and cried out in alarm.

The bleeper was ruined. Wrecked. Smashed.

The button wouldn't even push.

I must have landed on it when I fell.

It was useless.

I was all alone down here.

Alone with the ancient mummies, staring facelessly, silently, at me through the deep, dark shadows.

All alone.

I stared in horror at the worthless bleeper.

The torch trembled in my hand.

Suddenly, everything seemed to move in on me. The walls. The ceiling. The darkness.

The mummies.

"Huh?"

I stumbled back a step. Then another.

I realized I was gripping the torch so tightly, my hand hurt.

The light played over the faceless figures.

They weren't moving.

Of *course* they weren't moving.

I took another step back. The sour odour seemed to grow stronger, thicker. I held my breath, but the smell was in my nostrils, in my mouth. I could taste it, taste the decay, taste the four-thousand-year-old aroma of death.

I tossed the worthless bleeper on the floor and

took another step back, keeping my eyes on the hovering mummies.

What was I going to do?

The smell was making me sick. I had to get out of there, had to phone Uncle Ben.

Another step back.

"Help!"

I tried to shout, but my voice sounded weak, muffled by the heavy, foul air.

"Help! Can anybody hear me?" A little louder.

Tucking the torch under my arm, I cupped my hands around my mouth to form a megaphone. "*Can anybody hear me?*" I screamed.

I listened, desperate for a reply.

Silence.

Where *were* Sari and Uncle Ben? Why couldn't they hear me? Why weren't they looking for me?

"*Help! Somebody–please help!*"

I screamed as loud as I could, tilting my head up to the hole in the ceiling, the hole I had fallen through.

"*Can't anybody hear me?*" I shrieked.

I could feel the panic grip my chest, freeze my legs.

The panic swept over me, wave after paralyzing wave.

"Help me! *Somebody*—please!"

I took another step back.

And something crunched under my foot.

I uttered a high-pitched yelp and stumbled forward.

Whatever it was slithered away.

I exhaled loudly, a long sigh of relief.

And then I felt something brush against my ankle.

I cried out, and the torch dropped from under my arm. It clattered noisily to the floor.

The light went out.

Again, something scraped silently against me.

Something hard.

I heard soft, scrabbling sounds down on the floor. Something snapped at my ankle.

I kicked hard, but hit only air.

"Ohh, help!"

There were creatures down there. A lot of them.

But what *were* they?

Again, something snapped at my ankle, and kicked wildly.

Frantically, I bent down, grabbing for the torch in the darkness.

And touched something hard and warm.

"Ohh, no!"

I jerked my hand up with a startled cry.

In the darkness, groping for the torch, I had the feeling that the whole floor had come to life. The floor was moving in waves, rolling and tossing, seething beneath me.

Finally, I found the torch. I grabbed it up in my trembling hand, climbed to my feet, and struggled to turn it back on.

As I stepped backwards, something slid against my leg.

It felt hard. And prickly.

I heard clicking sounds. Snapping. Creatures bumping into each other.

Panting loudly, my chest heaving, my entire body gripped with terror, I jumped up, tried to dance away as I fiddled with the torch.

Something crunched loudly beneath my trainer. I danced away, hopping over something that scuttled through my legs.

Finally, the light flickered on.

My heart thudding, I lowered the yellow beam of light to the floor.

And saw the scrabbling, snapping creatures.

Scorpions!

I had stumbled into a disgusting nest of them.

"Ohh—help!"

I didn't recognize my tiny, frightened voice as I cried out. I didn't even realize I had cried out.

The light darted over the slithering creatures, their tails raised as if ready to attack, their claws snapping silently as they moved. Crawling over each other. Slithering past my ankles.

"Somebody—help!"

I leapt backwards as a pair of claws grabbed at the leg of my jeans—into another of the creatures whose tail snapped against the back of my trainer.

Struggling to escape from the poisonous creatures, I tripped.

"No! *Please-no!*"

I couldn't save myself.

I started to fall.

My hands shot out, but there was nothing to grab on to.

I was going to plunge right into the middle of them.

"*Nooooo!*"

I uttered a frantic cry as I toppled forward.

And felt two hands grab me by the shoulders from behind.

A mummy! I thought.

My entire body was convulsed with fear.

The scorpions snapped and scrabbled at my feet.

The strong hands gripped my shoulders, pulled me hard.

The ancient, bandaged hands.

I couldn't breathe. I couldn't think.

Finally, I managed to spin round.

"Sari!" I cried.

She gave me one more tug. We both stumbled backwards, claws snapping up at us.

"Sari—how—?"

We moved together now, making our way towards the centre of the vast chamber.

Safe. Safe from the disgusting nest of snapping scorpions.

"Saved your life," she whispered. "Yuck. Those are gross!"

"Tell me about it," I said weakly. I could still

feel the hideous creatures sliding along my ankles, still feel them slithering between my legs, crunching under my trainers.

I don't think I'll ever forget that crunching sound.

"What are you *doing* down here?" Sari cried impatiently, as if scolding a child. "Daddy and I have been looking everywhere for you."

I pulled her even farther from the scorpions, into the centre of the chamber. "How did you get down here?" I cried, struggling to calm my breathing, struggling to stop the pounding in my chest.

She pointed with her torch, to a tunnel in the corner that I hadn't seen. "I was searching for you. Daddy and I got separated. Can you believe it? He stopped to talk to a worker, and I didn't realize it. By the time I turned back, he'd gone. Then I saw the light moving around in here. I thought it was Daddy."

"You got lost, too?" I asked, wiping beads of cold sweat off my forehead with the back of my hand.

"I'm not lost. *You're* lost," she insisted. "How could you *do* that, Gabe? Daddy and I were totally freaked."

"Why didn't you wait for me?" I demanded angrily. "I called to you. You just disappeared."

"We didn't hear you," she replied, shaking her head. I was really glad to see her. But I hated the way she was looking at me, as if I was some kind of hopeless idiot. "I suppose we got involved in our argument. We thought you were right behind us. Then when we turned round, you were gone." She sighed and shook her head. "What a day!"

"What a day?" I cried shrilly. "What a day?"

"Gabe, why did you *do* that?" she demanded. "You know we were supposed to stay close together."

"Hey—it wasn't my fault," I insisted angrily.

"Daddy is so angry," Sari said, shining her light in my face.

I raised my arm to shield my eyes. "Cut it out," I snapped. "He won't be angry when he sees what I've discovered. Look."

I shone my light onto a mummy crouching near the tar pit, then moved it to another mummy, this one lying down, then to the row of mummy cases against the wall.

"Wow." Sari mouthed the word silently. Her eyes grew wide with surprise.

"Yeah. Wow," I said, starting to feel a bit more like normal. "The chamber is filled with mummies. And there are all kinds of tools and cloth and everything you need to make a mummy. It's all in perfect shape, as if it hasn't been touched for thousands of years." I couldn't hide my excitement. "And I discovered it all," I added.

"This must be where they prepared the

mummies for burial," Sari said, her eyes darting from mummy to mummy. "But why are some of them standing up like that?"

I shrugged. "Beats me."

She walked over to admire the stacks of neatly folded linen. "Wow. This is amazing, Gabe."

"Outstanding!" I agreed. "And if I hadn't stopped to tie my trainer lace, I never would have discovered it."

"You're going to be famous," Sari said, a smile spreading across her face. "Thanks to *me* saving your life."

"Sari—" I started.

But she had moved across the room and was admiring one of the upright mummies close up. "Wait till Daddy sees all this," she said, suddenly sounding as excited as me.

"We have to call him," I said eagerly. I glanced back at the scorpion nest and felt a chill of fear tighten the back of my neck.

"People were so tiny back then," she said, holding her torch up close to the mummy's covered face. "Look—I'm taller than this one."

"Sari, use your bleeper," I said impatiently, walking over to her.

"Yuck. There are bugs crawling in this one's face," she said, stepping back and lowering the light. She made a disgusted face. "Gross."

"Come on. Use your bleeper. Call Uncle Ben,"

I said. I reached for the bleeper at her waist, but she pulled away.

"Okay, okay. Why didn't you use *yours*?" She eyed me suspiciously. "You forgot about it, didn't you, Gabe!" she accused.

"No way," I replied sharply. "Mine broke when I fell into this place."

She made a face and pulled the bleeper off her belt loop. I shone my light on it as she pushed the button. She pressed it twice, just to make sure, then clipped it back onto her jeans.

We stood with our arms crossed, waiting for Uncle Ben to follow the radio signals and find us.

"It shouldn't take him long," Sari said, her eyes on the tunnel in the corner. "He wasn't far behind me."

Sure enough, a few seconds later, we heard the sounds of someone approaching in the tunnel.

"Uncle Ben!" I called excitedly. "Look what I've found!"

Sari and I both started to run to the tunnel, our lights zigzagging over the low entrance.

"Daddy, you won't believe—" Sari started.

She stopped when the stooped figure leaned out of the darkness and straightened up.

We both gaped in horror, our torches making his moustached face glow eerily.

"It's Ahmed!" Sari cried, grabbing my arm.

I swallowed hard.

Sari and I stared at each other. I saw her features tighten in fear.

Ahmed.

He had tried to kidnap us. And now he had us all alone down here.

He stepped forward, a flaming torch held high in one hand. His black hair glowed in the flickering flames. His eyes narrowed at us in menace.

"Ahmed, what are you doing here?" Sari called, grasping my arm so hard, I winced.

"What are *you* doing here?" he asked softly, his voice as cold as his eyes.

Holding the torch in front of him, he stepped into the chamber. His eyes went around the room, as if inspecting it, making sure that nothing had been moved.

"My dad will be here in a second," Sari warned him. "I've just bleeped him."

"I tried to warn your father," Ahmed said, staring hard at Sari. The flickering orange light from the torch made him grow bright, then fade into shadow.

"Warn him?" Sari asked.

"About the curse," Ahmed said without emotion.

"Uncle Ben mentioned some kind of curse to me," I said, glancing nervously at Sari. "I don't think he takes that kind of thing seriously."

"*He should*!" Ahmed replied, screaming the words, his eyes glowing with anger in the torch light.

Sari and I stared back at him in silence.

Where is Uncle Ben? I wondered.

What's keeping him?

Hurry, I urged silently. *Please—hurry*!

"The curse must be carried out," Ahmed said softly again, almost sadly. "I have no choice. You have violated the priestess's chamber."

"Priestess?" I stammered.

Sari was still squeezing my arm. I tugged it away. She crossed her arms resolutely over her chest.

"This chamber belongs to the Priestess Khala," Ahmed said, lowering the torch. "This is the Sacred Preparation Chamber of the Priestess Khala, and you have violated it."

"Well, we didn't know," Sari snapped. "I really don't see what the big deal is, Ahmed."

"She's right," I said quickly. "We didn't touch anything. We didn't move anything. I don't think—"

"*Shut up, you fools!*" Ahmed screamed. He swung the torch angrily as if trying to hit us.

"Ahmed, my dad will be here any second," Sari repeated, her voice trembling.

We both turned our eyes to the tunnel. I was dark and silent.

No sign of Uncle Ben.

"Your father is a clever man," Ahmed said. "It's too bad he wasn't clever enough to heed my warnings."

"Warnings?" Sari asked.

I realized she was stalling for time, trying to keep Ahmed talking until Uncle Ben arrived.

"I frightened the two workers," Ahmed confessed to Sari. "I frightened them to show your father that the curse was alive, that I was prepared to carry out Khala's wishes."

"How did you frighten them?" Sari demanded.

He smiled. "I gave them a little demonstration. I showed them what it might feel like to be boiled alive." He turned his eyes to the tar pit. "They didn't like it," he added quietly.

"But, Ahmed—" Sari started.

He cut her off. "Your father should have known better than to return here. He should have believed me. He should have believed in the Priestess's curse. The Priestess cursed all who would violate her chamber."

"But, come on, you don't really believe—" I started.

He raised the torch menacingly. "It was decreed by Khala more than four thousand years ago that this sacred chamber would not be violated," he cried, gesturing with the torch, leaving a trail of orange light against the darkness. "Since that time, from generation to generation, descendants of Khala have made sure that the Priestess's command was obeyed."

"But, Ahmed—" Sari cried.

"It has come to me," he continued, ignoring her, ignoring us both, staring at the ceiling as he spoke, as if speaking directly to the Priestess up in the heavens. "It has come to me as a descendant of Khala to make sure the curse is carried out."

I stared past Ahmed to the tunnel. Still no sign of Uncle Ben.

Was he coming? Had Sari's bleeper worked? What was keeping him?

"I volunteered to work for your father to make sure that Khala's sacred sanctuary was not violated," Ahmed continued, shadows flickering over his menacing face. "When he would not heed my warnings, I had to take action. I frightened the two workers. Then I planned to take you away, to hide you until he agreed to stop his work."

He lowered the torch. His face filled with sadness. "Now, I have no choice. I must carry out my sacred duties. I must keep the ancient promise to Khala."

"But what does that *mean*?" Sari cried. The orange torchlight revealed her frightened expression.

"What does it mean?" Ahmed repeated. He gestured with the torch. "Look around you."

We both turned and glanced quickly around the chamber. But we didn't understand.

"The mummies," he explained.

We still didn't understand. "What about the mummies?" I managed to stammer.

"They were all violators of the Priestess's chamber," Ahmed revealed. The thin smile that formed on his face could only be described as a proud smile.

"You mean—they're not from ancient Egypt?" Sari cried, raising her hands in horror to her face.

"A few of them," Ahmed replied, still smiling that frightening, cold smile. "A few of them were ancient intruders. Some are quite recent. But they all have one thing in common. They all became victims of the curse. And they were all mummified *alive!*"

"No!" I screamed without realizing it.

Ahmed ignored my terrified outburst. "I did that one myself," he said, pointing to a mummy standing stiffly to attention at the edge of the tar pit.

"Oh, how awful!" Sari cried, her voice trembling.

I stared hopefully at the tunnel opening behind Ahmed. But there was still no sign of Uncle Ben.

"Today, I must go to work again," Ahmed announced. Today there will be new mummies. New trophies of Khala."

"You can't *do* that!" Sari shrieked.

I grabbed her hand.

To my horror, I understood perfectly now. I understood why some of the mummies were in such good condition.

They were new.

All the tools, the tar, the linen—they had been used by descendants of Khala, descendants like Ahmed. Since the time of Khala, anyone who had entered the chamber—the chamber we were now standing in—had been mummified.

Alive.

And now Sari and I were about to become mummies, too.

"Ahmed, you *can't!*" Sari cried. She let go of my hand and balled her hands into angry fists at her side.

"It is the will of Khala," he replied softly, his dark eyes glowing in the light of the torch.

I saw a long-bladed dagger appear in his free hand. The blade caught the light from the torch.

Sari and I both took a step back as Ahmed began moving towards us with quick, determined strides.

As Ahmed approached, Sari and I shrank back to the centre of the chamber.

Run, I thought.

We can run away from him.

My eyes searched frantically for a place we could escape through.

But there was no way out.

The tunnel in the corner appeared to be the only opening. And we'd have to run right past Ahmed to get to it.

Sari, I saw, was frantically pressing the bleeper at her waist. She glanced at me, her features tight with fear.

"Yowwww!"

I cried out as I suddenly backed into someone.

I turned and stared into the bandaged face of a mummy.

With a loud gasp, I lurched away from it.

"Let's make a run for the tunnel," I whispered to Sari, my throat so dry and tight, I could barely make myself heard. "He can't get both of us."

Sari stared back at me, confused. I don't know if she heard me or not.

"There is no escape," Ahmed said softly, as if reading my thoughts. "There is no escape from Khala's curse."

"He—he's going to *kill* us!" Sari screamed.

"You have violated her sacred chamber," Ahmed said, raising the torch high, holding the dagger at his waist.

He stepped nearer. "I saw you climb into the sacred sarcophagus yesterday. I saw you two *playing* in Khala's holy chamber. It was then that I knew I had to carry out my sacred duties. I—"

Sari and I both cried out as something dropped from the chamber ceiling.

All three of us looked up to see a rope ladder dangling from the hole I had fallen through. It swung back and forth as it was lowered, nearly to the floor.

"Are you down there? I'm coming down!" Uncle Ben shouted down to us.

"Uncle Ben—no!" I screamed.

But he was already moving down the ladder, making his way quickly, the ladder steadying under his weight.

Halfway down, he stopped and peered into the chamber. "What on earth—?" he cried, his eyes roaming over the amazing scene.

112

And then he saw Ahmed.

"Ahmed, what are *you* doing here?" Uncle Ben cried in surprise. He quickly lowered himself to the floor, jumping down the last three rungs.

"Merely carrying out Khala's wishes," Ahmed said, his face expressionless now, his eyes narrowed in anticipation.

"Khala? The Priestess?" Uncle Ben wrinkled his features in confusion.

"He's going to kill us!" Sari cried, rushing up to her dad, throwing her arms around his waist. "Daddy—he's going to kill us! And then turn us into *mummies!*"

Uncle Ben held Sari and looked over her shoulder accusingly at Ahmed. "Is this true?"

"The chamber has been violated. It has fallen to me, Doctor, to carry out the curse."

Uncle Ben put his hands on Sari's trembling shoulders and gently moved her aside. Then he began to make his way slowly, steadily, towards Ahmed.

"Ahmed, let's go out of here and discuss this," he said, raising his right hand as if offering it in friendship.

Ahmed took a step back, raising the torch menacingly. "The Priestess's will must not be ignored."

"Ahmed, you are a scientist, and so am I," Uncle Ben said. I couldn't believe how calm he sounded. I wondered if it was an act.

The scene was tense. We were in such terrifying danger.

But I felt just a little bit calmer knowing that my uncle was here, knowing that he'd be able to handle Ahmed and get us out of here—alive.

I glanced reassuringly at Sari, who was staring hard, biting her lower lip in tense concentration as her father approached Ahmed.

"Ahmed, put down the torch," Uncle Ben urged, his hand extended. "The dagger, too. Please. Let's discuss this, scientist to scientist."

"What is there to discuss?" Ahmed asked softly, his eyes studying Uncle Ben intently. "The will of Khala must be carried out, as it has been for four thousand years. That cannot be discussed."

"As scientist to scientist," Uncle Ben repeated, returning Ahmed's stare as if challenging him. "The curse is ancient. Khala has had her way for many centuries. Perhaps it is time to let it rest. Lower your weapons, Ahmed. Let's talk about this. Scientist to scientist."

It's going to be okay, I thought, breathing a long sigh of relief. It's all going to be okay. We're going to get out of here.

But then Ahmed moved with startling quickness.

Without warning, without a word, he pulled back his arms and, gripping the torch handle

114

with both hands, swung it as hard as he could at Uncle Ben's head.

The torch made a loud *thonk* as it connected with the side of Uncle Ben's face.

The orange flames danced up.

A swirl of bright colour.

And then shadows.

Uncle Ben groaned. His blue eyes bulged wide with surprise.

With pain.

The torch hadn't set him aflame. But the blow had knocked him out.

He slumped to his knees. Then his eyes closed, and he dropped limply to the floor.

Ahmed raised the torch high, his eyes gleaming with excitement, with triumph.

And I knew we were doomed.

"Daddy!"

Sari rushed to her father and knelt at his side.

But Ahmed moved quickly, thrusting the torch towards her, holding the dagger ready, forcing her to back away.

A thin trickle of blood, glowing darkly in the light of the fire, rolled down the side of Uncle Ben's face. He groaned, but didn't stir.

I glanced quickly at the mummies scattered around the room. It was hard to believe that we would soon be one of them.

I thought of leaping at Ahmed, trying to knock him over. I imagined grabbing the torch, swinging it at him, forcing him against the wall. Forcing him to let us escape.

But the blade of the dagger glowed, as if warning me to stay back.

I'm just a kid, I thought.

Thinking I could beat a grown man with a knife and a torch was just crazy.

Crazy.

The whole scene was crazy. And terrifying.

I suddenly felt sick. My stomach tightened, and a wave of nausea swept over me.

"Let us go—*now*!" Sari screamed at Ahmed.

To my surprise, he reacted by swinging back the flaming torch and heaving it across the room.

It landed with a soft *plop* in the centre of the tar pit. Instantly, the surface of the tar burst into flames. The flames spread, leaping up towards the chamber ceiling, until the entire square was aflame.

As I stared in amazement, the tar popped and bubbled beneath the orange and red covering of flames.

"We must wait for it to boil," Ahmed said calmly, the shadows cast by the flames flickering across his face and clothing.

The chamber grew thick with smoke. Sari and I both started to cough.

Ahmed bent down and put his hands under Uncle Ben's shoulders. He began to drag him across the floor.

"Leave him alone!" Sari screamed, running frantically towards Ahmed.

I saw that she was going to try to fight him.

I grabbed her shoulders and held her back.

We were no match for Ahmed. He had already

knocked Uncle Ben unconscious. There was no telling what he would do to us.

Holding onto Sari, I stared at him. What did he plan to do now?

It didn't take long to find out.

With surprising strength, he pulled Uncle Ben across the floor to one of the open mummy cases against the wall. Then he hoisted him over the side and shoved him into the case. Not even the slightest bit out of breath, Ahmed slid the lid closed over my unconscious uncle.

Then he turned to us. "You two—into that one." He pointed to an enormous mummy case on a tall pedestal next to Uncle Ben's. It was nearly as tall as I was, and at least three metres wide. It must have been built to hold a mummified person—and all of his or her possessions.

"Let us go!" Sari insisted. "Let us out of here. We won't tell anyone what happened. Really!"

"Please climb into the case," Ahmed insisted patiently. "We must wait for the tar to be ready."

"We're not going in there," I said.

I was shaking all over. I could feel the blood pulsing at my temples. I didn't even realize I was saying what I was saying. I was so scared, I didn't even hear myself.

I glanced at Sari. She stood defiantly with her arms crossed tightly over her chest. But despite her brave pose, I could see her chin trembling and her eyes beginning to fill with tears.

118

"Into the coffin," Ahmed repeated, "to await your fate. Khala will not be kept waiting. The ancient curse will be carried out in her name."

"No!" I cried angrily.

I stood on tiptoe and peered into the enormous mummy case. It smelled so sour in there, I nearly threw up.

The case was made of wood. It was warped and stained and peeling inside. In the flickering light, I was sure I saw dozens of insects crawling around in there.

"Get into the case *now*!" Ahmed demanded.

Sari climbed up over the side and lowered herself
into the ancient mummy case. She always had to
be first at everything. But this was one time I
didn't mind.

I hesitated, resting my hand on the rotting
wood on the side of the case. I glanced at the case
next to it, the case with Uncle Ben inside. It was
carved of stone, and the heavy stone lid was
closed, sealing it up tight.

Did Uncle Ben have any air in there? I wondered, gripped with fear. Was he able to breathe?

And, then, I thought glumly, what difference
does it make? All three of us are going to be dead
soon. All three of us are going to be mummies,
locked away in this hidden chamber forever.

"Get in—now!" Ahmed ordered, his dark eyes
burning into mine.

"I—I'm just a *kid*!" I cried. I don't know where
the words came from. I was so scared, I really
didn't know what I was saying.

An unpleasant sneer formed on Ahmed's face. "Many of the pharaohs were your age at death," he said.

I wanted to keep him talking. I had the desperate idea that if I could keep the conversation going, I could get us out of this mess.

But I couldn't think of anything to say. My brain just froze.

"Get in," Ahmed ordered, moving towards me menacingly.

Feeling totally defeated, I slid one leg over the side of the rotting coffin, raised myself up, and then dropped down beside Sari.

She had her head bowed, and her eyes shut tight. I think she was praying. She didn't glance up, even when I touched her shoulder.

The coffin lid began to slide over us. The last thing I saw were the red flames leaping up over the pit of tar. Then the lid closed us into complete blackness.

"Gabe . . ." Sari whispered a few seconds after the lid was closed. "I'm frightened."

For some reason, her confession made me snigger. She said it with such *surprise*. As if being frightened was a startling new experience.

"I'm too frightened to be frightened," I whispered back.

She grabbed my hand and squeezed it. Her hand was even colder and clammier than mine.

"He's insane," she whispered.

"Yeah. I know," I replied, still holding onto her hand.

"I think there are bugs in here," she said with a shudder. "I can feel them crawling on me."

"Me, too," I told her. I realized I was gritting my teeth. I always do that when I'm nervous. And now I was more nervous than I thought was humanly possible.

"Poor Daddy," Sari said.

The air in the coffin was already beginning to feel stuffy and hot. I tried to ignore the disgustingly sour smell, but it had crept into my nostrils, and I could even taste it. I held my breath to keep from gagging.

"We're going to suffocate in here," I said glumly.

"He's going to kill us before we can suffocate," Sari wailed. "Ow!" I could hear her slap at a bug on her arm.

"Maybe something will happen," I told her. Pretty hopeless. But I couldn't think of what else to say. I couldn't *think*.

"All I keep thinking about is how he's going to reach in and pull my brain out through my nose," Sari wailed. "Why did you have to tell me that, Gabe?"

It took me a while to reply. Then, all I could say was, "Sorry." I began to picture the same thing, and another wave of nausea swept over me.

"We can't just sit here," I said. "We have to

escape." I tried to ignore the thick, sour smell.

"Huh? How?"

"Let's try to push up the lid," I said. "Maybe if we both push together . . ."

I counted to three in a low whisper, and we both flattened our hands against the coffin top and pushed up as hard as we could.

No. The lid wouldn't budge.

"Maybe he's locked it or put something heavy on top of it," Sari suggested with a miserable sigh.

"Maybe," I replied, feeling just as miserable.

We sat in silence for a while. I could hear Sari breathing. She was sort of sobbing as she breathed. I realized my heart was racing. I could feel my head throbbing.

I imagined the long hook that Ahmed would use to pull our brains out of our heads. I tried to force the thought out of my mind, but it wouldn't go away.

I remembered being a mummy two Hallowe'ens ago, and how the costume had unravelled in front of my friends.

Little did I know then that I'd soon have a mummy costume that would *never* unravel.

Time passed. I don't know how long.

I realized I'd been sitting with my legs crossed. Now they were beginning to fall asleep. I uncrossed them and stretched them out. The mummy case was so big, Sari and I could both lie down if we wanted to.

But we were too tense and terrified to lie down.

I was the first to hear the scrabbling sound. Like something climbing quickly around inside the mummy case.

At first I thought it was Sari. But she grabbed my hand with her icy hand, and I realized she hadn't moved from in front of me.

We both listened hard.

Something near us, something right next to us, bumped the side of the case.

A mummy?

Was there a mummy in the case with us?

Moving?

I heard a soft groan.

Sari squeezed my hand so tightly, it hurt, and I uttered a sharp cry.

Another sound. Closer.

"Gabe—" Sari whispered, her voice tiny and shrill. "Gabe—there's *something* in here with us!"

It's not a mummy, I told myself.

It *can't* be.

It's a beetle. A very large beetle. Moving across the coffin door.

It's not a mummy. It's not a mummy.

The words repeated in my mind.

I didn't have too long to think about it. Whatever it was crept closer.

"Hey!" a voice whispered.

Sari and I both shrieked.

"Where *are* you two?"

We recognized the voice immediately.

"Uncle Ben!" I cried, swallowing hard, my heart pounding.

"Daddy!" Sari lunged over me to get to her father.

"But how?" I stammered. "How did you get in here?"

"Easy," he replied, squeezing my shoulder reassuringly.

125

"Daddy—I don't *believe* it!" Sari wailed. I couldn't see in the blackness of the closed coffin, but I think she was crying.

"I'm okay. I'm okay," he repeated several times, trying to calm her down.

"How did you get out of that case and into this one?" I asked, totally confused and amazed.

"There's an escape hatch," Uncle Ben explained. "A small opening with a doorway. The Egyptians built hidden doorways and escape hatches into many of their mummy cases. For the corpse's soul to be able to leave."

"Wow," I said. I didn't know *what* to say.

"Ahmed is so caught up in his ancient curse mumbo jumbo, he's forgotten about this little detail," Uncle Ben said. I felt his hand on my shoulder again. "Come on, you two. Follow me."

"But he's out there—" I started.

"No," Uncle Ben replied quickly. "He's slipped away. When I climbed out of my case, I looked for him. I didn't see him anywhere. Maybe he went somewhere else while waiting for the tar to get hot enough. Or maybe he decided to just leave us in the mummy cases to suffocate."

I felt a bug slither up my leg. I slapped at it, then tried to pull it out from inside the leg of my jeans.

"Out we go," Uncle Ben said.

I heard him groan as he turned in the enormous coffin. Then I could hear him crawling to the back.

I saw a small rectangle of light as he pushed open the hidden door in the back of the case. It was a very small escape hatch, just big enough for us to squeeze through.

I followed Uncle Ben and Sari out of the case, flattening myself to crawl out of the small opening, then dropping onto all fours on the chamber floor.

It took a while for my eyes to adjust to the brightness.

The red flames still danced over the pit of bubbling tar, casting eerie blue shadows on all four chamber walls. The mummies stood as before, frozen in place around the room, shadows flickering over their faceless forms.

As my eyes began to focus, I saw that Uncle Ben had an enormous, dark bruise on the side of his head. A wide ribbon of dried blood streaked down his cheek.

"Let's get out of here before Ahmed comes back," he whispered, standing between us, one hand on each of our shoulders.

Sari looked pale and trembly. Her lower lip was bleeding from her chewing on it so hard.

Uncle Ben started towards the rope ladder in the centre of the chamber, but then stopped.

"It'll take too long," he said, thinking out loud. "Come on. To the tunnel. Hurry."

All three of us started jogging towards the tunnel in the corner. Looking down, I saw that my stupid shoelace had come untied again. But there was *no way* I was going to stop to tie it!

We were about to get *out* of there!

A few seconds before, I had given up all hope. But now, here we were out of the mummy case and heading to freedom.

We were just a few metres in front of the tunnel entrance when the tunnel suddenly filled with orange light.

Then, from out of the tunnel, Ahmed emerged, holding a new torch in front of him, the flames revealing a startled look on his face.

"No!" Sari and I cried in unison.

All three of us skidded to a halt right in front of him.

"You cannot escape!" Ahmed said softly, quickly regaining his composure, his startled expression tightening to anger. "You *will not* escape!"

He thrust the torch towards Uncle Ben, who was forced to fall backwards, out of reach of the hissing flames. He landed hard on his elbows and cried out in pain.

His cry brought a grim smile to Ahmed's lips. "You have made Khala angry," he announced, raising the torch above his head and reaching for the dagger sheathed at his waist. "You will not join the other violators of this chamber."

Whew. I breathed a sigh of relief.

Ahmed had changed his mind. He wasn't going to turn us into mummies after all.

"All three of you will die in the tar pit," he declared.

Sari and I exchanged horrified glances. Uncle Ben had climbed back to his feet and put his arms around us. "Ahmed, can't we talk about this calmly and rationally as scientists?" he asked.

"To the tar pit," Ahmed ordered, thrusting the flaming torch angrily at us.

"Ahmed—*please!*" Uncle Ben cried in a whining, frightened tone I'd never heard from him before.

Ahmed ignored Uncle Ben's desperate pleas. Pushing the torch at our backs and gesturing with the long-bladed dagger, he forced us to make our way to the edge of the pit.

The tar was bubbling noisily now, making ugly popping and sucking sounds. The flames across the top were low and red.

I tried to pull back. It smelled so bad. And the steam coming off it was so hot, it made my face burn.

"One by one, you will jump," Ahmed said.

He was standing a few metres behind us as we stared down into the bubbling tar. "If you don't jump, I will be forced to push you."

"Ahmed—" Uncle Ben began. But Ahmed brushed the torch against Ben's back.

"It has come to me," Ahmed said solemnly. "The honour of carrying out Khala's wishes."

The tar fumes were so overwhelming, I thought I was going to faint. The pit started to tilt in front of me. I felt very dizzy.

I shoved my hands into my jeans pockets, to steady myself, I suppose. And my hand closed around something I had forgotten about.

The Summoner.

The mummy hand that I carry around everywhere.

I'm not sure why—I wasn't thinking clearly, if at all—but I pulled out the little mummy hand.

I spun round quickly. And I held the mummy hand up high.

I can't really explain what was going through my mind. I was so terrified, so overwhelmed with fear, that I was thinking a hundred things at once.

Maybe I thought the mummy hand would distract Ahmed.

Or interest him.

Or confuse him.

Or frighten him.

Maybe I was just stalling for time.

Or maybe I was unconsciously remembering

the legend behind the hand that the kid at the garage sale had told me.

The legend of why it was called The Summoner.

How it was used to call up ancient souls and spirits.

Or maybe I wasn't thinking anything at all.

But I spun round and, gripping it by its slender wrist, held the mummy hand up high.

And waited.

Ahmed stared at it.

But nothing happened.

I waited, standing there like the Statue of Liberty with the little hand raised high above my head.

It seemed as if I were standing like that for hours.

Sari and Uncle Ben stared at the hand.

Lowering the torch a few centimetres, Ahmed squinted at the mummy hand. Then his eyes grew wider, and his mouth dropped open in surprise.

He cried out. I couldn't understand what he was saying. The words were in a language I'd never heard. Ancient Egyptian, maybe.

He took a step back, his surprised expression quickly replaced by a wide-eyed look of fear.

"The hand of the Priestess!" he cried.

At least, that's what I *think* he cried— because I was suddenly distracted by what was going on behind him.

Sari uttered a low cry.

All three of us stared over Ahmed's shoulder in disbelief.

A mummy propped against the wall appeared to lean forward.

Another mummy, lying on its back, slowly sat up, creaking as it raised itself.

"No!" I cried, still holding the mummy hand high.

Sari and Uncle Ben were gaping wide-eyed as the vast chamber filled with motion. As the mummies creaked and groaned to life.

The air filled with the odour of ancient dust, of decay.

In the shadowy light, I saw one mummy, then another, straighten up, stand tall. They stretched their bandaged arms above their featureless heads. Slowly. Painfully.

Staggering, moving stiffly, the mummies lumbered forward.

I watched, frozen in amazement, as they climbed out of mummy cases, raised themselves from the floor, leaned forward, took their first slow, heavy steps, their muscles groaning, dust rising up from their dry, dead bodies.

They're dead, I thought.

All of them. Dead. Dead for so many years.

But now they were rising up, climbing from their ancient coffins, struggling towards us on their heavy, dead legs.

Their bandaged feet scraped across the chamber floor as they gathered in a group.

Scrape. Scrape. Scrape.

A dry, shuffling sound I knew I'd never forget.

Scrape. Scrape.

The faceless army approached. Bandaged arms outstretched, they lumbered towards us, creaking and groaning. Moaning softly with ancient pain.

Ahmed caught the astonishment on our faces and spun round.

He cried out again in that strange language as he saw the mummies advancing on us, scraping so softly, so deliberately, across the chamber floor.

And then, with a furious scream, Ahmed heaved the torch at the mummy in the lead.

The torch hit the mummy in the chest and bounced to the floor. Flames burst from the mummy's chest, immediately spreading over the arms and down the legs.

But the mummy kept advancing, didn't slow down, didn't react at all to the fire that was quickly consuming it.

Gaping in open-mouthed horror, babbling an endless stream of words in that mysterious language, Ahmed tried to run.

But he was too late.

The burning mummy lunged at him. The ancient figure caught Ahmed up by the throat, lifted him high above its flaming shoulders.

Ahmed uttered a high-pitched shriek of terror as the other mummies lumbered forwards. Moaning and wailing through their yellowed bandages they moved in to help their burning colleague.

They raised Ahmed high above their moaning heads.

And then held him over the burning tar pit.

Squirming and kicking, Ahmed uttered a piercing scream as they held him over the boiling, bubbling, steaming tar.

I closed my eyes. The heat and tar fumes swirled around me. I felt as if I were being swallowed up, pulled down into the steaming blackness.

When I opened my eyes, I saw Ahmed fleeing to the tunnel, staggering clumsily, shrieking in open-mouthed terror as he ran. The mummies remained by the pit, enjoying their victory.

I realized I was still holding the mummy hand over my head. I lowered it slowly, and gazed at Sari and Uncle Ben. They were standing beside me, their faces filled with confusion. And relief.

"The mummies—" I managed to utter.

"Look," Sari said, pointing.

I followed the direction of her gaze. The mummies were all back in place. Some were leaning, some propped at odd angles, some lying down.

They were exactly as they had been when I'd entered the chamber.

"Huh?" My eyes darted rapidly around the room.

Had they all moved? Had they raised themselves, stood up, and staggered towards us? Or had we imagined it all?

No.

We *couldn't* have imagined it.

Ahmed had gone. We were safe.

"We're okay," Uncle Ben said gratefully, throwing his arms around Sari and me. "We're okay. We're okay."

"We can go now!" Sari cried happily, hugging her dad. Then she turned to me. "You saved our lives," she said. She had to choke out the words. But she said them.

Then Uncle Ben turned his gaze on me and the object I still gripped tightly in front of me. "Thanks for the helping hand," Uncle Ben said.

We had an enormous dinner at a restaurant back in Cairo. It's a miracle any of us got any food down since we were all talking at once, chattering excitedly, reliving our adventure, trying to make sense of it all.

I was spinning The Summoner around on the table.

Uncle Ben grinned at me. "I had no idea *how* special that mummy hand was!"

He took it from me and examined it closely. "Better not play with it," he said seriously. "We must treat it carefully." He shook his head. "Some great scientist *I* am!" he exclaimed scornfully. "When I saw it, I thought it was just a toy, some kind of reproduction. But this hand may be my biggest discovery of all!"

"It's my good luck charm," I said, handling it gently as I took it back.

"You can say *that* again!" Sari said appreciatively. The nicest thing she'd ever said to me.

Back at the hotel, I surprised myself by falling asleep instantly. I thought I'd be up for hours, thinking about all that had happened. But I suppose all the excitement had exhausted me.

The next morning, Sari, Uncle Ben, and I had a big breakfast in the room. I had a plate of scrambled eggs and a bowl of Frosties. As I ate, I fiddled with the little mummy hand.

All three of us were feeling good, happy that our frightening adventure was over. We were kidding around, teasing each other, laughing a lot.

After I'd finished my cereal, I raised the little mummy hand high. "O, Summoner," I chanted in a deep voice, "I summon the ancient spirits. Come alive. Come alive again!"

"Stop it, Gabe," Sari snapped. She grabbed for the hand, but I swung it out of her reach.

"That isn't funny," she said. "You shouldn't fool around like that."

"Are you a chicken?" I asked, laughing at her. I could see that she was really frightened, which made me enjoy my little joke even more.

Keeping it away from her, I raised the hand high. "I summon thee, ancient spirits of the dead," I chanted. "Come to me. Come to me now!"

And there was a loud knock on the door.

All three of us gasped.

Uncle Ben knocked over his glass full of orange juice. It clattered onto the table and spilled.

I froze with the little hand in the air.

Another loud knock.

We heard a scrabbling at the door. The sound of ancient, bandaged fingers struggling with the lock.

Sari and I exchanged horrified glances.

I slowly lowered the hand as the door swung open.

Two shadowy figures lumbered into the room.

"Mum and Dad!" I cried.

I bet they were surprised at how glad I was to see them.

Let's Get Invisible!

I went invisible for the first time on my twelfth birthday.

It was all Whitey's fault, in a way. Whitey is my dog. He's just a mongrel, part terrier, part everything else. He's all black, so of course we named him Whitey.

If Whitey hadn't been sniffing around in the attic . . .

Well, maybe I'd better slow down a bit and start at the beginning.

My birthday was on a rainy Saturday. It was a few minutes before kids would start arriving for my birthday party, so I was getting ready.

Getting ready means brushing my hair.

My brother is always on my case about my hair. He gives me a hard time because I spend so much time in front of the mirror brushing it and checking on it.

The thing is, I just happen to have great hair. It's very thick and sort of a golden brown, and just a little bit wavy. My hair is my best feature, so I like to make sure it looks okay.

Also, I have very big ears. They stick out a lot. So I have to keep making sure that my hair covers my ears. It's important.

"Max, it's messed up at the back," my brother, Lefty said, standing behind me as I studied my hair in the front hall mirror.

His name is really Noah, but I call him Lefty because he's the only left-handed person in our family. Lefty was tossing a softball up and catching it in his left hand. He knew he wasn't supposed to toss that softball around in the house, but he always did it anyway.

Lefty is two years younger than me. He's not a bad kid, but he has too much energy. He always has to be tossing a ball around, drumming his hands on the table, hitting something, running around, falling down, leaping into things, wrestling with me. You get the idea. Dad says that Lefty has ants in his pants. It's a stupid expression, but it sort of describes my brother.

I turned and twisted my neck to see the back of my hair. "It is *not* messed up, liar," I said.

"Think fast!" Lefty shouted, and he tossed the softball at me.

I made a grab for it and missed. It hit the wall just below the mirror with a loud *thud*. Lefty and I held our breath, waiting to see if Mum had heard the sound. But she hadn't. I think she was in the kitchen doing something to the birthday cake.

"That was pretty stupid," I whispered to Lefty. "You almost broke the mirror."

"*You're* stupid," he said. Typical.

"Why don't you learn to throw right-handed? Then maybe I could catch it sometimes," I told him. I liked to tease him about being left-handed because he really hated it.

"You stink," he said, picking up the softball.

I was used to it. He said it a hundred times a day. I suppose he thought it was clever or something.

He's okay for a ten-year-old, but he doesn't have much of a vocabulary.

"Your ears are sticking out," he said.

I knew he was lying. I started to answer him, but the doorbell rang.

He and I raced down the narrow hallway to the front door. "Hey, it's *my* party!" I told him.

But Lefty got to the door first and pulled it open.

My best friend, Zack, pulled open the screen door and hurried into the house. It was starting to rain pretty hard, and he was already soaked.

He handed me a present, wrapped in silver paper, raindrops dripping off it. "It's a load of comics," he said. "I've already read 'em. The *X-Force* graphic novel is pretty cool."

143

"Thanks," I said. "They don't look too wet."

Lefty grabbed the present from my hand and ran into the living room with it. "Don't open it!" I shouted. He said he was just starting a pile.

Zack took off his Red Sox cap, and I got a look at his new haircut. "Wow! You look . . . different," I said, studying his new look. His black hair was shaved really short on the left side. The rest of it was long, brushed straight to the right.

"Did you invite any girls?" he asked me, "or is it just boys?"

"Some girls are coming," I told him. "Erin and April. Maybe my cousin Debra." I knew he liked Debra.

He nodded thoughtfully. Zack has a really serious face. He has these little blue eyes that always look far away, as if he's thinking hard about something. As if he's really deep.

He's quite an intense boy. Not nervous. Just keyed up. And very competitive. He has to win at everything. If he comes in second place, he gets really upset and kicks the furniture. You know the kind.

"What are we going to do?" Zack asked, shaking the water off his Red Sox cap.

I shrugged. "We were supposed to be in the back garden. Dad put the volleyball net up this morning. But that was before it started to rain. I got out some videos. Maybe we'll watch them."

The doorbell rang. Lefty appeared again from out of nowhere, pushed Zack and me out of the way, and made a dive for the door. "Oh, it's you," I heard him say.

"Thanks for the welcome." I recognized Erin's squeaky voice. Some kids call Erin "Mouse" because of that voice, and because she's tiny like a mouse. She has short, straight blonde hair, and I think she's cute, but of course I'd never tell anyone that.

"Can we come in?" I recognized April's voice next. April is the other girl in our group. She has curly black hair and dark, sad eyes. I always thought she was really sad, but then I realized that she's just shy.

"The party's tomorrow," I heard Lefty tell them.

"Huh?" Both girls uttered cries of surprise.

"No, it isn't," I shouted. I stepped into the doorway and shoved Lefty out of the way. I pushed open the screen door so Erin and April could come in. "You know Lefty's little jokes," I said, squeezing my brother against the wall.

"Lefty *is* a little joke," Erin said.

"You're stupid," Lefty told her. I pressed him into the wall a little harder, leaning against him with all my weight. But he ducked down and scooted away.

"Happy birthday," April said, shaking the rain from her curly hair. She handed me a

145

present, wrapped in Christmas wrapping paper. "It's the only paper we had," she explained, seeing me staring at it.

"Merry Christmas to you, too," I joked. The present felt like a CD.

"I forgot your present," Erin said.

"What is it?" I asked, following the girls into the living room.

"I don't know. I haven't bought it yet."

Lefty grabbed April's present out of my hand and ran to put it on top of Zack's present in the corner behind the sofa.

Erin plopped down on the white leather ottoman in front of the armchair. April stood at the window, staring out at the rain.

"We were going to barbecue hot dogs," I said.

"They'd be pretty soggy today," April replied.

Lefty stood behind the sofa, tossing his softball up and catching it one-handed.

"You're going to break that lamp," I warned him.

He ignored me, of course.

"Who else is coming?" Erin asked.

Before I could answer, the doorbell rang again. Lefty and I raced to the door. He tripped over his own trainers and went skidding down the hall on his stomach. So typical.

By two-thirty everyone had arrived, fifteen kids in all, and the party got started. Well, it didn't really get started because we couldn't

146

decide what to do. I wanted to watch the *Terminator* film I'd got out. But the girls wanted to play Twister.

"It's *my* birthday!" I insisted.

We compromised. We played Twister. Then we watched some of the *Terminator* video until it was time to eat.

It was a pretty good party. I think everyone had an okay time. Even April seemed to be having fun. She was usually really quiet and nervous-looking at parties.

Lefty spilled his Coke and ate his slice of chocolate birthday cake with his hands because he thought it was funny. But he was the only animal in the group.

I told him the only reason he was invited was because he was family and there was nowhere else we could stash him. He replied by opening his mouth up really wide so everyone could see his chewed-up chocolate cake inside.

After I'd opened my presents, I put the *Terminator* video back on. But everyone started to leave. I think it was about five o'clock. It looked much later. It was dark as night out, still storming.

My parents were in the kitchen clearing up. Erin and April were the only ones left. Erin's mother was supposed to pick them up. She phoned and said she'd be a little late.

Whitey was standing at the living room

window, barking his head off. I looked outside. I couldn't see anyone there. I grabbed him with both hands and wrestled him away from the window.

"Let's go up to my room," I suggested when I finally got the stupid dog quiet. "I've got a new Super Nintendo game I want to try."

Erin and April gladly followed me upstairs. They didn't like the *Terminator* film, for some reason.

The upstairs landing was pitch black. I clicked the light switch, but the overhead light didn't come on. "The bulb must have gone," I said.

My room was at the end of the hall. We made our way slowly through the darkness.

"It's spooky up here," April said quietly.

And just as she said it, the airing cupboard door swung open and, with a deafening howl, a dark figure leapt out at us.

As the girls cried out in horror, the howling creature grabbed me round the waist and wrestled me to the floor.

"Lefty—*let go*!" I screamed angrily. "You're not funny!"

He was laughing like a lunatic. He thought he was a riot. "Gotcha!" he cried. "I gotcha good!"

"We weren't scared," Erin insisted. "We knew it was you."

"Then why'd you scream?" Lefty asked.

Erin didn't have an answer.

I shoved him off me and climbed to my feet. "That was stupid, Lefty."

"How long have you been waiting in the airing cupboard?" April asked.

"A long time," Lefty told her. He started to get up, but Whitey ran up to him and began furiously licking his face. It tickled so much, Lefty fell onto his back, laughing.

"You scared Whitey, too," I said.

"No, I didn't. Whitey's cleverer than you lot."
Lefty pushed Whitey away.

Whitey began sniffing at the door across the hall.

"Where does that door lead to, Max?" Erin asked.

"To the attic," I told her.

"You've got an attic?" Erin cried. As if it was some kind of big deal. "What's up there? I *love* attics!"

"Huh?" I squinted at her in the dark. Sometimes girls are really weird. I mean, how could anyone *love* attics?

"Just a lot of old junk my grandparents left," I told her. "This house used to be theirs. Mum and Dad stored a lot of their stuff in the attic. We hardly ever go up there."

"Can we go up and take a look?" Erin asked.

"I suppose so," I said. "I don't think it's too big a thrill or anything."

"I love old junk," Erin said.

"But it's so dark . . ." April said softly. I think she was a bit scared.

I opened the door and reached for the light switch just inside. A ceiling light clicked on in the attic. It cast a pale yellow light down at us as we stared up the steep wooden stairs.

"See? There's light up there," I told April. I started up the stairs. They creaked under my feet. My shadow was really long. "You coming?"

"Erin's mum will be here any minute," April said.

"We'll just go up for a second," Erin said. She gave April a gentle push. "Come on."

Whitey trotted past us as we climbed the stairs, his tail wagging excitedly, his toenails clicking loudly on the wooden steps. About halfway up, the air grew hot and dry.

I stopped on the top step and looked around. The attic stretched on both sides. It was one long room, filled with old furniture, cardboard boxes, old clothes, fishing rods, stacks of yellowed magazines—all kinds of junk.

"Ooh, it smells so musty," Erin said, moving past me and taking a few steps into the vast space. She took a deep breath. "I love that smell!"

"You're definitely weird," I told her.

Rain drummed loudly against the roof. The sound echoed through the low room, a steady roar. It sounded as if we were inside a waterfall.

All four of us began walking around, exploring. Lefty kept tossing his softball up against the ceiling rafters, then catching it as it came down. I noticed that April stayed close to Erin. Whitey was sniffing furiously along the wall.

"Think there are mice up here?" Lefty asked, a devilish grin crossing his face. I saw April's eyes

151

widen. "Big fat mice who like to climb up girls' legs?" Lefty teased.

My little brother has a great sense of humour.

"Could we go now?" April asked impatiently. She started back towards the stairs.

"Look at these old magazines," Erin exclaimed, ignoring her. She picked one up and started flipping through it. "Check this out. The clothes these models are wearing are a riot!"

"Hey—what's Whitey doing?" Lefty asked suddenly.

I followed his gaze to the far wall. Behind a tall stack of boxes, I could see Whitey's tail wagging. And I could hear him scratching furiously at something.

"Whitey—come!" I commanded.

Of course he ignored me. He began scratching harder.

"Whitey, what are you scratching at?"

"Probably pulling a mouse apart," Lefty suggested.

"I'm outta here!" April exclaimed.

"Whitey?" I called. Stepping round an old dining room table, I made my way across the cluttered attic. I quickly saw that he was scratching at the bottom of a door.

"Hey, look," I called to the others. "Whitey's found a hidden door."

"Cool!" Erin cried, hurrying over. Lefty and April were right behind.

"I didn't know this was up here," I said.

"We've got to explore," Erin urged. "Let's see what's on the other side."

And that's when the trouble all began.

You can understand why I say it was all Whitey's fault, right? If that stupid dog hadn't started sniffing and scratching there, we might never have found the hidden attic room.

And we never would have discovered the exciting—and frightening—secret behind that wooden door.

"Whitey!" I knelt down and pulled the dog away from the door. "What's your problem, doggie?"

As soon as I moved him aside, Whitey lost all interest in the door. He trotted off and started sniffing another corner. Talk about your short attention span. But I suppose that's the difference between dogs and people.

The rain continued to pound down, a steady roar just above our heads. I could hear the wind whistling around the corner of the house. It was a real spring storm.

The door had a rusted latch about halfway up. It slid off easily, and the warped wooden door started to swing open before I even pulled at it.

The door hinges squeaked as I pulled the door towards me, revealing solid darkness on the other side.

Before I had got the door open halfway, Lefty scooted under me and darted into the dark room.

"A *dead body*!" he shrieked.

"Nooo!" April and Erin both cried out with squeals of terror.

But I knew Lefty's stupid sense of humour. "Nice try, Lefty," I said, and followed him through the doorway.

Of course he was just teasing.

I found myself in a small, windowless room. The only light came from the pale yellow ceiling light behind us in the middle of the attic.

"Push the door all the way open so the light can get in," I instructed Erin. "I can't see a thing in here."

Erin pushed open the door and slid a box over to hold it in place. Then she and April crept in to join Lefty and me.

"It's too big to be a cupboard," Erin said, her voice sounding even squeakier than usual. "So what is it?"

"Just a room, I suppose," I said, still waiting for my eyes to adjust to the dim light.

I took another step into the room. And as I did, a dark figure stepped towards me.

I screamed and jumped back.

The other person jumped back, too.

"It's a mirror, dork!" Lefty said, and started to laugh.

Instantly, all four of us were laughing. Nervous, high-pitched laughter.

It *was* a mirror in front of us. In the pale yellow light filtering into the small, square room, I could see it clearly now.

It was a big, rectangular mirror, about half a metre taller than me, with a dark wood frame. It rested on a wooden base.

I moved closer to it and my reflection moved once again to greet me. To my surprise, the reflection was clear. No dust on the glass, despite the fact that no one had been in here for ages.

I stepped in front of it and started to examine my hair.

I mean, that's what mirrors are for, right?

"Who would put a mirror in a room all by itself?" Erin asked. I could see her dark reflection in the mirror, a metre or so behind me.

"Maybe it's a valuable piece of furniture or something," I said, reaching into my jeans pocket for my comb. "You know. An antique."

"Did your parents put it up here?" Erin asked.

"I don't know," I replied. "Maybe it belonged to my grandparents. I just don't know." I ran the comb through my hair a few times.

"Can we go now? This isn't too thrilling," April said. She was still lingering reluctantly in the doorway.

"Maybe it was a carnival mirror," Lefty said, pushing me out of the way and making faces in the mirror, bringing his face just centimetres from the glass. "You know. One of those fun house mirrors that makes your body look as if it's shaped like an egg."

"You're already shaped like an egg," I joked, pushing him aside. "At least, your head is."

"You're a *rotten* egg," he snapped back. "You stink."

I peered into the mirror. I looked perfectly normal, not distorted at all. "Hey, April, come in," I urged. "You're blocking most of the light."

"Can't we just leave?" she asked, whining. Reluctantly, she moved from the doorway, taking a few small steps into the room. "Who cares about an old mirror, anyway?"

"Hey, look," I said, pointing. I had spotted a light attached to the top of the mirror. It was oval-shaped, made of brass or some other kind of metal. The bulb was long and narrow, almost like a fluorescent bulb, only shorter.

I gazed up at it, trying to make it out in the dim light. "How do you turn it on, I wonder."

"There's a chain," Erin said, coming up beside me.

Sure enough, a slender chain descended from the right side of the lamp, hanging down about twenty centimetres from the top of the mirror.

"Wonder if it works," I said.

"The bulb's probably dead," Lefty remarked. Good old Lefty. Always an optimist.

"Only one way to find out," I said. Standing on tiptoe, I stretched my hand up to the chain.

157

"Be careful," April warned.

"Huh? It's just a light," I told her.

Famous last words.

I reached up. Missed. Tried again. I grabbed the chain on the second try and pulled.

The light came on with a startlingly bright flash. Then it dimmed down to normal light. Very white light that reflected brightly in the mirror.

"Hey—that's better!" I exclaimed. "It lights up the whole room. Pretty bright, huh?"

No one said anything.

"I *said*, pretty bright, huh?"

Still silence from my companions.

I turned round and was surprised to find looks of horror on all three faces.

"Max?" Lefty cried, staring hard at me, his eyes practically popping out of his head.

"Max—where are you?" Erin cried. She turned to April. "Where'd he go?"

"I'm right here," I told them. "I haven't moved."

"*But we can't see you!*" April cried.

All three of them were staring in my direction with their eyes bulging and looks of horror still on their faces. But I could tell they were teasing.

"Give me a break, you lot," I said. "I'm not as stupid as I look. No way am I falling for your pathetic joke."

"But, Max—" Lefty insisted. "We're *serious*!"

"We can't see you!" Erin repeated.

Stupid, stupid, stupid.

Suddenly, the light started to hurt my eyes. It seemed to grow brighter. It was shining right in my face.

Shielding my eyes with one hand, I reached up with the other hand and pulled the chain.

The light went out, but the white glare stayed with me. I tried to blink it away, but I still saw large bright spots before my eyes.

"Hey—you're back!" Lefty cried. He stepped up and grabbed my arm and squeezed it, as if he were testing it, making sure I was real or something.

"What's your problem?" I snapped. I was starting to get angry. "I didn't fall for your stupid joke, Lefty. So why keep it up?"

To my surprise, Lefty didn't back away. He held onto my arm as if he were afraid to let go.

"We weren't joking, Max," Erin insisted in a low voice. "We really couldn't see you."

"It must have been the light in the mirror," April said. She was pressed against the wall next to the doorway. "It was so bright. I think it was just an optical illusion or something."

"It *wasn't* an optical illusion," Erin told her. "I was standing right next to Max. And I couldn't see him."

"He was invisible," Lefty added solemnly.

I laughed. "You lot are trying to scare me," I said. "And you're doing a pretty good job of it!"

"You scared *us!*" Lefty exclaimed. He let go of my arm and stepped up to the mirror.

I followed his gaze. "There I am," I said, pointing to my reflection. A strand of hair was poking up at the back of my head. I carefully slicked it down.

"Let's get out of here," April pleaded.

Lefty started to toss his softball up, studying himself in the mirror.

Erin made her way round to the back of the

mirror. "It's too dark back here. I can't see anything," she said.

She stepped round to the front and stared up at the oval-shaped lamp on top. "You disappeared as soon as you pulled the chain on that lamp."

"You're really serious!" I said. For the first time I began to believe they weren't joking.

"You were invisible, Max," Erin said. "Poof. You were gone."

"She's right," Lefty agreed, tossing the softball up and catching it, admiring his form in the mirror.

"It was just an optical illusion," April insisted. "Why are you all making such a big deal about it?"

"It *wasn't*!" Erin insisted.

"He clicked on the light. Then he disappeared in a flash," Lefty said. He dropped the softball. It bounced loudly on the hardwood floor, then rolled behind the mirror.

He hesitated for a few seconds. Then he went after it, diving for the ball in the darkness. A few seconds later, he came running back.

"You really were invisible, Max," he said.

"Really," Erin added, staring hard at me.

"Prove it," I told them.

"Let's *go*!" April pleaded. She had moved to the doorway and was standing half in, half out of the room.

"What do you mean *prove it*?" Erin asked,

talking to my dark reflection in the mirror.

"Show me," I said.

"You mean do what you did?" Erin asked, turning to talk to the real me.

"Yeah," I said. "You go invisible, too. Just like I did."

Erin and Lefty stared at me. Lefty's mouth dropped open.

"This is just silly," April called from behind us.

"I'll do it," Lefty said. He stepped up to the mirror.

I pulled him back by the shoulders. "Not you," I said. "You're too young."

He tried to pull out of my grasp, but I held onto him. "How about you, Erin?" I urged, wrapping my arms around Lefty's waist to keep him back from the mirror.

She shrugged. "Okay. I'll try, I suppose."

Lefty stopped struggling to get away. I loosened my grip a little.

We watched Erin step up in front of the mirror. Her reflection stared back at her, dark and shadowy.

She stood on tiptoe, reached up, and grabbed the lamp chain. She glanced over at me and smiled. "Here goes," she said.

The chain slipped from Erin's hand.

She reached up and grabbed it again.

She was just about to tug at it when a woman's voice interrupted from downstairs. "Erin! are you up there? April?"

I recognized the voice. Erin's mum.

"Yeah. We're up here," Erin shouted. She let go of the chain.

"Hurry down. We're late!" her mum called. "What are you doing up in the attic, anyway?"

"Nothing," Erin called down. She turned to me and shrugged.

"Good. I'm *outta* here!" April exclaimed, and hurried to the stairs.

We all followed her down, clumping noisily down the creaking wooden stairs.

"What were you doing up there?" my mum asked when we were all in the living room. "It's so dusty in that attic. It's a wonder you're not filthy."

"We were just messing about," I told her.

"We were playing with an old mirror," Lefty said. "It was fun."

"Playing with a mirror?" Erin's mum flashed my mum a bewildered glance.

"See you two," Erin said, pulling her mum to the door. "Great party, Max."

"Yeah. Thanks," added April.

They headed out of the front door. The rain had finally stopped. I stood at the screen door and watched them step around the puddles on the path as they made their way to the car.

When I turned back into the living room, Lefty was tossing the softball up to the ceiling, trying to catch it behind his back. He missed. The ball bounced up from the floor onto a side table, where it knocked over a large vase of tulips.

What a crash!

The vase shattered. Tulips went flying. All the water poured down onto the carpet.

Mum threw up her hands and said something silently up to the sky, the way she always does when she's been pushed too far about something.

Then she really got on Lefty's case. She started screaming: "How many times do I have to tell you not to throw that ball in the house?" Stuff like that. She kept it up for quite a while.

Lefty shrank into a corner and tried to make himself tinier and tinier. He kept saying he was sorry, but Mum was yelling so loud, I don't think she heard him.

I bet Lefty wanted to be invisible right at that moment.

But he had to stand and take his punishment.

Then he and I helped clear up the mess.

A few minutes later, I saw him tossing the softball up in the living room again.

That's the thing about Lefty. He never learns.

I didn't think about the mirror again for a couple of days. I was so busy with school and other things. Rehearsing for the spring concert. I'm only in the chorus, but I still have to go to every rehearsal.

I saw Erin and April at school a lot. But neither of them mentioned the mirror. I suppose maybe it had slipped their minds, too. Or maybe we all just shut it out of our minds.

It was pretty scary, if you stopped to think about it.

I mean, *if* you believed what they said happened.

Then that Wednesday night I couldn't get to sleep. I was lying there, staring up at the ceiling, watching the shadows sway back and forth.

I tried counting sheep. I tried shutting my eyes

really tight and counting backwards from one thousand.

But I was really wound up, for some reason. Not at all sleepy.

Suddenly I found myself thinking about the mirror up in the attic.

What was it doing up there? I asked myself. Why was it closed up in that hidden room with the door carefully latched?

Who did it belong to? My grandparents? If so, why would they hide it in that tiny room?

I wondered if Mum and Dad even knew it was up there.

I started thinking about what had happened on Saturday after my birthday party. I pictured myself standing in front of the mirror. Combing my hair. Then reaching for the chain. Pulling it. The flash of bright light as the lamp went on. And then . . .

Did I see my reflection in the mirror after the light went on?

I couldn't remember.

Did I see myself at all? My hands? My feet?

I couldn't remember.

"It was a joke," I said aloud, lying in my bed, kicking the covers off me.

It had to be a joke.

Lefty was always playing stupid jokes on me, trying to make me look bad. My brother was a joker. He'd always been a joker. He was never serious. Never.

So what made me think he was serious now?

Because Erin and April had agreed with him?

Before I realized it, I had climbed out of bed. Only one way to find out if they were serious or not, I told myself. I searched in the dark for my bedroom slippers. I buttoned my pyjama shirt which had come undone from all my tossing and turning.

Then, as silent as I could be, I crept out onto the landing.

The house was dark except for the tiny night-light down by the floor just outside Lefty's bedroom. Lefty was the only one in the family who ever got up in the middle of the night. He insisted on having a night-light in his room and one on the landing, even though I made fun of him about it as often as I could.

Now I was grateful for the light as I made my way on tiptoe to the attic stairs. Even though I was being so careful, the floorboards squeaked under my feet. It's just impossible not to make a noise in an old house like this.

I stopped and held my breath, listening hard, listening for any sign that I had been heard.

Silence.

Taking a deep breath, I opened the attic door, fumbled around till I found the light switch, and clicked on the attic light. Then I made my way slowly up the steep stairs, leaning all my weight on the banister, trying my hardest not to make the stairs creak.

It seemed to take forever to get all the way up. Finally, I stopped at the top step and gazed around, letting my eyes adjust to the yellow glare of the ceiling light.

The attic was hot and stuffy. The air was so dry, it made my nose burn. I had a sudden urge to turn round and go back.

But then my eyes stopped at the doorway to the small, hidden room. In our hurry to leave, we had left the door wide open.

Staring at the darkness beyond the open doorway, I stepped onto the landing and made my way quickly across the cluttered floor. The floorboards creaked and groaned beneath me, but I barely heard them.

I was drawn to the open doorway, drawn to the mysterious room as if being pulled by a powerful magnet.

I had to see the tall mirror again. I had to examine it, study it closely.

I had to know the truth about it.

I stepped into the small room without hesitating and walked up to the mirror.

I paused for a moment and studied my shadowy reflection in the glass. My hair was totally messed up, but I didn't care.

I stared at myself, stared into my eyes. Then I

took a step back to get a different view.

The mirror reflected my entire body from head to foot. There wasn't anything special about the reflection. It wasn't distorted or weird in any way.

The fact that it was such a normal reflection helped to calm me. I hadn't realized it, but my heart was fluttering like a nervous butterfly. My hands and feet were cold as ice.

"Calm down, Max," I whispered to myself, watching myself whisper in the dark mirror.

I did a funny little dance for my own benefit, waving my hands above my head and shaking my whole body.

"Nothing special about this mirror," I said aloud.

I reached out and touched it. The glass felt cool despite the warmth of the room. I ran my hand along the glass until I reached the frame. Then I let my hand wander up and down the wood frame. It also felt smooth and cool.

It's just a mirror, I thought, finally feeling more relaxed. Just an old mirror that someone stored up here long ago and forgot about.

Still holding onto the frame, I walked around to the back. It was too dark to see clearly, but it didn't seem too interesting back here.

Well, I might as well turn on the light at the top, I thought.

I returned to the front of the mirror. Standing

just centimetres back from it, I began to reach up for the lamp chain when something caught my eye.

"Oh!"

I cried out as I saw two eyes, down low in the mirror. Two eyes staring out at me.

My breath caught in my throat. I peered down into the dark reflection.

The two eyes peered up at me. Dark and evil eyes.

Uttering a cry of panic, I turned away from the mirror.

"Lefty!" I cried. My voice came out shrill and tight, as if someone were squeezing my throat.

He grinned at me from just inside the doorway.

I realized that it had been Lefty's eyes reflected in the mirror.

I ran over to him and grabbed him by the shoulders. "You scared me to death!" I half-screamed, half-whispered.

His grin grew wider. "You're stupid," he said.

I wanted to strangle him. He thought it was a riot.

"Why'd you sneak up behind me?" I demanded, giving him a shove back against the wall.

He shrugged.

"Well, what are you doing up here, anyway?" I spluttered.

I could still see those dark eyes staring out at me in the mirror. So creepy!

"I heard you," he explained, leaning back against the wall, still grinning. "I was awake. I heard you walk past my room. So I followed you."

"Well, you shouldn't be up here," I snapped.

"Neither should you," he snapped back.

"Get back downstairs and go to bed," I said. My voice was finally returning to normal. I tried to sound as if I meant business.

But Lefty didn't move. "Make me," he said. Another classic argument-winner.

"I mean it," I insisted. "Go back to bed."

"Make me," he repeated nastily. "I'll tell Mum and Dad you're up here," he added.

I hate being threatened. And he knows it. That's why he threatens me every hour of the day.

Sometimes I just wish I could pound him.

But we live in a non-violent family.

That's what Mum and Dad say every time Lefty and I start a fight. "Break it up, you two. We live in a non-violent family."

Sometimes non-violence can be really frustrating. Know what I mean?

This was one of those times. But I could see

172

that I wasn't going to get rid of Lefty so easily. He was determined to stay up in the attic with me and see what I was doing with the mirror.

My heart had finally slowed down to normal. I was starting to feel calmer. So I decided to stop arguing with him and let him stay. I turned back to the mirror.

Luckily, there wasn't *another* pair of eyes in there staring out at me!

"What are you doing?" Lefty demanded, stepping up behind me, his arms still crossed over his chest.

"Just checking out the mirror," I told him.

"Are you going to go invisible again?" he asked. He was standing right behind me, and his breath smelled sour, like lemons.

I turned and shoved him back a few steps. "Get out of my face," I said. "Your breath stinks."

That started another stupid argument, of course.

I was sorry I'd ever come up here. I should have stayed in bed, I realized.

Finally, I persuaded him to stand some way away from me. A major victory.

Yawning, I turned back to the mirror. I was starting to feel sleepy. Maybe it was because of the heat of the attic. Maybe it was because I was tired of arguing with my dopey brother. Or maybe it was because it was really late at night, and I was tired.

"I'm going to turn on the light," I told him, reaching for the chain. "Tell me if I go invisible again."

"No." He shoved his way right next to me again. "I want to try it, too."

"No way," I insisted, shoving back.

"Yes *way*." He pushed me hard.

I pushed back. Then I had a better idea. "How about if we *both* stand in front of the mirror, and I pull the light chain?"

"Okay. Go ahead." Standing centimetres in front of it, practically nose to nose with his reflection, Lefty stiffened until he was standing to attention.

He looked ridiculous, especially in those awful green pyjamas.

I stepped up beside him. "Here goes nothing," I said.

I stretched my hand up, grabbed the light chain, and pulled.

The light on top of the mirror flashed.

"Ow!" I cried out. The light was so bright, it hurt my eyes.

Then it quickly dimmed, and my eyes started to adjust.

I turned to Lefty and started to say something. I don't remember what it was. It completely flew out of my mind when I realized that Lefty had disappeared.

"L-Lefty?" I stammered.

"I'm right here," he replied. His voice sounded nearby, but I couldn't see him. "Max—where are *you*?"

"You can't see me?" I cried.

"No," Lefty said. "No, I can't."

I could smell his sour breath, so I knew he was there. But he was invisible. Gone. Out of sight.

So they *weren't* teasing! Erin, April, and Lefty had been telling the truth on Saturday after my birthday party. I really had gone invisible.

And now I was invisible again, along with my brother.

"Hey, Max," his voice sounded tiny, shaky. "This is weird."

"Yeah. It's weird, okay," I agreed. "You really can't see me, Lefty?"

"No. And I can't see myself," he said.

The mirror. I had forgotten to check in the mirror.

Did I have a reflection?

I turned and stared into the mirror. The light was pouring down from the top of the frame, casting a bright glare over the glass.

Squinting into the glare, I saw . . . *nothing*.

No me.

No Lefty.

Just the reflection of the wall behind us and the open doorway leading to the rest of the attic.

"We—we don't have reflections," I said.

"It's kind of cool," Lefty remarked. He grabbed my arm. I jumped in surprise.

"Hey!" I cried.

It felt creepy to be grabbed by an invisible person.

I grabbed him back. I tickled his ribs. He started to laugh.

"We still have our bodies," I said. "We just can't see them."

He tried to tickle me, but I danced away from him.

"Hey, Max, where'd you go?" he called, sounding frightened again.

"Try and find me," I teased, backing towards the wall.

"I—I can't," he said shakily. "Come back over here, okay?"

"No way," I said. "I don't want to be tickled."

"I won't," Lefty swore. "I promise."

I stepped back in front of the mirror.

"Are you here?" Lefty asked timidly.

"Yeah. I'm right beside you. I can smell your bad breath," I told him.

And he started to tickle me again. The little liar.

We wrestled around for a bit. It was just so strange wrestling with someone you couldn't see.

Finally, I pushed him away. "I wonder if we could go downstairs and still be invisible," I said. "I wonder if we could leave the house like this."

"And go and spy on people?" Lefty suggested.

"Yeah," I said. I yawned. I was starting to feel a little strange. "We could go and spy on girls and stuff."

"Cool," Lefty replied.

"Remember that old film Mum and Dad were watching on TV?" I asked him. "About the ghosts who kept appearing and disappearing all the time? They had a lot of fun scaring people.

You know, playing jokes on them, driving them crazy."

"But we're not ghosts," Lefty replied in a trembling voice. I think the idea kind of frightened him.

It frightened me, too!

"Could we go back to normal now?" Lefty asked. "I don't feel right."

"Me, neither," I told him. I was feeling very light. Kind of fluttery. Just . . . weird.

"How can we get back visible again?" he asked.

"Well, the last time, I just pulled the chain. I clicked the light off, and I was back. That's all it took."

"Well, do it," Lefty urged impatiently. "Right now. Okay?"

"Yeah. Okay." I started to feel pretty dizzy. Kind of light. As if I could float away or something.

"Hurry," Lefty said. I could hear him breathing hard.

I reached up and grabbed the light chain. "No problem," I told him. "We'll be back in a second."

I pulled the chain.

The light went out.

But Lefty and I didn't return.

"Max—I can't see you!" Lefty whined.

"I know," I replied quietly. I felt so frightened. I had chills running down my back, chills that wouldn't stop. "I can't see you, either."

"What happened?" Lefty cried. I could feel him tug at my invisible arm.

"I—I don't know," I stammered. "It worked before. I clicked off the light and I was back."

I gazed into the mirror. No reflection. Nothing. No me. No Lefty.

I stood there, staring at the spot where our reflections should be, frozen with fear. I was glad Lefty couldn't see me because I wouldn't want him to see how frightened I looked.

"Try it again, Max," he whined. "Please. Hurry!"

"Okay," I said. "Just try to stay calm, okay?"

"Stay calm? How?" Lefty wailed. "What if we *never* get back? What if *no one* can ever see us again?"

I suddenly felt so sick. My stomach just sort of heaved.

Get a grip, I told myself. You've *got* to keep calm, Max. For Lefty's sake.

I stretched up for the light chain, but it seemed to be out of my reach.

I tried again. Missed.

And then suddenly, I was back. And so was Lefty.

We could see each other. And we could see our reflections in the mirror.

"We're *back*!" We both shouted it in unison.

And then we both fell on the floor, laughing. We were so relieved. So happy.

"Ssshh!" I grabbed Lefty and shoved my hand over his mouth. I'd just remembered it was the middle of the night. "If Mum and Dad catch us up here, they'll kill us," I warned, whispering.

"Why did it take so long for us to come back?" Lefty asked, turning serious, gazing at his reflection.

I shrugged. "Beats me." I thought about it. "Maybe if you stay invisible longer, it takes longer for you to get back," I suggested.

"Huh? What do you mean?"

"The first time I went invisible," I told him, "it was only for a few seconds. And I came back instantly, as soon as I clicked off the light. But tonight—"

"We stayed invisible a lot longer. So it took

longer to come back. I get it," Lefty said.

"You're not as thick as you look," I said, yawning.

"*You* are!" he snapped back.

Feeling totally exhausted, I started to lead the way out of the tiny room, motioning for Lefty to follow me. But he hesitated, glancing back at his reflection in the mirror.

"We have to tell Mum and Dad about the mirror," he whispered thoughtfully.

"No way!" I told him. "No way are we telling them. If we tell them about it, they'll take it away. They won't let us use it."

He stared at me thoughtfully. "I'm not sure I *want* to use it," he said softly.

"Well, I do," I said, turning at the doorway to look back at it. "I want to use it just one more time."

"What for?" Lefty asked, yawning.

"To scare Zack," I said, grinning.

Zack couldn't come over until Saturday. As soon as he arrived, I wanted to take him up to the attic and give him a demonstration of the mirror's powers.

Mainly, I wanted to scare the life out of him!

But Mum insisted that we sit down for lunch first. Tinned chicken noodle soup and peanut butter-and-jam sandwiches.

I gulped my soup down as fast as I could, not

181

even bothering to chew the noodles. Lefty kept giving me meaningful glances across the table. I could see that he was as eager as I was to scare Zack.

"Where'd you get that haircut?" my mum asked Zack. She walked around the table, staring at Zack's head, frowning. I could tell she *hated* it.

"At Quick Cuts," Zack told her after swallowing a mouthful of peanut butter and jam. "You know. At the shopping centre."

We all studied Zack's haircut. I thought it was pretty cool. The way it was shaved so short on the left, then hung down long on the right.

"It's different, all right," my mum said.

We could all tell she hated it. But I suppose she thought she was covering up by calling it *different*. If I ever came home with a haircut like that, she'd *murder* me!

"What did your mum say about it?" she asked Zack.

Zack laughed. "Not much."

We all laughed. I kept glancing up at the clock. I was so eager to get upstairs.

"How about some chocolate cupcakes?" Mum asked when we'd finished our sandwiches.

Zack started to say yes, but I interrupted him. "Can we have dessert later? I'm full."

I pushed back my chair and got up quickly,

motioning for Zack to follow me. Lefty was already running to the stairs.

"Hey—where are you going so fast?" Mum called after us, following us into the hall.

"Uh . . . upstairs . . . to the attic," I told her.

"The attic?" She wrinkled her face, puzzled. "What's so interesting up there?"

"Uh . . . just a pile of old magazines," I lied. "They're funny. I want to show them to Zack." That was pretty fast thinking, for me. I'm usually not very quick at making up stories.

Mum stared at me. I don't think she believed me. But she turned back to the kitchen. "Have fun, boys. Don't get too dirty up there."

"We won't," I told her. I led Zack up the steep stairs. Lefty was already waiting for us in the attic.

It was about a hundred degrees hotter up there. I started to sweat the second I stepped into the room.

Zack stopped a few metres behind me and looked around. "It's just a lot of old junk. What's so interesting up here?" he asked.

"You'll see," I said mysteriously.

"This way," Lefty called eagerly, running to the little room against the far wall. He was so excited he dropped his softball. It rolled in front of him, and he tripped over it and fell face down on the floor with a *thud*.

"I *meant* to do that!" Lefty joked, climbing up

quickly and leaping after the ball, which had rolled across the floor.

"Your brother must be made of rubber or something," Zack laughed.

"Falling over is his hobby," I said. "He falls over about a hundred times a day." I wasn't exaggerating.

A few seconds later, the three of us were in the hidden room standing in front of the mirror. Even though it was a sunny afternoon, the room was as dark and shadowy as ever.

Zack turned from the mirror to me, a bewildered look on his face. "*This* is what you wanted to show me?"

"Yeah." I nodded.

"Since when are you into furniture?" he asked.

"It's an interesting mirror, don't you think?" I asked.

"No," he said. "Not really."

Lefty laughed. He bounced his softball off the wall and caught it.

I was deliberately taking my time. Zack was in for the surprise of his life, but I wanted to confuse him a little bit first. He was always doing things like that to me. He always acted as if he knew everything there was to know, and if I was good, he'd share a little bit of his knowledge with me.

Well, now I knew something he didn't know. I wanted to stretch this moment out, make it last.

But at the same time, I couldn't wait to watch the look on Zack's face when I disappeared right in front of his eyes.

"Let's go outside," Zack said impatiently. "It's too hot up here. I brought my bike. Why don't we cycle to the playground behind school, see who's there?"

"Maybe later," I replied, grinning at Lefty. I turned to my brother. "Should I show Zack our secret or not?"

Lefty grinned back at me. He shrugged.

"What secret?" Zack demanded. I knew he couldn't stand to be left out of anything. He couldn't *bear* it if anyone had a secret he didn't know about.

"What secret?" he repeated when I didn't answer.

"Show him," Lefty said, tossing up the softball.

I rubbed my chin, pretended to be thinking about it. "Well . . . okay." I motioned for Zack to stand behind me.

"You're going to make funny faces in the mirror?" Zack guessed. He shook his head. "Big deal!"

"No. That's not the secret," I told him. I stood in front of the mirror, admiring my reflection, which stared back at me in the glass.

"Watch!" Lefty urged, stepping up beside Zack.

"I'm watching. I'm watching," Zack said impatiently.

"I bet you I can disappear into thin air," I told Zack.

"Yeah. Sure," he muttered.

Lefty laughed.

"How much do you want to bet?" I asked.

"Two cents," Zack said. "Is this some kind of trick mirror or something?"

"Something like that," I told him. "How about ten dollars? Bet me ten dollars?"

"Huh?"

"Forget the bet. Just show him," Lefty said, bouncing up and down impatiently.

"I have a magic kit at home," Zack said. "I can do over a thousand tricks. But it's kids' stuff," he sneered.

"You don't have any tricks like this," I said confidently.

"Just get it over with so we can go outside," he grumbled.

I stood facing the middle of the mirror. "Ta*daa!*" I sang myself a short fanfare. Then I reached up and grabbed the light chain.

I pulled it. The lamp above the mirror flashed on, blindingly bright at first, then dimming as before.

And I was gone.

"Hey!" Zack cried. He stumbled backwards. He actually stumbled out of shock!

Invisible, I turned away from the mirror to enjoy his stunned reaction.

"Max?" he cried out. His eyes searched the room.

Lefty was laughing his head off.

"Max?" Zack sounded really worried. "Max? How'd you do that? Where *are* you?"

"I'm right here," I said.

He jumped at the sound of my voice. Lefty laughed even harder.

I reached out and took the softball from Lefty's hand. I glanced at the reflection in the mirror. The ball seemed to float in midair.

"Here. Catch, Zack." I tossed it at him.

He was so stunned, he didn't move. The ball bounced off his chest. "Max? How do you do this trick?" he demanded.

"It isn't a trick. It's real," I said.

"Hey, wait..." He got a suspicious look on his face. He ran around to the back of the mirror. I think he expected me to be hiding back there.

He looked very disappointed when he didn't see me. "Is there a trapdoor or something?" he asked. He walked back in front of the mirror, got down on his hands and knees, and started searching the floorboards for a trapdoor.

I leaned over and pulled his T-shirt up over his head.

"Hey—stop it!" he yelled, climbing angrily to his feet.

I tickled his stomach.

"Stop, Max." He squirmed away, thrashing his arms, trying to hit me. He looked really frightened now. He was breathing hard, and his face was bright red.

I pulled his T-shirt up again.

He jerked it down. "You're really invisible?" His voice rose up so high, only dogs could hear it. "Really?"

"Good trick, huh?" I said right in his ear.

He jumped and spun away. "What does it feel like? Does it feel weird?"

I didn't answer him. I crept out of the room and picked up a cardboard box just outside the door. I carried it up to the mirror. It looked great. A box floating all by itself.

"Put it down," Zack urged. He sounded really scared. "This is really freaking me out, Max. Stop it, okay? Come back so I can see you."

I wanted to torture him some more, but I could see he was about to lose patience. Besides, I was starting to feel weird again. Sort of dizzy and lightheaded. And the bright light was hurting my eyes, starting to blind me.

"Okay, I'm coming back," I announced. "Watch."

I leaned against the mirror and reached up for the chain. I suddenly felt very tired, very weak. It took all my strength to wrap my hand around the chain.

I had the strangest sensation that the mirror was pulling me, tugging me towards it, holding me down.

With a determined burst of strength, I pulled the chain.

The lamp went out. The room darkened.

"Where are you? I still can't see you!" Zack cried, his voice revealing panic.

"Just wait!" I told him. "It takes a few seconds. The longer I stay invisible, the longer it takes to come back." And then I added, "I think."

Staring into the blank mirror, waiting for my reflection to return, I suddenly realized that I didn't know anything at all about this mirror, about turning invisible. About coming back.

My mind suddenly whirred with all sorts of terrifying questions:

What made me think that reappearing was automatic?

What if you could only come back twice? And after the third time you went invisible, you stayed invisible?

What if the mirror was broken? What if it was locked away in this hidden room because it didn't work properly and it made people stay invisible forever?

What if I never came back?

No, that can't be, I told myself.

But the seconds were ticking by. And my body was still not visible.

I touched the mirror, rubbing my invisible hand over the smooth, cool glass.

"Max, what's taking so long?" Zack asked, his voice trembling.

"I don't know," I told him, sounding as frightened and upset as he did.

And then suddenly, I was back.

I was staring at my reflection in the mirror, watching intently, gratefully, as a wide smile crossed my face.

"Ta-*daaa!*" I sang my triumphant fanfare, turning to my still shaken friend. "Here I am!"

"Wow!" Zack exclaimed, and his mouth remained in a tight O of surprise and wonder. "Wow."

"I know," I said, grinning. "Pretty cool, huh?"

I felt very shaky, kind of trembly all over. My knees felt all weak and sweaty. You know the feeling.

But I ignored it. I wanted to enjoy my moment of glory. It wasn't often that I got to do something that Zack hadn't already done ten times.

"Amazing," Zack said, staring hard at the mirror. "I've *got* to try it!"

"Well..." I wasn't so sure I wanted Zack to do it. It was such a big responsibility. I mean, what if something went wrong?

"You've *got* to let me do it!" Zack insisted.

"Hey—where's Lefty?" I asked, glancing quickly around the small room.

"Huh? Lefty?" Zack's eyes searched, too.

"I was so busy being invisible, I forgot he was here," I said. And then I called, "Hey, Lefty?"

No reply.

"Lefty?"

Silence.

I walked quickly around to the back of the mirror. He wasn't there. Calling his name, I made my way to the door and peered out into the attic.

No sign of him.

"He was standing right here. In front of the mirror," Zack said, suddenly pale.

"Lefty?" I called. "Are you here? Can you hear me?"

Silence.

"Weird," Zack said.

I swallowed hard. My stomach suddenly felt as if I'd swallowed a stone.

"He was right here. Standing right here," Zack said in a shrill, frightened voice.

"Well, he's gone now," I said, staring at the dark, shadowy reflection of the mirror. "Lefty's gone."

"Maybe Lefty went invisible, too," Zack suggested.

"Then why doesn't he answer us?" I cried. I tried calling my brother again. "Lefty—are you here? Can you hear me?"

No reply.

I walked up to the mirror and angrily slapped the frame. "Stupid mirror."

"Lefty? Lefty?" Zack had his hands cupped around his mouth like a megaphone. He stood at the door to the little room, calling out into the attic.

"I don't believe this," I said weakly. My legs were shaking so much, I dropped down onto the floor.

And then I heard giggling.

"Huh? Lefty?" I jumped to my feet.

More giggling. Coming from behind the box I'd carried into the little room.

I lunged towards the box just as Lefty popped

up from behind it. "Gotcha!" he cried, and collapsed over the box, slapping the floor, laughing his head off.

"Gotcha! Gotcha both!"

"You little creep!" Zack screamed.

He and I both pounced on Lefty at the same time. I pulled his arm back until he screamed. Zack messed up his hair, then tickled him.

Lefty was screaming and laughing and squirming and crying all at the same time. I gave him a hard punch on the shoulder. "Don't ever do that again," I shouted angrily.

Lefty laughed, so I gave him a hard shove and climbed to my feet.

Zack and I, both breathing hard, both red in the face, glared angrily at Lefty. He was rolling around on the floor, covered in dust, still laughing like a lunatic.

"You scared us to death. You really did!" I exclaimed heatedly.

"I know," Lefty replied happily.

"Let's beat him up some more," Zack suggested, balling his hands into tight fists.

"Okay," I agreed.

"You'll have to catch me first!" Lefty cried. He was on his feet in a flash, and out of the door.

I chased after him, tripped over a stack of old clothes, and went flying headfirst to the floor. "Ow!" I banged my leg hard. The pain shot up through my body.

Pulling myself up slowly, I started after Lefty again. But voices on the attic staircase made me stop.

Erin's head popped up first. Then April appeared.

Lefty was sitting on the windowsill at the far end of the attic, red-faced and sweaty, catching his breath.

"Hey, how's it going?" I called to the two girls, brushing dust off my jeans, then straightening my hair with one hand.

"Your mum said you were up here," Erin explained, looking from Lefty to me.

"What are you lot *doing* up here?" April asked.

"Oh . . . just messing about," I said, casting an angry glance at my brother, who stuck his tongue out in reply.

April picked up an old *Life* magazine from a stack of yellowed magazines and began flipping through it. But the pages crumbled as she looked at them. "Yuck," she said, putting it down. "This stuff is so old."

"That's what attics are for," I said, starting to feel a little more normal. "Whoever heard of keeping *new* stuff in an attic?"

"Ha-ha," Lefty laughed sarcastically.

"Where's that mirror?" Erin asked, stepping into the centre of the room. "The one that made that weird optical illusion last Saturday."

"It wasn't an optical illusion," I blurted out. I

didn't really feel like messing about with the mirror any more. I'd had enough scares for one afternoon. But the words just tumbled out of me.

I can never keep a secret. It's a real character flaw.

"What do you mean?" Erin asked, very interested. She walked past me, heading for the open doorway of the little room.

"You mean that wasn't an optical illusion last week?" April asked, following her.

"No, not really," I said, glancing at Lefty, who hadn't budged from the windowsill across the large room. "The mirror has strange powers or something. It really can turn you invisible."

April laughed scornfully. "Yeah. Right," she said. "And I'm going to Mars in a flying saucer tonight after dinner."

"Give me a break," I muttered. I turned my eyes to Erin. "I'm serious."

Erin stared back at me, her face filled with doubt. "You're trying to tell us that you've gone in that room and become invisible?"

"I'm not *trying* to tell you," I replied heatedly. "I *am* telling you!"

April laughed.

Erin continued to stare at me, studying my face. "You *are* serious," she decided.

"It's a trick mirror," April told her. "That's all. That light on top of it is so bright, it makes your eyes go weird."

"Show us," Erin said to me.

"Yeah. Show them!" Lefty exclaimed eagerly. He jumped up from the windowsill and started running to the little room. "I'll go this time! Let me do it!"

"No way," I said.

"Let *me* try it," Erin volunteered.

"Hey, do you know who else is here?" I asked the girls, following them to the room. "Zack is here." I called to him. "Hey, Zack. Erin wants to go invisible. Think we should let her?"

I stepped into the room. "Zack?"

"Where's he hiding?" Erin asked.

I uttered a silent gasp.

The mirror light was on. Zack had gone.

"Oh, no!" I cried. "I don't believe this!"

Lefty laughed. "Zack's invisible," he told Erin and April.

"Zack—where are you?" I demanded angrily.

Suddenly, the softball floated up from Lefty's hand. "Hey, give that back!" Lefty shouted, and grabbed for it. But invisible Zack pulled the ball out of Lefty's reach.

Erin and April were both gaping at the ball as it floated in midair, their eyes bulging, their mouths wide open.

"Hi, girls," Zack called in a booming, deep voice that floated from in front of the mirror.

April screamed and grabbed Erin's arm.

"Zack, stop kidding around. How long have you been invisible?" I asked.

"I don't know." The ball flew back to Lefty, who dropped it and had to chase it out into the attic.

"How long, Zack?" I repeated.

"About five minutes, maybe," he replied. "When you chased after Lefty, I turned on the light and went invisible. Then I heard you talking to Erin and April."

"You've been invisible the whole time?" I asked, feeling really nervous and upset.

"Yeah. This is awesome!" he exclaimed. But then his tone grew doubtful. "I—I'm starting to feel kinda funny, though, Max."

"Funny?" Erin asked, staring at where Zack's voice seemed to be coming from. "What do you mean 'funny'?"

"Kinda dizzy," Zack replied weakly. "Everything's kind of breaking up. You know. Like a bad TV picture. I mean, you're starting to fade, to seem far away."

"I'm bringing you back," I said. And without waiting for Zack to reply, I reached up and pulled the light chain.

The light clicked off. Darkness seemed to roll into the room, filling the mirror with grey shadows.

"Where *is* he?" April cried. "It didn't work. He isn't back."

"It takes a while," I explained.

"How long?" April asked.

"I don't really know," I said.

"Why aren't I back?" Zack asked. He was standing right beside me. I could feel his breath on my neck. "I can't see myself." He sounded very frightened.

"Don't get tense," I said, forcing myself to sound calm. "You know it takes a while. Especially since you stayed invisible so long."

"But how long?" Zack wailed. "Shouldn't I be back by now? *You* were back by now. I remember."

"Just stay cool," I told him, even though my stomach was churning and my throat was dry.

"This is too scary. I *hate* this!" April moaned.

"Be patient," I repeated softly. "Everybody just be patient."

We all stared from the spot where we thought Zack was standing to the mirror, then back again.

"Zack, how do you feel?" Erin asked, her voice trembling.

"Weird," Zack replied. "As if I'm never coming back."

"Don't say that!" I snapped.

"But that's how I feel," Zack said sadly. "Like I'm never coming back."

"Just chill out," I said. "Everybody. Just calm down."

We stood in silence. Watching. Watching.

Waiting.

I had never been so frightened in all my life.

"Do something!" Zack, still invisible, pleaded. "Max—you've *got* to do something!"

"I—I'd better get Mum," Lefty stammered. He dropped the softball to the floor and started for the door.

"Mum? What could Mum do?" I cried in a panic.

"But I'd better get *somebody*!" Lefty declared.

At that moment, Zack shimmered back into view. "Wow!" He uttered a long, breathless sigh of relief and slumped to his knees on the floor.

"Yaaaay!" Erin cried happily, clapping her hands as we all gathered around Zack.

"How do you feel?" I asked, grabbing his shoulders. I think I wanted to know for sure that he was really back.

"I'm back!" Zack proclaimed, smiling. "That's all I care about."

"That was really scary," April said quietly,

200

hands shoved into the pockets of her white tennis shorts. "I mean, really."

"I wasn't scared," Zack said, suddenly changing his tune. "I knew there was no problem."

Do you *believe* this guy?

One second, he's whining and wailing, begging me to do something.

The next second, he's pretending he had the time of his life. Mister Confident.

"What did it feel like?" Erin asked, resting one hand on the wooden mirror frame.

"Awesome," Zack replied. He climbed unsteadily to his feet. "Really. It was totally awesome! I want to get invisible again before school on Monday so I can go and spy on the girls' cloakroom!"

"Zack, you're a pig!" Erin declared disgustedly.

"What's the point of being invisible if you can't spy on girls?" Zack asked.

"Are you sure you're okay?" I asked, genuinely concerned. "You look pretty shaky to me."

"Well, I started to feel a little strange at the end," Zack confessed, scratching the back of his head.

"How do you mean?" I asked.

"Well, as if I was being pulled away. Away from the room. Away from all of you."

"Pulled where?" I demanded.

He shrugged. "I don't know. I only know one thing." A smile began to form on his face, and his blue eyes seemed to light up.

Uh-oh, I thought.

"I only know one thing," Zack repeated.

"What?" I had to ask.

"I'm the new invisible champ. I stayed invisible longer than you. At least five minutes. Longer than anybody."

"But I haven't had a turn!" Erin protested.

"I don't *want* a turn!" April declared.

"Chicken?" Zack teased her.

"I think you're stupid for messing around with this," April said heatedly. "It isn't a toy, you know. You don't know anything about it. You don't know what it really does to your body."

"I feel fine!" Zack told her, and pounded his chest with both hands like a gorilla to prove it. He glanced at the dark mirror. "I'm ready to go back—even longer."

"I want to get invisible and go outside and play tricks on people," Lefty said enthusiastically. "Can I go next, Max?"

"I—I don't think so . . ."

I was thinking about what April had said. We really were messing around with something that could be dangerous, something we didn't know anything about.

"Max has to go again," Zack said, slapping me

hard on the back, nearly sending me sprawling against the mirror. "To beat my record." He grinned at me. "Unless you're chicken, too."

"I'm *not* chicken!" I insisted. "I just think—"

"You're chicken," Zack accused, laughing scornfully. He started clucking loudly, flapping his arms like a chicken.

"*I'm* not chicken. Let *me* go," Lefty pleaded. "I can break Zack's record."

"It's my turn," Erin insisted. "You boys have all had turns. I haven't gone once yet!"

"Okay," I said with a shrug. "You go first, Erin. Then me." I was glad Erin was so eager to do it. I really didn't feel like getting invisible again just yet.

To be honest, I felt very fluttery and nervous.

"Me next!" Lefty insisted. "Me next! Me next!" He started chanting the words over and over.

I clamped my hand over his mouth. "Maybe we should all go downstairs," I suggested.

"Chicken?" Zack teased. "You're chickening out?"

"I don't know, Zack," I replied honestly. "I think—" I saw Erin staring at me. Was that disappointment on her face? Did Erin think I was a chicken, too?

"Okay," I said. "Go ahead, Erin. You go. Then I'll go. Then Lefty. We'll all beat Zack's record."

Erin and Lefty clapped. April groaned and rolled her eyes. Zack grinned.

It's no big deal, I told myself. I've done it three times already. It's perfectly painless. And if you just stay cool and wait patiently, you come right back the way you were.

"Does anyone have a watch?" Erin asked. "We need to keep time so I know what time I have to beat."

I could see that Erin was really into this competition.

Lefty seemed really excited, too. And of course Zack would compete in *anything*.

Only April was unhappy about the whole thing. She walked silently to the back of the room and sat down on the floor with her back against the wall, her arms folded over her knees.

"Hey, you're the only one with a watch," Erin called to April. "So you be the timer, okay?"

April nodded without enthusiasm. She raised her wrist and stared down at her watch. "Okay. Get ready."

Erin took a deep breath and walked up to the mirror. She closed her eyes, reached up, and tugged the light chain.

The light came on with a bright flash. Erin disappeared.

"Oh, wow!" she cried. "This is really cool!"

"How does it feel?" April called from behind us, her eyes glancing from the mirror to her watch.

"I don't feel any different at all," Erin said. "What a great way to lose weight!"

"Fifteen seconds," April announced.

Lefty's hair suddenly stood straight up in the air. "Cut it out, Erin!" he shouted, twisting away from her invisible hands.

We heard Erin laugh from somewhere near Lefty.

Then we heard her footsteps as she walked out of the room and into the attic. We saw an old coat rise up into the air and dance around. After it dropped back into its box, we saw an old magazine fly up and its pages appear to flip rapidly.

"This is so much fun!" Erin called to us. The magazine dropped back onto the stack. "I can't *wait* to go outside like this and really scare people!"

"One minute," April called. She hadn't moved from her sitting position against the wall.

Erin moved around the attic for a while, making things fly and float. Then she returned to the little room to admire herself in the mirror.

"I'm really invisible!" we heard her exclaim excitedly. "Just like in a film or something!"

"Yeah. Great special effects!" I said.

"Three minutes," April announced.

Erin continued to enjoy herself until about four minutes had passed. Then her voice suddenly changed. She started to sound doubtful, frightened.

"I—I don't like this," she said. "I feel pretty strange."

April jumped to her feet and ran up to me. "Bring her back!" she demanded. "Hurry!"

I hesitated.

"Yes. Bring me back," Erin said weakly.

"But you haven't beaten my record!" Zack declared. "Are you sure—?"

"Yes. Please. I don't feel right." Erin suddenly sounded far away.

I stepped up to the mirror and pulled the chain. The light clicked off.

We waited for Erin to return.

"How do you feel?" I asked.

"Just...weird," she replied. She was standing right next to me, but I still couldn't see her.

It took nearly three minutes for Erin to reappear. Three very tense minutes.

When she shimmered back into view, she shook herself like a dog shaking water off after a bath. Then she grinned at us reassuringly. "I'm okay. It was really terrific. Except for the last few seconds."

"You didn't beat my record," Zack reported happily. "You came so close. But you wimped out. Just like a girl."

"Hey—" Erin gave Zack a hard shove. "Stop being such a jerk."

"But you only had fifteen seconds to go, and you wimped out!" Zack told her.

"I don't care," Erin insisted, frowning angrily at him. "It was really cool, anyway. I'll beat your record next time, Zack."

"I'm going to be the winner," Lefty announced. "I'm going to stay invisible for a whole day. Maybe two!"

"Whoa!" I cried. "That might be dangerous, Lefty."

"It's Max's turn next," Zack announced. "Unless you want to forfeit a go, Max."

"No way," I said, glancing at Erin. Reluctantly, I stepped up to the mirror and took a deep breath. "Okay, Zack, say goodbye to your record," I said, trying to sound calm and confident.

I didn't really want to do it, I admitted to myself. But I didn't want to look like a chicken in front of the others. For one thing, if I did wimp out, I knew that Lefty would only remind me of it twenty or thirty times a day for the rest of my life.

So I decided to go ahead and do it.

"One thing," I said to Zack. "When I call out 'ready', that means I want to come back. So when I say 'ready', you pull the light chain as fast as you can—okay?"

"Gotcha," Zack replied, his expression turning serious. "Don't worry. I'll bring you back

207

instantly." He snapped his fingers. "Like that. Remember, Max, you've got to beat five minutes."

"Okay. Here goes," I said, staring at my reflection in the mirror.

I suddenly had a bad feeling about this.

A really bad feeling.

But I reached up and pulled on the light anyway.

When the glaring light dimmed, I stared hard into the mirror.

The reflections were bright and clear. Against the back wall, I could see April, slumped on the floor, staring intently at her watch.

Lefty stood near the wall to the right, gaping at the spot where I had stood, a silly grin on his face. Zack stood next to him, his arms crossed over his chest, also staring into the mirror. Erin leaned against the wall to the left. Her eyes were on the light above the mirror frame.

And where was I?

Standing right in front of the mirror. Right in the centre of it. Staring at their reflections. Staring at the spot where my reflection should be.

Only it wasn't.

I felt perfectly normal.

Experimenting, I kicked the floor. My invisible trainers made the usual scraping sound.

I grabbed my left arm with my right hand and squeezed it. It felt perfectly normal.

"Hi, everyone," I said. I sounded the same as ever.

Only I was invisible.

I glanced up at the light, casting a yellow rectangle down onto the mirror. What was the light's power? I wondered.

Did it do something to your molecules? Make them break apart somehow so you couldn't be seen?

No. That wasn't a good theory. If your molecules broke up, you'd *have* to feel it. And you wouldn't be able to kick the floor, or squeeze your arm, or talk.

So what did the light do? Did it cover you up, somehow? Did the light form some kind of blanket? A covering that hid you from yourself and everyone else?

What a mystery!

I had the feeling I'd never be able to work it out, never know the answer.

I turned away from the light. It was starting to hurt my eyes.

I closed my eyes, but the bright glare stayed with me. Two white circles that refused to dim.

"How do you feel, Max?" Erin's voice broke into my thoughts.

"Okay, I suppose," I said. My voice sounded weird to me, sort of far away.

210

"Four minutes, thirty seconds," April announced.

"The time went so fast," I said.

At least, I thought I said it. I realized I couldn't tell if I was saying the words or just thinking them.

The bright yellow light glowed even brighter.

I had the sudden feeling that it was pouring over me, surrounding me.

Pulling me.

"I—I feel weird," I said.

No response.

Could they hear me?

The light folded over me. I felt myself begin to float.

It was a frightening feeling. As if I were losing control of my body.

"Ready!" I screamed. "Zack—ready! Can you hear me, Zack?"

It seemed to take Zack hours to reply. "Okay," I heard him say. His voice sounded so tiny, so far away.

Miles and miles away.

"Ready!" I cried. "Ready!"

"Okay!" Again I heard Zack's voice.

But the light was so bright, so blindingly bright. Waves of yellow light rolling over me. Ocean waves of light.

Sweeping me away with it.

"Pull the chain, Zack!" I screamed. At least,

211

I *think* I was screaming.

The light was tugging me so hard, dragging me away, far, far away.

I knew I would float away. Float forever.

Unless Zack pulled the chain and brought me back.

"Pull it! Pull it! *Please*—pull it!"

"Okay."

I saw Zack step up to the mirror.

He was blurred in shadows. He stepped through dark shadows, on the other side of the light.

So far away.

I felt so feather light.

I could see Zack in the shadows. He jumped up. He grabbed the lamp chain.

He pulled it down hard.

The light didn't click off. It glowed even brighter.

And then I saw Zack's face fill with horror.

He held up his hand. He was trying to show me something.

He had the chain in his hand.

"Max, the chain—" he stammered. "It's broken off. I can't turn off the light!"

Beyond the shimmering wall of yellow light, Zack's outstretched hand came clearly into my view. The dark chain dangled from his hand like a dead snake.

"It broke off!" he was crying, sounding very alarmed.

I stared through the light at the chain, feeling myself hovering beside Zack, floating, fading.

Somewhere far in the distance, April was screaming. I couldn't make out her words.

Lefty stood frozen in the middle of the room. It seemed strange to see him standing so still. He was always moving, always bouncing, running, falling. But now he, too, stood staring at the chain.

The light shimmered brighter.

I saw sudden movement.

Someone was crossing the room. I struggled to focus.

It was Erin. She was dragging a large cardboard box across the floor. The scraping sound it made seemed so far away.

Feeling myself being pulled away, I struggled to watch her. She pulled the box next to the mirror. Then she climbed up onto it.

I saw her reaching up to the lamp. I saw her staring into the light.

I wanted to ask her what she was doing, but I was too far away. I was floating off. I felt so light, so feather light.

And as I floated, the yellow light spread over me. It covered me. Pulled me.

And then with startling suddenness it was gone.

And all was darkness.

"I did it!" Erin proclaimed.

I heard her explaining to the others. "There was a little bit of chain left up there. I pulled it and turned off the light." Her eyes darted frantically around the room, searching for me. "Max—are you okay? Can you hear me?"

"Yeah. I'm okay," I replied.

I felt better. Stronger. Closer.

I stepped up to the mirror and searched for my reflection.

"That was scary," Lefty said behind me.

"I can feel myself coming back," I told them.

"What was his time?" Zack asked April.

April's features were tight with worry. Sitting

214

against the wall, she looked pale and uncomfortable. "Five forty-eight," she told Zack. And then quickly added, "I really think this stupid competition is a big mistake."

"You beat my record!" Zack groaned, turning to where he thought I was standing. "I don't believe it! Almost six minutes!"

"I'm going for longer than that," Lefty said, pushing past Zack and stepping up to the mirror.

"We have to fix the chain first," Erin told him. "It's too hard to keep climbing up on a box to pull that little piece of chain."

"I felt pretty strange at the end," I told them, still waiting to reappear. "The light grew brighter and brighter."

"Did you feel as if you were being pulled away?" Erin asked.

"Yeah," I replied. "As if I was fading or something."

"That's how *I* started to feel," Erin cried.

"This is just so dangerous," April said, shaking her head.

I popped back.

My knees buckled and I almost fell to the floor. But I grabbed the mirror and held myself up. After a few seconds, my legs felt strong again. I took a few steps and regained my balance.

"What if we couldn't turn off the light?" April demanded, climbing to her feet, brushing the dust off the back of her jeans with both hands.

"What if the chain completely broke and the light stayed on? What then?"

I shrugged. "I don't know."

"You broke my record," Zack said, making a disgusted face. "That means I have to have another turn."

"No way!" Lefty shouted. "It's my turn next!"

"None of you are listening to me!" April cried. "Answer my question. What if one of you is invisible and the light won't go out!"

"That won't happen," Zack told her. He pulled a string from his pocket. "Here. I'm going to tie this tightly to the chain." He climbed up onto the box and began to work. "Pull the string. The light goes out," he told April. "No problem."

"Which one of us is going to be first to get invisible and then go outside?" Erin asked.

"I want to go to school and terrorize Miss Hawkins," Lefty said, sniggering. Miss Hawkins is his social studies teacher. "She's been terrorizing me ever since school started. Wouldn't it be cool just to sneak up behind her and say, 'Hi, Miss Hawkins'? And she'd turn round and there'd be no one there?"

"That's the best you can do?" Erin scoffed. "Lefty, where's your imagination? Don't you want to make the chalk fly out of her hand, and the blackboard rubbers fly across the room, and the wastebasket spill everything out on her desk, and her yoghurt fly into her face?"

216

"Yeah! That *would* be cool!" exclaimed Lefty.

I laughed. It was a funny idea. The four of us could go around, completely invisible, doing whatever we wanted. We could wreck the whole school in ten minutes! Everyone would be screaming and running out of the doors. What a laugh!

"We can't do it now," Lefty said, interrupting my thoughts. "Because it's my turn to beat the record." He turned back to April, who was standing tensely by the door, pulling at a strand of her black hair, a worried frown on her face. "Ready to time me?"

"I suppose so," she replied, sighing.

Lefty pushed me out of the way. He stepped in front of the mirror, stared at his reflection, and reached for the string.

"Lefty!" a voice shouted from behind us. "Lefty!"

Startled by the interruption, I uttered an alarmed cry. Lefty stepped back from the mirror.

"Lefty, tell your brother his friends have to leave! It's dinnertime. Grammy and Poppy are here. They're eager to see you!"

It was Mum, calling up from downstairs.

"Okay, Mum. We'll be right down!" I shouted quickly. I didn't want her to come up.

"But that's not *fair*!" Lefty whined. "I didn't get my turn."

He stepped back up to the mirror and angrily grabbed for the string again.

"Put it down," I told him sternly. "We have to go downstairs. Quick. We don't want Mum or Dad coming up here and seeing the mirror, do we?"

"Okay, okay," Lefty grumbled. "But next time, I get to go first."

218

"And then me," Zack said, heading for the stairs. "I get a chance to beat your record, Max."

"Everybody, stop talking about it," I warned as we all clomped down the stairs. "Talk about something else. We don't want them to overhear anything."

"Can we come over tomorrow?" Erin asked. "We could start up the contest again."

"I'm busy tomorrow," April said.

"We can't do it tomorrow," I replied. "We're visiting my cousins in Springfield." I was sorry they'd reminded me. My cousins have this humongous sheepdog that likes to run through the mud and then jump on me and wipe its hairy paws all over my clothes. Not my idea of a good time.

"There's no school on Wednesday," Zack said. "Teachers' meetings, I think. Maybe we could all come over on Wednesday."

"Maybe," I said.

We stepped into the hallway. Everyone stopped talking. I could see that my grandparents and parents were already sitting at the dining room table. Grammy and Poppy liked to eat promptly. If their dinner came one minute late, it made them really bad tempered for the rest of the day.

I ushered my friends out quickly, reminding them not to tell anyone about what we'd been doing. Zack asked again if Wednesday would be okay, and again I told him I wasn't sure.

Getting invisible was really exciting, really thrilling. But it also made me nervous. I wasn't sure I wanted to do it again so soon.

"Please!" Zack begged. He couldn't wait to get invisible again and beat my record. He couldn't stand it that he wasn't the champ.

I closed the front door behind them and hurried to the dining room to greet my grandparents. They were already slurping their soup when I came in.

"Hi, Grammy. Hi, Poppy." I walked around the table and gave them each a kiss on the cheek. Grammy smelled of oranges. Her cheek felt soft and mushy.

Grammy and Poppy are the names I gave them when I was a kid. It's really embarrassing to call them that now, but I still do. I don't have much choice. They even call *each other* Grammy and Poppy!

They look alike, almost like brother and sister. I suppose that's what happens when you've been married a hundred years. They both have long, thin faces and short white hair. They both wear thick glasses with silver wire frames. They're both really skinny. And they both have sad eyes and sad expressions.

I didn't feel like sitting there at dinner and making small talk with them today. I was still really stunned about what we'd been doing all afternoon.

Being invisible was just so weird and exciting.

I wanted to be by myself and think about it. You know. Try to relive it, relive what it felt like.

A lot of times after I've done something really exciting or interesting, I like to go up to my room, lie down on my bed, and just think about it. Analyse it. Tear it apart.

Dad says I have a very scientific mind. I think he's right.

I walked over to my place at the table.

"You're looking much shorter," Poppy said, wiping his mouth with his serviette. That was one of his standard jokes. He said it every time he saw me.

I forced a laugh and sat down.

"Your soup must be ice cold by now," Grammy said, clicking her tongue. "Nothing I hate more than cold soup. I mean, what's the point of having soup if it isn't steaming hot?"

"It tastes okay," I said, taking a spoonful.

"We had some delicious cold soup last summer," Poppy said. He loved to contradict Grammy and start arguments with her. "Strawberry soup, remember? You wouldn't want *that* hot, would you?"

"It wasn't strawberry," Grammy told him,

frowning. "It wasn't even soup. It was some kind of fancy yoghurt."

"No, it wasn't," Poppy insisted. "It was definitely cold soup."

"You're wrong, as usual," Grammy snapped.

This could get ugly, I thought. "What kind of soup is this?" I asked, trying to stop their arguing.

"Chicken noodle," Mum answered quickly. "Didn't you recognize it?"

"Poppy and I had soup a few weeks ago that we couldn't recognize," my grandmother said, shaking her head. "I had to ask the waiter what it was. It didn't look like what we'd ordered at all. Some kind of potato-leek soup, wasn't it, Poppy?"

Poppy took a long time swallowing some noodles. "No. Tomato," he answered.

"Where's your brother?" Dad asked, staring at the empty chair next to me.

"Huh?" I reacted with surprise. I had been so busy listening to my grandparents' silly soup arguments, I had forgotten all about Lefty.

"His soup is getting cold," Poppy said.

"You'll have to heat it up for him," Grammy said, tutting again.

"So where is he?" Dad asked.

I shrugged. "He was right behind me," I said. I turned towards the dining room doorway and shouted, "Lefty! *Lef-teeeee!*"

"Don't shout at the table," Mum scolded. "Get up and go and find him."

"Is there any more soup?" Poppy asked. "I didn't really get enough."

I put down my serviette and started to get up. But before I was out of my chair, I saw Lefty's soup bowl rise up into the air.

Oh no! I thought.

I knew instantly what was happening.

My idiot brother had made himself invisible, and now he thought he was being funny, trying to scare the daylights out of everyone at the table.

The soup bowl floated up over Lefty's place.

I stood up and lunged for it and pulled it down as fast as I could.

"Get out!" I whispered loudly to Lefty.

"What did you say?" my mum asked, gaping at me.

"I said I'm getting out and going to find Lefty," I told her, thinking quickly.

"Get out—now!" I whispered to Lefty.

"Stop talking about finding him. Just go and do it," my mum said impatiently.

I stood up just as my stupid, invisible brother raised his water glass. The glass floated up over the table.

I gasped and grabbed for it.

But I grabbed too hard. I jerked the glass, and water spilled all over the table.

"Hey!" Mum screamed.

I pulled the glass down to its place.

Then I looked up. Dad was glaring at me, his eyes burning angrily into mine.

He knows, I thought, a heavy feeling of dread sweeping over me.

He saw what just happened, and he knows.

Lefty has spoiled it for everyone.

Dad glared angrily across the table at me.

I waited for him to say, "Max, why is your brother invisible?" But instead, he yelled, "Stop fooling about, Max. We don't appreciate your comedy act. Just get up and find your brother."

I was so relieved. Dad hadn't realized what was really happening, after all. He thought I was just playing up.

"Is there seconds of the soup?" I heard Poppy ask again as I gratefully pushed away from the table and hurried out of the dining room.

"You've had enough," Grammy scolded.

"No, I haven't!"

I made my way quickly through the living room, taking long strides, climbed to the second floor, and stopped in the hallway at the door to the attic stairs. "Lefty!" I whispered. "I hope you've followed me."

"I'm here," Lefty whispered back. I couldn't see him, of course, but he was right beside me.

"What's the big idea?" I demanded angrily. I wasn't angry. I was *furious*. "Are you trying to win the stupid championship?"

Lefty didn't care that I was upset. He started to giggle.

"Shut up!" I whispered. "Just shut up! You really are a nerd!"

I clicked on the attic light and stomped angrily up the stairs. I could hear his trainers stomping up behind me.

He was still giggling at the top of the stairs. "I win!" he declared. I felt a hand slap me hard on the back.

"Stop it, idiot!" I screamed, storming into the little room that housed the mirror. "Don't you realize you nearly spoiled it for everybody?"

"But I win!" he repeated gleefully.

The lamp over the mirror was shining brightly, the reflection glaring sun-yellow in the mirror.

I really couldn't believe Lefty. He was usually a pretty selfish kid. But not *this* selfish!

"Don't you realize the trouble you could have got us into?" I cried.

"I win! I win!" he chanted.

"Why? How long have you been invisible?" I asked. I stepped up to the mirror and pulled the string. The light went out. The glare remained in my eyes.

"Ever since you lot went downstairs," Lefty, still invisible, bragged.

"That's almost ten minutes!" I exclaimed.

"I'm the champ!" Lefty proclaimed.

I stared into the mirror, waiting for him to reappear.

"The stupidity champ," I repeated. "This is the dumbest thing you've ever done."

He didn't say anything. Finally, he asked in a quiet voice, "Why is it taking so long for me to come back?"

Before I could answer, I heard Dad calling from downstairs: "Max? Are you two up there?"

"Yeah. We'll be right down," I shouted.

"What are you two *doing* up there?" Dad demanded. I heard him start to climb the stairs.

I ran to the top of the stairs to head him off. "Sorry, Dad," I said. "We're coming."

Dad stared up at me on the staircase. "What on earth is so interesting up there?"

"Just a lot of old stuff," I muttered. "Nothing, really."

Lefty appeared behind me, looking like his old self. Dad disappeared back to the dining room. Lefty and I started down the stairs.

"Wow, that was *awesome*!" Lefty exclaimed.

"Didn't you start to feel weird after a while?" I asked him, whispering even though we were alone.

"No." He shook his head. "I felt fine. It was

227

really *awesome*! You should have seen the look on your face when I made the soup bowl float up in the air!" He started giggling again, that high-pitched giggle of his that I hate.

"Listen, Lefty," I warned, stopping at the bottom of the stairs, blocking his way to the hallway. "Getting invisible is fun, but it could be dangerous. You—"

"It's awesome!" he repeated. "And I'm the new champ."

"Listen to me," I said heatedly, grabbing him by the shoulders. "Just listen. You've got to promise me that you won't go up there and get invisible by yourself again. I mean it. You've got to wait till someone else is around. Promise?" I squeezed his shoulders hard.

"Okay, okay," he said, trying to squirm away. "I promise."

I looked down. He had his fingers crossed on both hands.

Erin phoned me later that night. It was about eleven. I was in my pyjamas, reading a book in bed, thinking about going downstairs and begging my parents to let me stay up and watch *Saturday Night Live*.

Erin sounded really excited. She didn't even say hello. Just started talking a mile a minute in that squeaky mouse voice, so fast I had trouble understanding her.

"What about the science fair?" I asked, holding the phone away from my ear, hoping that would help me understand her better.

"The winning project," Erin said breathlessly. "The prize is a silver trophy and a gift token for Video World. Remember?"

"Yeah. So?" I still wasn't following her. I think I was sleepier than I'd thought. It had been a nervous, tiring day, after all.

"Well, what if you brought the mirror to school?" Erin asked excitedly. "You know. I would make you go invisible. Then I'd bring you back, and I'd get invisible. That could be our project."

"But, Erin—" I started to protest.

"We'd win!" she interrupted. "We'd *have* to win! I mean, what else could beat it? We'd win first prize. And we'd be famous!"

"Whoa!" I cried. "Famous?"

"Of course. Famous!" she exclaimed. "Our picture would be in *People* magazine and everything!"

"Erin, I'm not so sure about this," I said softly, thinking hard.

"Huh? Not so sure about *what*?"

"Not so sure I want to be famous," I replied. "I mean, I really don't know if I want the whole world to know about the mirror."

"Why not?" she demanded impatiently. "*Everyone* wants to be famous. And rich."

"But they'll take away the mirror," I explained. "It's an amazing thing, Erin. I mean, is it magic? Is it electronic? Is it someone's invention? Whatever it is, it's unbelievable! And they're not going to let a kid keep it."

"But it's *yours*!" she insisted.

"They'll take it away to study it. Scientists will want it. Government people will want it. Army people. They'll probably want to use it to make the army invisible or something."

"Scary," Erin mumbled thoughtfully.

"Yeah. Scary," I said. "So I don't know. I've got to think about this. A lot. In the meantime, it's got to be a secret."

"Yeah, I suppose so," she said doubtfully. "But think about the science fair, Max. We could win the prize. We really could."

"I'll think about it," I told her.

I haven't thought about anything else! I realized.

"April wants to try it," she said.

"Huh?"

"I convinced her. I told her it didn't hurt or anything. So she wants to try it on Wednesday. We *are* going to do it on Wednesday, aren't we, Max?"

"I suppose so," I replied reluctantly. "Since everyone wants to."

"Great!" she exclaimed. "I think I'll beat your record."

"The new record is ten minutes," I informed her. I explained about Lefty and his dinnertime adventure.

"Your brother really is a nutcase," Erin remarked.

I agreed with her, then said goodnight.

I couldn't get to sleep that night. I tried sleeping on one side, then the other. I tried counting sheep. Everything.

I knew I was sleepy. But my heart was racing. I just couldn't get comfortable. I stared up at the ceiling, thinking about the mirror in the little room above me.

It was nearly three in the morning when I crept barefoot out of my room, wide awake, and headed for the attic. As before, I leaned heavily on the banister as I climbed, trying to keep the wooden stairs from their usual symphony of creaks and groans.

In my hurry to get to the little room, I stubbed my toe on the corner of a wooden crate.

"Ow!" I screamed as quietly as possible. I wanted to hop up and down, but I forced myself to stand still, and waited for the pain to fade.

As soon as I could walk again, I made my way into the little room. I pulled a box in front of the mirror and sat down on it.

My toe still throbbed, but I tried to ignore it. I stared at my dark reflection in the mirror, studying my hair first, of course. It was totally messed up, but I really didn't care.

Then I peered beyond my reflection, behind it. I think I was trying to look deep into the glass. I don't really know what I was doing or why I was up there.

I was so tired and wound up at the same time, so curious and confused, sleepy and nervous.

I ran a hand along the glass, surprised again at how cool it felt in the hot, nearly airless little room. I pushed my open hand against the glass, then pulled it away. It left no handprint.

I moved my hand to the wooden frame, once again rubbing the smooth wood. I stood up and slowly walked around to the back of the mirror. It was too dark back here to really examine it carefully. But there wasn't anything to examine. The back of the frame was smooth, plain, and uninteresting.

I came back around to the front and gazed up at the light. It looked like an ordinary lamp. Nothing at all special about it. The bulb was an odd shape, long and very thin. But it looked like an ordinary light bulb.

Sitting back down on the box, I rested my head in my hands and stared drowsily into the mirror. I yawned silently.

I knew I should go back downstairs and go to sleep. Mum and Dad were going to wake us up early the next morning to drive to Springfield.

But something was holding me there.

My curiosity, I suppose.

I don't know how long I sat there, still as a statue, watching my own unmoving reflection. It may have been just a minute or two. Or it might have been half an hour.

But after a while, as I stared into the mirror, the reflection seemed to lose its sharpness. Now I found myself staring at vague shapes, blurred colours, deepening shadows.

And then I heard the soft whisper.

"*Maaaaaaaax.*"

Like the wind through the trees. The hushed shaking of leaves.

Not a voice at all. Not even a whisper.

Just the hint of a whisper.

"*Maaaaaaaaax.*"

At first, I thought it was inside my own head.

So faint. So soft. But so near.

I held my breath, listened hard.

Silence now.

So it *was* inside my head, I told myself. I *was* imagining it.

I took a deep breath, let it out slowly.

"*Maaaaax.*"

Again, the whisper.

Louder this time. Sad, somehow. Almost a plea. A call for help. From far, far away.

"*Maaaaaaaax.*"

I raised my hands to my ears. Was I trying to shut it out? To see if I could make it go away?

Inside the mirror, the dark reflected shapes shifted slowly. I stared back at myself, my expression tense, frightened. I realized I was chilled from head to foot. My whole body shivered from the cold.

"*Maaaaax.*"

The whisper, I realized, was coming from the mirror.

From my own reflection? From somewhere behind my reflection?

I leapt to my feet, turned away, and ran. My bare feet slapped against the hardwood floor. I plunged down the stairs, flew across the hall, and dived into my bed.

I shut my eyes tight and prayed that the frightening whisper wouldn't follow me.

I pulled the covers up to my chin. I felt so cold. My whole body was trembling.

I was breathing hard, gripping the top of the blanket with both hands, waiting, listening.

Would the whispers follow me into my room? Were they real, or only in my head?

Who was calling to me, whispering my name in that sad, desperate voice?

Suddenly I heard panting louder than mine. I felt hot breath on my face. Sour-smelling and moist.

It reached for me. It grabbed my face.

I opened my eyes in terror.

"Whitey!" I cried.

The stupid dog was standing on his hind paws, leaning over the blanket, furiously licking my face.

"Whitey, good dog!" I cried, laughing. His scratchy tongue tickled. I was never so glad to see him.

I hugged him and pulled him up into the bed. He whimpered excitedly. His tail was wagging like crazy.

"Whitey, what's got you so worked up?" I asked, hugging him. "Do you hear voices, too?"

He uttered a low bark, as if answering the question. Then he hopped off the bed and shook himself. He turned three times in a tight circle, making a place for himself on the carpet, and lay down, yawning loudly.

"You're definitely weird tonight," I said. He curled himself into a tight ball and chewed softly on his tail.

Accompanied by the dog's gentle snores, I eventually drifted into a restless sleep.

When I awoke, the morning sky outside my bedroom window was still grey. The window was open just a crack, and the curtains were swaying in a strong breeze.

I sat up quickly, instantly alert. I have to stop going up to the attic, I thought.

I have to forget about the stupid mirror.

I stood up and stretched. I've got to stop. And I've got to get everyone else to stop.

I thought of the whispered cry from the night before. The dry, sad voice, whispering my name.

"Max!"

The voice from outside my room startled

236

me out of my chilling thoughts.

"Max—time to wake up! We're going to Springfield, remember?" It was my mum out on the landing. "Hurry. Breakfast is on the table."

"I'm already up!" I shouted. "I'll be down in a minute."

I heard her footsteps going down the stairs. Then I heard Whitey downstairs barking at the door to be let out.

I stretched again.

"Whoa!" I cried out as my wardrobe door swung open.

A red Gap T-shirt rose up off the top shelf and began to float across the room.

I heard giggling. Familiar giggling.

The T-shirt danced in front of me.

"Lefty, you're ridiculous!" I yelled angrily. I swiped at the T-shirt, but it danced out of my reach. "You promised you wouldn't do this again!"

"I had my fingers crossed," he said, giggling.

"I don't care!" I cried. I lunged forward and grabbed the shirt. "You've got to stop. I mean it."

"I just wanted to surprise you," he said, pretending his feelings were hurt. A pair of jeans floated up from the wardrobe shelf and began to parade back and forth in front of me.

"Lefty, I'm going to *murder* you!" I shouted.

237

Then I lowered my voice, remembering that Mum and Dad might hear. "Put that down—now. Go upstairs and turn off the mirror light. Hurry!"

I shook my fist at where the jeans were marching. I was so angry.

Why did he have to be so stupid? Didn't he realize that this wasn't just a game?

Suddenly, the jeans collapsed in a heap on the carpet.

"Lefty, toss them to me," I instructed him. "Then get upstairs and get yourself visible again."

Silence.

The jeans didn't move.

"Lefty—don't mess about," I snapped, feeling a stab of dread in the pit of my stomach. "Give me the jeans and get out of here."

No reply.

The jeans remained crumpled on the carpet.

"Stop this stupid game!" I screamed. "You're not funny! So just stop it. Really. You're *scaring* me!"

I knew that's what he wanted to hear. Once I admitted that he was scaring me, I was sure he'd giggle and go and do as I said.

But no. The room was still silent. The curtains fluttered towards me, then pulled back with a gentle rustling sound. The jeans lay crumpled on the carpet.

"Lefty? Hey, Lefty?" I called, my voice trembling.

No reply.

"Lefty? Are you here?"

No.

Lefty had gone.

"Lefty?" My voice came out weak and trembling.

He wasn't there. It wasn't a game. He had gone.

Without thinking, I ran out of my room, down the hall, and up the stairs to the attic. My bare feet pounded on the steep wooden steps. My heart was pounding even louder.

As I stepped into the heat of the attic, a wave of fear crept over me.

What if Lefty had disappeared *forever*?

With a frightened cry, I lunged into the tiny room.

The bright light reflected in the mirror shone into my eyes.

Shielding my eyes with one hand, I made my way to the mirror and pulled the string. The light went out immediately.

"Lefty?" I called anxiously.

No reply.

"Lefty? Are you up here? Can you hear me?" Fear clogged my throat. I was panting loudly, barely able to speak.

"Lefty?"

"Hi, Max. I'm here." My brother's voice came from right beside me.

I was so happy to hear it, I turned and gave him a hug, even though I couldn't see him.

"I'm okay," he said, startled by my emotion. "Really, Max. I'm okay."

It took a few minutes for him to reappear.

"What happened?" I asked, looking him up and down as if I hadn't seen him for months. "You were clowning around in my room. Then you were gone."

"I'm fine," he insisted with a shrug.

"But where did you go?" I demanded.

"Up here," he repeated.

"But Lefty—" Something about him looked different. I couldn't quite put my finger on it. But staring at his face, I was sure that something was weird.

"Stop staring at me like that, Max." He shoved me away. "I'm fine. Really." He started dancing away from me, heading for the stairs.

"But, Lefty—" I followed him out of the room.

"No more questions. Okay? I'm all right."

"Stay away from the mirror," I said sternly. "Do you hear me?"

He started down the stairs.

"I mean it, Lefty. *Don't* get invisible again."

"Okay, okay," he snapped. "I won't do it any more."

I checked to make sure his fingers weren't crossed. This time they weren't.

Mum was waiting for us in the hall. "So *there* you are," she said impatiently. "Max, you're not dressed!"

"I'll hurry," I told her, and bolted into my room.

"Lefty, what have you done to your hair?" I heard Mum ask my brother. "Have you brushed it differently or something?"

"No," I heard Lefty reply. "It's the same, Mum. Really. Maybe your eyes are different."

"Stop being so cheeky and get downstairs," Mum told him.

Something was definitely weird about Lefty. Mum had noticed it, too. But I couldn't work out what.

As I picked my jeans up off the floor and pulled them on, I started to feel a little better. I had been so frightened, frightened that something terrible had happened to my brother. Frightened that he'd disappeared for good, and I'd never see him again.

All because of that stupid mirror.

All because it was such a thrill to get invisible.

I suddenly thought about Erin, April, and Zack.

They were so excited about Wednesday. About the big competition. Even April was going to get invisible this time.

No, I thought.

I have to call them. I have to tell them.

I've really made up my mind.

No more mirror. No more getting invisible.

I'll call all three of them when I get back from Springfield. And I'll tell them the competition is cancelled.

I sat down on my bed to tie my trainer laces.

Whew, I thought. That's a load off my mind.

And it was. Having decided not to use the mirror ever again made me feel much, much better. All of my fear seemed to float away.

Little did I know that the most frightening time was still to come.

Imagine my surprise when Zack, Erin, and April appeared at my front door on Wednesday morning.

"I told you lot the competition is off," I spluttered, staring at them in astonishment through the screen door.

"But Lefty phoned us," Erin replied. "He said you'd changed your mind." The other two agreed.

My mouth dropped open to my knees. "Lefty?"

They nodded. "He phoned us yesterday," April said.

"But Lefty isn't even here this morning," I told them as they marched into the house. "He's at the playground playing softball with some of his friends."

"Who's here?" my mum called. She came walking into the hall, drying her hands on a tea towel. She recognized my friends, then turned to me, a bewildered look on her face.

"Max, I thought you were going to help me down in the basement. I didn't know you'd made plans with Zack, Erin, and April."

"I didn't," I replied weakly. "Lefty—"

"We just dropped in," Zack told Mum, coming to my rescue.

"If you're busy, Max, we can go," Erin added.

"No, that's okay," Mum told them. "Max was complaining about how boring it would be to help me. It's good that you three have turned up."

She disappeared back into the kitchen. As soon as she had gone, my three friends practically pounced on me.

"Upstairs!" Zack cried eagerly, pointing to the stairs.

"Let's get invisible!" Erin whispered.

"I get to go first since I've never gone," April said.

I tried to argue with them, but I was outnumbered and outvoted. "Okay, okay," I reluctantly agreed. I started to follow them up the stairs when I heard scratching noises at the door.

I recognized the sound. It was Whitey, back from his morning walk. I pushed open the screen door and he trotted in, wagging his tail.

The silly dog had some burrs stuck to his tail. I chased him into the kitchen and managed to get him to stand still long enough to pull them off. Then I hurried up to the attic to join my friends.

By the time I got up there, April was already standing in front of the mirror, and Zack was standing beside her, ready to pull the light on.

"Whoa!" I called.

They turned to look at me. I could see that April had a frightened expression on her face. "I have to do this right away. Or else I might wimp out," she explained.

"I just think we should get the rules straight first," I said sternly. "This mirror really isn't a toy, and—"

"We know, we know," Zack interrupted, grinning. "Come on, Max. No lectures today, okay? We know you're nervous because you're going to lose. But that's no reason—"

"I don't want to compete," April said nervously. "I just want to see what it's like to be invisible. For just a minute. Then I want to come back."

"Well, I'm going for the world record," Zack boasted, leaning against the mirror frame.

"Me, too," Erin said.

"I really don't think it's a very good idea," I told them, staring at my reflection in the mirror. "We should just get invisible for a short time. It's too dangerous to—"

"What a wimp!" Zack declared, shaking his head.

"We'll be careful, Max," Erin said.

"I just have a really bad feeling," I confessed. My hair was standing up at the back. I stepped closer to the mirror to see better, and smoothed it down with my hand.

"I think we should all get invisible at the same time," Zack said to me, his blue eyes lighting up with excitement. "Then we could go to the playground and scare your brother to death!"

Everyone laughed except April. "I just want to try it for a minute," she insisted. "That's all."

"First we compete," Erin told Zack. "Then we go out and scare people."

"Yeah! All *right*!" Zack exclaimed.

I decided to give up. There was no sense in trying to reason with Zack and Erin. They were too excited about this competition. "Okay, let's get it over with," I told them.

"But I go first," April said, turning back to the mirror.

Zack reached up for the string again. "Ready? After three," he said.

I turned to the door as Whitey came sniffing his way in, his nose lowered to the floor, his tail straight out behind him.

"Whitey, what are *you* doing up here?" I asked.

He ignored me and continued sniffing furiously.

"One . . . two . . ." Zack started.

"When I say 'ready', bring me back. Okay?" April asked, standing stiffly, staring straight ahead into the mirror. "No jokes or anything, Zack."

"No jokes," Zack replied seriously. "As soon as you want to come back, I'll turn off the light."

"Good," April replied softly.

Zack began his count again. "One . . . two . . . three!"

As he said three and pulled the string, Whitey stepped up beside April.

The light flashed on.

"Whitey!" I screamed. "Stop!"

But it was too late.

With a *yelp* of surprise, the dog vanished along with April.

"The dog!" Erin screamed.

"Hey—I'm gone! I'm invisible!" April exclaimed at the same time.

I could hear Whitey whimpering. He sounded really frightened.

"Pull the string!" I shouted to Zack.

"Not yet!" April protested.

"Pull it!" I insisted.

Zack pulled the string. The light went out. April reappeared first, with an angry expression on her face.

Whitey reappeared, and fell down. He jumped up quickly, but his legs were all wobbly.

He looked so funny, we all started to laugh.

"What's going on up there?" My mum's voice from the stairs startled us into instant silence. "What are you doing?"

"Nothing, Mum," I answered quickly, signalling for my friends to remain silent. "Just messing about."

"I don't understand what's so interesting up there in that dusty old attic," she called up.

I crossed my fingers, hoping she wouldn't come upstairs to find out.

"We just like it up here," I replied. Pretty pathetic, but it was the only thing I could think of to say.

Whitey, having recovered his balance, went running to the stairs. I heard the dog's toenails click on the wooden stairs as he went down to join my mum.

"That wasn't fair," April complained after Mum and Whitey had gone. "I didn't get any time."

"I think we should get out of here," I pleaded. "You see how unpredictable it is. You never know what's going to happen."

"That's half the fun of it," Erin insisted.

"I want another turn," April said.

We argued for about ten minutes. Once again, I lost.

It was time to start the competition. Erin was going first.

"Ten minutes is the time to beat," Zack instructed her.

"No problem," Erin said, making funny faces at herself in the mirror. "Ten minutes is too easy."

April had resumed her position, sitting on the floor with her back against the wall, studying her watch. We had agreed that she would take another turn after the competition was over.

After it was over . . .

Standing there watching Erin get ready, I wished it was over already. I felt cold all over. I had a heavy feeling of dread weighing me down.

Please, please, I thought to myself, let everything go okay.

Zack pulled the string.

Erin disappeared in the flash of light.

April studied her watch.

Zack took a step back from the mirror and crossed his arms in front of his chest. His eyes glowed with excitement.

"How do I look?" Erin teased.

"You've never looked better," Zack joked.

"I like what you did with your hair," April teased, glancing up from the watch.

Even April was joking and having a good time. Why couldn't I relax, too? Why was I suddenly so frightened?

"You feel okay?" I asked Erin. The words nearly caught in my throat.

"Fine," Erin replied.

I could hear her footsteps as she walked around the room.

"If you start to feel weird, just say 'ready', and Zack'll pull the string," I said.

"I know," she replied impatiently. "But I won't be ready to come back until I break the record."

"I'm going next," Zack told Erin, arms still crossed in front of him. "So your record won't last for long."

Suddenly Zack's arms uncrossed. His hands flew wildly up in the air, and he began slapping his face with both hands.

"Ow! Stop it, Erin!" he yelled, trying to squirm away. "Let go!"

We heard Erin laugh as Zack slapped himself a few more times, then finally managed to wrestle out of her grip.

"One minute," April announced from behind us.

"Ow! You hurt me!" Zack said, scowling and rubbing his red cheeks.

Erin laughed again.

"You still feel okay?" I asked, glancing into the mirror.

"Fine. Stop worrying, Max," Erin scolded.

My T-shirt suddenly pulled up over my head. Erin laughed.

"Give me a break!" I cried, spinning away.

"Two minutes," April announced.

I heard the attic stairs creaking. A few seconds later, Whitey poked his head in. This time, he stopped in the doorway and peered into the room without coming in.

"Go back downstairs, boy," I told him. "Go down."

He stared back at me as if considering my request. But he didn't budge from the doorway.

I didn't want to take another chance of him getting too close to the mirror. So I grabbed him by the collar and guided him to the stairs. Then it took a while for the stupid dog to get the idea that he was supposed to go *down* the stairs!

When I returned to the little room, April had just called out four minutes. Zack was pacing impatiently back and forth in front of the mirror. I suppose he couldn't wait for it to be his turn.

I found myself thinking about Lefty. Lefty knew I had phoned everyone and cancelled the competition. So why had *he* called Zack, Erin, and April and told them it was back on?

Just one of his practical jokes, I decided.

I'd have to find a way to pay him back for this.

Something really evil . . .

"Eight minutes," April said, stretching.

"Pretty good," Zack told Erin. "Sure you don't want to quit now? There's no way you can win. Why not save everyone the time?"

"Do you still feel okay?" I asked anxiously.

No reply.

"Erin?" I called, searching around as if I had a chance of spotting her. "You feel okay?"

253

No reply.

"Erin—don't mess about. It's not funny!" I cried.

"Yeah. Answer us!" Zack demanded.

Still no reply.

Glancing into the mirror, I saw April's reflection, caught her horrified expression. "Erin's gone," she uttered, her voice a frightened whisper.

"Erin—where *are* you?" I shouted.

When she didn't reply, I ran over to the string. Just as I grabbed it, I heard footsteps outside the room. A few seconds later, a can of Coke came floating through the door.

"Miss me?" Erin asked playfully.

"You scared us to death!" I cried, my voice squeaking.

Erin laughed. "I didn't know you cared."

"That wasn't funny, Erin," Zack said sternly. For once he was agreeing with me. "You really did scare us."

"I got thirsty," Erin replied. The Coke can tilted up. We saw Coke start to pour out of it. The liquid abruptly disappeared as it flowed into Erin's mouth.

"I think being invisible must make you really thirsty," Erin explained. "So I slipped downstairs and got a Coke."

"But you should've told us," scolded April,

her eyes turned back to her watch. "Nine minutes."

"You shouldn't go downstairs," I added heatedly. "I mean, what if my mum had seen you?"

"*Saw* me?"

"Well . . . you know what I mean," I muttered.

Erin laughed. I didn't think it was funny.

Why was I the only one taking this seriously?

Erin beat Lefty's record and kept going. When April called out twelve minutes, Zack asked Erin if she wanted to come back.

No reply.

"Erin? Are you winding us up again?" I demanded.

Still no reply.

I could feel my throat tighten once again with fear. I walked over and pulled the string. My hand was shaking as I pulled it. I prayed silently to myself that Erin would return okay.

The light went out. The three of us waited tensely for Erin to come back.

After what seemed an endless wait, she shimmered back into view. She turned quickly away from the mirror, a triumphant smile on her face. "The new champ!" she declared, raising her fists in a gesture of victory.

"You're okay?" I asked, my feeling of fear refusing to leave.

She nodded. "Just fine, worryguts." She

stepped away from the mirror, walking unsteadily.

I stared at her. Something about her looked
different.

She looked perfectly okay. Not pale or sick-
looking or anything. But something was different. Her smile? Her hair? I wished I could work
out what.

"Max, pull the string." Zack's eager voice
jerked me away from my thoughts. "Let's go,
man. I'm going for *fifteen* minutes."

"Okay. Get ready," I said, glancing at Erin as
I grabbed for the string. She flashed me a
reassuring smile.

But something about her smile was different.
Something.

But what?

I pulled the string. Zack vanished in the flash
of bright light.

"Return of the Invisible Man!" he cried in a
deep voice.

"Not so loud," I warned him. "My mum'll hear
you downstairs."

Erin had lowered herself to the floor beside
April. I walked over and stood over her. "You
sure you're okay?" I asked. "You don't feel dizzy
or weird or anything?"

She shook her head. "No. Really. Why don't
you believe me, Max?"

As I stared down at her, I tried to work out

what was different about her appearance. What a mystery! I just couldn't put my finger on it.

"Well, how come you didn't answer when I called you?" I demanded.

"Huh?" Her face filled with surprise. "When?"

"At about twelve minutes," I told her. "I called you and Zack called you. But you didn't answer us."

Erin's expression turned thoughtful. "I suppose I didn't hear you," she replied finally. "But I'm fine, Max. Really. I feel great. It was really awesome."

I joined them on the floor and leaned back against the wall to wait for Zack's turn to be over. "I really meant it. Don't turn off the light till fifteen minutes," he reminded me.

Then he messed up my hair, making it stand straight up in the air.

Both girls laughed.

I had to get up, walk over to the mirror, and comb it back down. I don't know why people think messed-up hair is such a riot. I really don't get it.

"Hey, follow me. I've got an idea," Zack said. His voice was coming from the doorway.

"Whoa—hold on!" I called. But I could hear his trainers stepping across the attic.

"Follow me outside," he called to us. We heard his footsteps on the attic stairs.

"Zack—don't do it," I pleaded. "Whatever it is, don't do it!"

But there was no way he was going to listen to me.

A few seconds later, we were out of the back door, following our invisible friend towards our neighbour Mr Evander's back garden.

This is going to be trouble, I thought unhappily. Big trouble.

Erin, April, and I hid behind the hedge that separated our two gardens. As usual, Mr Evander was out in his tomato garden, stooped over, pulling up weeds, his big belly hanging out under his T-shirt, his red bald head shiny under the sun.

What is Zack going to do? I wondered, holding my breath, my whole body heavy with dread.

And then I saw three tomatoes float up from the ground. They hovered in the air, then floated closer to Mr Evander.

Oh, no, I thought, groaning silently to myself. Please, Zack. Please don't do it.

Erin, April, and I were huddled together behind the hedge, staring in disbelief as the three tomatoes began to circle each other rapidly in the air.

Invisible Zack was juggling them. Showing off, as usual. He was always bragging about how he could juggle, and we couldn't.

It took a while for Mr Evander to notice.

259

But when he finally saw the three tomatoes spinning around in midair barely a metre in front of him, his eyes bugged out and his face turned as red as the tomatoes!

"Oh!" he cried. He let the weeds fall from his hands. And then he just stared at the spinning tomatoes, as if he was frozen.

Zack tossed the tomatoes higher as he juggled.

April and Erin held hands over their mouths to stifle their laughter. They thought Zack's stunt was a real hoot. But I just wanted to get Zack back up to the attic.

"Hey, Mary! Mary!" Mr Evander started calling to his wife. "Mary—come out here! You've *got* to see this! Mary!"

A few seconds later, his wife came running across the garden, a frightened expression on her face. "Mike, what's wrong? What's *wrong*?"

"Look—these tomatoes are twirling in the air!" Mr Evander cried, motioning wildly for her to hurry.

Zack let the tomatoes fall to the ground.

"Where?" Mrs Evander asked breathlessly, running as fast as she could.

"There. Look!" Mr Evander pointed.

"I don't see any tomatoes," Mrs Evander said, stopping in front of her husband, panting loudly.

"Yes! They're spinning. They're—"

"Those tomatoes?" Mrs Evander asked, pointing to the three tomatoes on the ground.

"Well . . . yes. They were twirling around, and—" Looking terribly confused, Mr Evander scratched the back of his neck.

"Mike, how long have you been out in the sun?" his wife scolded. "Didn't I tell you to wear a cap?"

"Uh . . . I'll be in in a few minutes," Mr Evander said softly, staring down at the tomatoes.

As soon as Mrs Evander turned and headed back to the house, the three tomatoes floated up from the ground and began twirling in the air again.

"Mary, look!" Mr Evander shouted excitedly. "Look—quick! They're doing it again!"

Zack let the tomatoes drop to the ground.

Mrs Evander spun round and stared into empty space. "Mike, you'd better come with me—*right now*," she insisted. She hurried back, grabbed Mr Evander by the arm, and pulled him away. The poor man looked totally bewildered, staring at the tomatoes on the ground, still scratching the back of his neck as his wife pulled him to the house.

"Hey, this is brilliant!" Zack cried, right in front of me.

Erin and April collapsed in giggles. I had to admit it was pretty funny. We laughed about it for a while. Then we sneaked back into the house and up to the attic.

In the safety of the little room, we laughed some more about Zack's juggling stunt. Zack bragged that he was the world's first invisible juggler.

Then, at twelve minutes, Zack suddenly stopped answering us.

Just as Erin had.

The three of us called his name over and over again.

Silence.

Zack didn't reply.

"I'm going to bring him back," I said, instantly gripped with fear once again. I ran to the string.

"Wait," Erin said, holding me back.

"Huh? What for?" I pulled away from her.

"He said to wait for fifteen minutes, remember?" she argued.

"Erin, he's completely disappeared!" I cried.

"But he'll be really angry," Erin pleaded.

"I say bring him back," April said anxiously.

"Give him until fifteen minutes," Erin insisted.

"No," I said. I pulled the string.

The light clicked off.

A few minutes later, Zack flickered back. He smiled at us. "How long?" he asked, turning to April.

"Thirteen minutes, twenty seconds," she told him.

His grin widened. "The new champ!"

"You're okay? You didn't answer us," I said, studying his face.

"I'm fine. I didn't hear you calling me. But I'm fine."

Zack looked different to me, too. Something was very different about him. But what?

"What's your problem, Max?" he demanded. "Why are you staring at me like I'm some kind of alien life-form or something?"

"Your hair," I said, studying him. "Was it like that before?"

"Huh? What are you talking about? Are you freaking out or something?" Zack asked, rolling his eyes.

"Was your hair like that before?" I repeated. "Shaved really short on the right hand and then combed long on the left? Wasn't it the other way round?"

"You're weird, Max," he said, grinning at Erin and April. "My hair is the same as it's always been. You've been staring in that mirror too long or something."

I could've sworn his hair had been short on the left, long on the right. But I suppose Zack would know his own hair.

"Are you going to go?" Erin asked, jumping up behind me.

"Yeah, are you going to beat fifteen minutes?" Zack asked.

I shook my head. "No, I really don't feel like it," I told them truthfully. "Let's declare Zack the winner and get out of here."

"No way!" Zack and Erin declared in unison.

"You've got to try," Zack insisted.

"Don't wimp out, Max. You can beat Zack. I know you can," Erin declared.

She and Zack both pushed me up to the mirror.

I tried to pull back. But they practically held me in place.

"No. Really," I said. "Zack can be the winner. I—"

"Go for it, Max!" Erin urged. "I'm betting on you!"

"Yeah. Go for it," Zack repeated, his hand firmly on my shoulder.

"No. Please—" I said.

But Zack reached up with his free hand and pulled the string.

I stared into the mirror for a moment, waiting for the glare to fade from my eyes. It was always such a shock. That first moment, when your reflection disappeared. When you stared at the spot where you knew you were standing—and realized you were looking right through yourself!

"How do you feel, Max? How do you feel?" Erin asked, imitating me.

"Erin, what's your problem?" I snapped. It wasn't like her to be so sarcastic.

"Just giving you a taste of your own medicine," she replied, grinning.

Something about her smile was lopsided, not normal.

"Think you can beat my record?" Zack demanded.

"I don't know. Maybe," I replied uncertainly.

Zack stepped up to the mirror and studied his reflection. I had the strangest feeling as I watched him. I can't really explain it. I'd never seen Zack stand in just that position and admire himself in just that way.

Something was different. I knew it. But I couldn't work out what.

Maybe it's just my nervousness, I told myself.

I'm just so stressed out. Maybe it's affecting the way I look at my friends. Maybe I'm making all this up.

"Two minutes," April announced.

"Are you just going to stand there?" Erin asked, staring into the mirror. "Aren't you going to move around or anything, Max?"

"No. I don't think so," I said. "I mean, I can't think of anything I want to do. I'm just going to wait till the time is up."

"You want to stop now?" Zack asked, grinning at the spot where he thought I was standing.

I shook my head. Then I remembered that no one could see it. "No. I might as well go the distance," I told him. "Since I'm here, I might as well make you look bad, Zack."

He laughed scornfully. "You won't beat thirteen-twenty," he said confidently. "No way."

"Well, you know what?" I said, angered by his smug tone of voice. "I'm just going to stand here until I do."

And that's what I did. I stood in place, leaning

266

against the mirror frame, while April counted off the minutes.

I did okay until a short while after she had called out eleven minutes. Then, suddenly, the glare of the light began to hurt my eyes.

I closed my eyes, but it didn't help. The light grew brighter, harsher. It seemed to sweep around me, surround me, fold over me.

And then I began to feel dizzy and light. As if I were about to float away, even though I knew I was standing still.

"Hey?" I called out. "I think I've had enough."

My voice sounded tiny and far away, even to me.

The light swirled around me. I felt myself grow lighter, lighter, until I had to struggle to keep my feet on the floor to keep from floating away.

I uttered a high-pitched cry. I was suddenly gripped by panic.

Cold panic.

"Zack—bring me back!" I shouted.

"Okay, Max. No problem," I heard Zack reply.

He seemed miles and miles away.

I struggled to see him through the blinding yellow light. He was a dark figure behind the wall of light, a dark figure moving quickly to the mirror.

"I'm bringing you back now, Max. Hold on," I heard Zack say.

The bright light glowed even brighter. It hurt so much. Even with my eyes closed, it hurt.

"Zack, pull the string!" I shouted.

I opened my eyes to see his dim shadow reaching up to the string.

Pull it, pull it, *pull it*! I urged silently.

I knew that in a second, the light would go off. And I'd be safe.

A second.

One tug of the string.

Pull it, pull it, *pull it, Zack*!

Zack reached for the string. I saw him grab it.

And then I heard another voice in the room. A new voice. A surprised voice.

"Hi. What's going on up here? What are you kids doing?"

I saw the shadowy figure of Zack drop the string and step away without pulling it.

My mum had burst into the room.

"Please—pull the string!" I called.

No one seemed to hear me.

"We're just messing about," I heard Zack tell my mum.

"But where's Max?" I heard her ask. "How did you find this little room? What are you all *doing* in here?" Her voice sounded as if it were coming from underwater, far, far away.

The whole room began to shimmer in the light, flickering on and off. I held on tightly to the frame of the mirror, struggling not to float away.

"Can you hear me?" I called. "Please, somebody—pull the string! Bring me back!"

They were just grey shadows in the wavering, rolling light. They didn't seem to hear me.

Gripping the frame tightly, I saw a shadow approach the mirror. My mum. She walked around it, admiring it.

"I can't *believe* we never knew about this

269

room. Where did this old mirror come from?" I heard her ask.

She was standing so close to me. They all were.

They were so close and so far away at the same time.

"Please bring me back!" I shouted.

I listened for an answer. But the voices faded away.

The shadows moved in a flickering blur. I tried to reach out to them, but they were too far away.

I let go of the mirror frame and began to float.

"Mum, I'm right here. Can't you hear me? Can't you *do* anything?"

So light, so completely weightless, I floated in front of the mirror.

My feet were off the floor. I couldn't see them in the blinding glare.

I floated to the mirror glass, under the light.

I could feel the light pull me closer. Closer.

Until it pulled me right into the mirror.

I knew I was inside the mirror. Inside a glistening blur of colours. The shapes shimmered and rolled together as if underwater.

And I floated through the glimmering shards of light and colour, floated silently away from my friends, away from my mum, floated away from the tiny attic room.

Into the centre of the mirror.

Into the centre of an undulating, rolling world of twisting lights and colours.

"Help me!" I cried.

But my voice was muffled by the blurred, shifting colours.

"Bring me back! Get me back!"

Floating deeper into this glimmering world, I could barely hear myself.

Deeper into the mirror. And still deeper.

The colours gave way to shapes of grey and black. It was cold here. Cold as glass.

And as I floated deeper, deeper, the greys and blacks faded, too. The world was white now. Pure white all around. Shadowless white as far as I could see.

I stared straight ahead, no longer calling out, too frightened to call out, too mystified by the cold, ivory world I had entered.

"Hello, Max," a familiar voice said.

"Ohh!" I cried out, realizing I was not alone.

A scream of terror escaped my lips. I tried to form words, but my brain seemed to be paralysed.

The figure approached quickly, silently, through the cold, white world of the mirror. He smiled at me, an eerie, familiar smile.

"You!" I managed to scream.

He stopped centimetres away from me.

I stared at him in disbelief.

I was staring at myself. Me. Smiling back at me. The smile as cold as the glass that surrounded us.

"Don't be afraid," he said. "I'm your reflection."

"No!"

His eyes—*my* eyes—studied me hungrily, like a dog staring at a meaty bone. His smile grew wider as I cried out my fear.

"I've been waiting here for you," my reflection said, his eyes locked on mine.

"No!" I repeated.

I turned away.

I knew I had to get away.

I started to run.

But I stopped short when I saw the faces in front of me. Distorted, unhappy faces, dozens of them, fun house mirror faces, with enormous, drooping eyes, and tiny mouths tight with sadness.

The faces seemed to hover just ahead of me. The gaping eyes staring at me, the tiny mouths moving rapidly as if calling to me, warning me, telling me to get away.

Who were these people, these faces?

Why were they inside the mirror with me?

Why did their distorted, twisted images reveal so much sadness, so much pain?

"No!"

I gasped as I thought I recognized two of the floating faces, their mouths working furiously, their eyebrows rising wildly up and down.

Erin and Zack?

No.

That was impossible, wasn't it?

I stared hard at them. Why were they talking so frantically? What were they trying to tell me?

"Help me!" I called. But they didn't seem to hear me.

The faces, dozens of them, bobbed and floated.

"Help me—please!"

273

And then I felt myself being spun round. I stared into the eyes of my reflection as he gripped my shoulders and held me in place.

"You're not leaving," he told me. His quiet voice echoed through the clear stillness, icicles scratching against glass.

I struggled to free myself, but his grip was strong.

"I'm the one to leave," he told me. "I've been waiting so long. Ever since you turned on the light. And now I'm going to step out from here and join the others."

"Others?" I cried.

"Your friends gave in easily," he said. "They did not resist. The switch was made. And now you and I will also make a switch."

"No!" I screamed, and my cry seemed to echo through the icy cold for miles.

"Why are you so afraid?" he asked, turning me round, still gripping my shoulders, bringing his face close to mine. "Are you so afraid of your other side, Max?"

He stared at me intently. "That's what I am, you know," he said. "I'm your reflection. Your other side. Your dark side. Don't be afraid of me. Your friends were not afraid. They made the switch without much of a struggle. Now they are inside the mirror. And their reflections . . ."

His voice trailed off. He didn't have to finish his sentence. I knew what he was saying.

Now I understood about Erin and Zack. Now I understood why they looked different to me. They were reversed. They were their own reflections.

And now I understood why they had pushed me into the mirror, why they had forced me to disappear, too.

If I didn't do something, I realized, my reflection would switch places with me. My reflection would step into the attic. And I'd be trapped inside the mirror forever, trapped forever with the sad, bobbing faces.

But what could I do?

Staring at myself, I decided to stall, to ask questions, to give myself a little time to think.

"Whose mirror is it? Who built it?" I demanded.

He shrugged. "How should I know? I'm only your reflection, remember?"

"But how—"

"It's time," he said eagerly. "Don't try to stall with foolish questions. Time to make the switch. Time for *you* to become *my* reflection!"

I pulled away.

I started to run.

The sad, distorted faces hovered in front of me.

I shut my eyes and dodged away from them.

I couldn't think. Couldn't breathe.

My legs pumped. My arms flew out at my sides. It was so clear and bright, I couldn't tell if I was moving or not. My feet couldn't feel a floor. There were no walls, no ceiling. There was no *air* brushing my face as I ran.

But my fear kept me moving. Through the clear, cold, shimmering light.

He was behind me.

I couldn't hear him.

He had no shadow.

But I knew he was right behind me.

And I knew that if he caught me, I'd be lost. Lost inside this blank world, unable to see, to hear, to smell, to touch anything, lost in the cold glass forever.

Another silent, bobbing face.

And so I kept running.

Until the colours returned.

Until light bent to form shapes.

And I saw shadows moving and shifting in front of me.

"Stop, Max!" I heard my reflection's voice right behind me. "Stop right there!"

But now *he* sounded worried.

And so I kept running, running into the colours and moving shapes.

Suddenly, Zack turned off the light.

I came bursting out of the mirror, into the tiny attic room, into an explosion of sound, of colour, of hard surfaces, of real things. The real world.

I stood up, panting, gasping for breath. I tested my legs. I stamped on the floor. The solid floor.

I turned my eyes to my friends, who were standing in front of me, startled expressions on their faces. My mum, I realized, must have retreated back downstairs.

"Did you make the switch?" Zack asked eagerly, his eyes glowing with excitement.

"Are you one of us?" Erin asked at the same time.

"No," said a voice—my voice—coming from just behind me.

We all stared into the mirror.

Inside, it, my reflection, red-faced and angry,

glared out at us, his hands pressed against the glass. "He got away," my reflection told my friends. "The switch wasn't made."

"I don't understand!" I heard April cry. "What's going on?"

Zack and Erin ignored her. They stepped up quickly and grabbed me by the arms. They spun me round roughly.

"The switch wasn't made," my reflection repeated from inside the glass.

"No problem," Erin told it.

She and Zack forced me up to the mirror.

"You're going back in, Max," Zack said heatedly.

He reached up and pulled the light cord.

The light flashed on.

I was invisible again.

My reflection remained in the mirror, open palms pressed against the inside of the glass, staring out.

"I'm waiting for you, Max," he said. "In a few minutes, you'll join me in here."

"No!" I shouted. "I'm leaving. I'm going downstairs."

"No, you're not," my reflection said, shaking his head. "Erin and Zack won't let you escape. But don't be so frightened, Max. It's all quite painless. Really." He smiled. It was my smile. But it was cold. Cruel.

"I don't get this," April was protesting back by the door. "Will someone tell me what's going on?"

"You'll see, April," Erin told her soothingly.

What am I going to do? I wondered, frozen in panic.

What *can* I do?

"Just a few more minutes," my reflection said calmly, already celebrating his victory. His freedom.

"April, get help!" I cried.

She spun round at the sound of my voice. "Huh?"

"Get help! Go downstairs. Get help! Hurry!" I screamed.

"But—I don't understand—" April hesitated.

Erin and Zack moved to block her path.

But the door suddenly swung open.

I saw Lefty stop at the doorway. He peered in. Saw my reflection.

He must have thought the reflection was me.

"Think fast!" he shouted, and he tossed a softball.

The ball smashed into the mirror.

I saw the startled look on Lefty's face. And then I heard the crash and saw the mirror crack and shatter.

My reflection didn't have time to react. He broke into shards of glass and fell to the floor.

"Nooooo!" Erin and Zack shrieked.

I popped back into view just as Erin's and Zack's reflections floated up off the floor. They were sucked into the broken mirror—screaming all the way—sucked into it as if a powerful vacuum cleaner were pulling them in.

The two reflections flew screaming into the mirror and appeared to crack into hundreds of pieces.

"Whoa!" Lefty cried, gripping the door with all his strength, pressing his body against the doorframe, struggling to keep himself from being sucked into the room.

And then Erin and Zack dropped onto the floor on their knees, looking dazed and confused, staring at the pieces of shattered mirror that littered the floor around them.

"You're back!" I cried happily. "It's really you!"

"Yeah. It's me," Zack said, climbing unsteadily to his feet, then turning to help Erin up.

The mirror was shattered. The reflections were gone.

Erin and Zack gazed round the room, still shaken and dazed.

April stared at me in total confusion.

Lefty remained outside the doorway, shaking his head. "Max," he said, "you should've caught the ball. That was an easy catch."

Erin and Zack were back. And they were okay.

It didn't take long to get everything back to normal.

We explained everything to April and Lefty as best we could.

April went home. She had to babysit for her little sister.

Erin and Zack—the *real* Erin and Zack—helped me sweep up the broken glass. Then we closed the door to the little room. I latched it tightly, and we all carried boxes over and stacked them up to block off the door.

We knew we'd never go in there again.

We vowed never to tell anyone about getting invisible or the mirror or what happened in that little room. Then Erin and Zack headed home.

Later, Lefty and I were hanging around out in the back garden. "That was so scary," I told Lefty with a shudder. "You just can't imagine what it was like."

"Sounds pretty scary," Lefty replied absently. He tossed his softball from hand to hand. "But at least everything is okay now. Want to play a little catch?"

"No," I shook my head. I wasn't in the mood. But then I changed my mind. "Maybe it'll take my mind off what happened this morning," I said.

Lefty tossed me the ball. We trotted behind the garage, our usual place for tossing the ball around.

I lobbed it back to him.

We were having a pretty good game of catch.

Until about five minutes had gone by.

Until . . .

282

Until I stopped and froze in place.

Were my eyes playing tricks on me?

"Here comes my fastball," he said. He heaved it at me.

No. No. No.

I gaped open-mouthed as the ball shot past me. I didn't even try to catch it. I couldn't move.

I could only stare in horror.

My brother was throwing *right-handed*.

Goosebumps

Night of the Living Dummy

"Mmmmm! Mmmm! Mmmmm!"

Kris Powell struggled to get her twin sister's attention.

Lindy Powell glanced up from the book she was reading to see what the problem was. Instead of her sister's pretty face, Lindy saw a round, pink bubble almost the size of Kris's head.

"Nice one," Lindy said without much enthusiasm. With a sudden move, she poked the bubble and popped it.

"Hey!" Kris cried as the pink bubble gum exploded onto her cheeks and chin.

Lindy laughed. "Gotcha."

Kris angrily grabbed Lindy's paperback and slammed it shut. "Whoops—lost your place!" she exclaimed. She knew her sister hated losing her place in a book.

Lindy grabbed the book back with a scowl. Kris struggled to pull the pink gum off her face.

"That was the biggest bubble I ever blew," she said angrily. The gum wasn't coming off her chin.

"I've blown much bigger ones than that," Lindy said with a superior sneer.

"I don't *believe* you two," their mother muttered, making her way into their bedroom and dropping a neatly folded pile of laundry at the foot of Kris's bed. "You even compete over bubble gum?"

"We're not competing," Lindy muttered. She tossed back her blonde ponytail and returned her eyes to her book.

Both girls had straight blonde hair. But Lindy kept hers long, usually tying it behind her head on one side in a ponytail. And Kris had hers cut very short.

It was a way for people to tell the twins apart, for they were nearly identical in every other way. Both had broad foreheads and round, blue eyes. Both had dimples in their cheeks when they smiled. Both blushed easily, large pink circles forming on their pale cheeks.

Both thought their noses were a little too wide. Both wished they were a little taller. Lindy's best friend, Alice, was nearly eight centimetres taller, even though she hadn't turned twelve yet.

"Did I get it all off?" Kris asked, rubbing her chin, which was red and sticky.

"Not all," Lindy told her, glancing up. "There's some in your hair."

"Oh, great," Kris muttered. She grabbed at her hair, but couldn't find any bubble gum.

"Gotcha again," Lindy said, laughing. "You're too easy!"

Kris uttered an angry growl. "Why are you always so mean to me?"

"Me? Mean?" Lindy looked up in wide-eyed innocence. "I'm an angel. Ask anyone."

Exasperated, Kris turned back to her mother, who was stuffing socks into the chest of drawers. "Mum, when am I going to get my own room?"

"On the Twelfth of Never," Mrs Powell replied, grinning.

Kris groaned. "That's what you always say."

Her mother shrugged. "You know we don't have enough space, Kris." She turned to the bedroom window. Bright sunlight streamed through the filmy curtains. "It's a beautiful day. What are you two doing inside?"

"Mum, we're not little girls," Lindy said, rolling her eyes. "We're twelve. We're too old to go out and play."

"Did I get it all?" Kris asked, still scraping pink patches of bubble gum off her chin.

"Leave it. It improves your complexion," Lindy told her.

"I wish you girls would be nicer to each other," Mrs Powell said with a sigh.

They suddenly heard shrill barking coming from downstairs. "What's Barky excited about now?" Mrs Powell fretted. The little black terrier was always barking about something. "Why not take Barky for a walk?"

"Don't feel like it," Lindy muttered, nose in her book.

"What about those beautiful new bikes you got for your birthdays?" Mrs Powell said, hands on hips. "Those bikes you just couldn't live without. You know, the ones that have been sitting in the garage since you got them."

"Okay, okay. You don't have to be sarcastic, Mum," Lindy said, closing her book. She stood up, stretched, and tossed the book onto her bed.

"You want to?" Kris asked Lindy.

"Want to what?"

"Go for a bike ride. We could ride to the playground, see if anyone's hanging around there."

"You just want to see if Robby is there," Lindy said, making a face.

"So?" Kris said, blushing.

"Go on. Get some fresh air," Mrs Powell urged. "I'll see you later. I'm off to the supermarket."

Kris peered into the dressing table mirror. She had got most of the gum off. She brushed her short hair back with both hands. "Come on. Let's go out," she said. "Last one out is a rotten egg." She darted to the doorway, beating her sister by half a step.

As they burst out of the back door, with Barky yipping shrilly behind them, the afternoon sun was high in a cloudless sky. The air was still and dry. It felt more like summer than spring.

Both girls were wearing shorts and sleeveless T-shirts. Lindy bent to pull open the garage door, then stopped. The house next door caught her eye.

"Look—they've got the walls up," she told Kris, pointing across their back garden.

"That new house is going up so quickly. It's amazing," Kris said following her sister's gaze.

The builders had knocked down the old house during the winter. The new concrete foundations had been put down in March. Lindy and Kris had walked around on it when no builders were there, trying to work out where the different rooms would go.

And now the walls had been built. The construction suddenly looked like a real house, rising up in the midst of tall stacks of timber, a big mound of red-brown dirt, a pile of concrete blocks, and an assortment of power saws, tools, and machinery.

"No one's working today," Lindy said.

They took a few steps towards the new house. "Who do you think will move in?" Kris wondered.

"Maybe some good-looking guy of our age. Maybe good-looking twin boys!"

"Yuck!" Lindy made a disgusted face. "Twin boys? How drippy can you get! I can't believe you and I belong to the same family."

Kris was used to Lindy's sarcasm. Both girls liked being twins and hated being twins at the same time. Because they shared nearly everything—their looks, their clothes, their room—they were closer than most sisters ever get.

But because they were so much alike, they also managed to drive each other crazy a lot of the time.

"No one's around. Let's explore the new house," Lindy said.

Kris followed her across the garden. A squirrel, halfway up the wide trunk of a maple tree, watched them warily.

They made their way through an opening in the low shrubs that divided the two gardens. Then, walking past the stacks of timber and the tall mound of earth, they climbed the concrete front steps.

A sheet of heavy plastic had been nailed over the opening where the front door would go. Kris pulled one end of the plastic up, and they slipped into the house.

It was dark and cool inside and had a fresh wood smell. The plaster walls were up but hadn't been painted.

"Careful," Lindy warned. "Nails." She pointed to the large nails scattered over the floor. "If you step on one, you'll get lockjaw and die."

"You wish," Kris said.

"I don't want you to die," Lindy replied. "Just get lockjaw." She sniggered.

"Ha-ha," Kris said sarcastically. "This must be the living room," she said, making her way carefully across the front room to the fireplace against the back wall.

"A cathedral ceiling," Lindy said, staring up at the dark, exposed wooden beams above their heads. "Cool."

"This is bigger than our living room," Kris remarked, peering out of the large window at the street.

"It smells great," Lindy said, taking a deep breath. "All the sawdust. It smells so piney."

They made their way through the hall and explored the kitchen. "Are those wires live?" Kris asked, pointing to a cluster of black electrical wires suspended from the ceiling beams.

"Why don't you touch one and find out?" Lindy suggested.

"You first," Kris shot back.

"The kitchen isn't very big," Lindy said, bending down to stare into the holes where the kitchen cabinets would go.

She stood up and was about to suggest they

explore upstairs when she heard a sound. "Huh?" Her eyes widened in surprise. "Is someone in here?"

Kris froze in the middle of the kitchen.

They both listened.

Silence.

Then they heard soft, rapid footsteps. Close by. Inside the house.

"Let's go!" Lindy whispered.

Kris was already ducking under the plastic, heading out of the doorway opening. She leapt off the back door steps and started running towards their back garden.

Lindy stopped at the bottom of the steps and turned back to the new house. "Hey—look!" she called.

A squirrel came flying out of a side window. It landed on the ground with all four feet moving and scrambled towards the maple tree in the Powells' garden.

Lindy laughed. "Just a stupid squirrel."

Kris stopped near the low bushes. "Are you sure?" She hesitated, watching the windows of the new house. "That was a pretty loud squirrel."

When she turned back from the house, she was surprised to find that Lindy had disappeared.

"Hey—where'd you go?"

"Over here," Lindy called. "I can see something!"

It took Kris a while to locate her sister. Lindy

was half-hidden behind a rubbish skip at the far end of the garden.

Kris shielded her eyes with one hand to see better. Lindy was bent over the side of the skip. She appeared to be rummaging through some rubbish.

"What's in there?" Kris called.

Lindy was tossing things around and didn't seem to hear her.

"What *is* it?" Kris called, taking a few reluctant steps towards the skip.

Lindy didn't reply.

Then, slowly, she pulled something out. She started to hold it up. Its arms and legs dangled down limply. Kris could see a head with brown hair.

A head? Arms and legs?

"Oh, no!" Kris cried aloud, raising her hands to her face in horror.

A child?

Kris uttered a silent gasp, staring in horror as Lindy lifted him out of the skip.

She could see his face, frozen in a wide-eyed stare. His brown hair stood stiffly on top of his head. He seemed to be wearing some sort of grey suit.

His arms and legs dangled lifelessly.

"Lindy!" Kris called, her throat tight with fear. "Is it—is he . . . *alive*?"

Her heart pounding, Kris started to run to her sister. Lindy was cradling the poor thing in her arms.

"Is he alive?" Kris repeated breathlessly.

She stopped short when her sister started to laugh.

"No. Not alive!" Lindy called gleefully.

And then Kris realized that it wasn't a child after all. "A dummy!" she shrieked.

Lindy held it up. "A ventriloquist's dummy,"

she said. "Someone threw him away. Can you believe it? He's in perfect condition."

It took Lindy a while to notice that Kris was breathing hard, her face bright red. "Kris, what's your problem? Oh, wow. Did you think he was a real kid?" Lindy laughed scornfully.

"No. Of course not," Kris insisted.

Lindy held the dummy up and examined his back, looking for the string to pull to make his mouth move. "I *am* a real kid!" Lindy made him say. She was speaking in a high-pitched voice through gritted teeth, trying not to move her lips.

"Stupid," Kris said, rolling her eyes.

"I am *not* stupid. You're stupid!" Lindy made the dummy say in a high, squeaky voice. When she pulled the string in his back, the wooden lips moved up and down, clicking as they moved. She moved her hand up his back and found the control to make his painted eyes shift from side to side.

"He's probably full of fleas," Kris said, making a disgusted face. "Throw him back, Lindy."

"No way," Lindy insisted, rubbing her hand tenderly over the dummy's wooden hair. "I'm keeping him."

"She's keeping me," she made the dummy say.

Kris stared suspiciously at the dummy. His brown hair was painted on his head. His blue eyes moved only from side to side and couldn't blink. He had bright red painted lips, curved up into an eerie smile. The lower lip had a chip on one side so that it didn't quite match the upper lip.

The dummy wore a grey, double-breasted suit over a white shirt collar. The collar wasn't attached to a shirt. Instead, the dummy's wooden chest was painted white. Big brown leather shoes were attached to the ends of his thin, dangling legs.

"My name is Slappy," Lindy made the dummy say, moving his grinning mouth up and down.

"Stupid," Kris repeated, shaking her head. "Why Slappy?"

"Come over here and I'll slap you!" Lindy made him say, trying not to move her lips.

Kris groaned. "Are we going to ride our bikes to the playground or not, Lindy?"

"Afraid poor Robby misses you?" Lindy made Slappy ask.

"Put that ugly thing down," Kris replied impatiently.

"I'm not ugly," Slappy said in Lindy's squeaky voice, sliding his eyes from side to side. "You're ugly!"

"Your lips are moving," Kris told Lindy. "You're a lousy ventriloquist."

"I'll get better," Lindy insisted.

"You mean you're really keeping it?" Kris cried.

"I like Slappy. He's cute," Lindy said, cuddling the dummy against the front of her T-shirt.

"I'm cute," she made him say. "And you're ugly."

"Shut up," Kris snapped at the dummy.

"You shut up!" Slappy replied in Lindy's tight, high-pitched voice.

"What do you want to keep him for?" Kris asked, following her sister towards the street.

"I've always liked puppets," Lindy recalled. "Remember those string puppets I used to have? I played with them for hours at a time. I made up long plays with them."

"I always played with the string puppets, too," Kris remembered.

"You got the strings all tangled up," Lindy said, frowning. "You weren't any good at it."

"But what are you going to *do* with this dummy?" Kris demanded.

"I don't know. Maybe I'll work up an act," Lindy said thoughtfully, shifting Slappy to her other arm. "I bet I could earn some money with him. You know. Appear at kids' birthday parties. Put on shows."

"Happy birthday!" she made Slappy declare. "Hand over some money!"

Kris didn't laugh.

The two girls walked along the street in front

of their house. Lindy cradled Slappy in her arms, one hand up his back.

"I think he's creepy," Kris said, kicking a large stone across the street. "You should put him back in the skip."

"No way," Lindy insisted.

"No way," she made Slappy say, shaking his head, his glassy blue eyes moving from side to side. "I'll put *you* in the skip!"

"Slappy certainly is nasty," Kris remarked, frowning at Lindy.

Lindy laughed. "Don't look at me," she teased. "Complain to Slappy."

Kris scowled.

"You're jealous," Lindy said. "Because I found him and you didn't."

Kris started to protest, but they both heard voices. Kris looked up to see the two Marshall kids from down the road running towards them. They were cute, red-headed kids that Lindy and Kris sometimes babysat for.

"What's that?" Amy Marshall asked, pointing at Slappy.

"Does he talk?" her younger brother, Ben, asked, staying at a distance, an uncertain expression on his freckled face.

"Hi, I'm Slappy!" Lindy made the dummy call out. She cradled Slappy in one arm, making him sit up straight, his arms dangling at his sides.

"Where'd you get him?" Amy asked.

300

"Do his eyes move?" Ben asked, still hanging back.

"Do *your* eyes move?" Slappy asked Ben.

Both Marshall kids laughed. Ben forgot his reluctance. He stepped up and grabbed Slappy's hand.

"Ouch! Not so hard!" Slappy cried.

Ben dropped the hand with a gasp. Then he and Amy collapsed in gleeful laughter.

"Ha-ha-ha-ha!" Lindy made Slappy laugh, tilting his head back and opening his mouth wide.

The two kids thought that was a riot. They laughed even harder.

Pleased by the response she was getting, Lindy glanced at her sister. Kris was sitting on the kerb, cradling her head in her hands, a dejected look on her face.

She's jealous, Lindy realized. Kris sees that the kids really like Slappy and that I'm getting all the attention. And she's totally jealous.

I'm *definitely* keeping Slappy! Lindy told herself, secretly pleased at her little triumph.

She stared into the dummy's bright blue painted eyes. To her surprise, the dummy seemed to be staring back at her, a twinkle of sunlight in his eyes, his grin wide and knowing.

"Who was that on the phone?" Mr Powell asked, shovelling another forkful of spaghetti into his mouth.

Lindy slipped back into her place at the table. "It was Mrs Marshall. Down the road."

"Does she want you to babysit?" Mrs Powell asked, reaching for the salad bowl. She turned to Kris. "Don't you want any salad?"

Kris wiped spaghetti sauce off her chin with her napkin. "Maybe later."

"No," Lindy answered. "She wants me to perform. At Amy's birthday party. With Slappy."

"Your first job," Mr Powell said, a smile crossing his slender face.

"Amy and Ben liked Slappy so much, they insisted on him," Lindy said. "Mrs Marshall is going to pay me twenty dollars."

"That's great!" their mother exclaimed. She passed the salad bowl across the table to her husband.

It was a week since Lindy had rescued Slappy from the skip. Every day after school, she had spent hours up in her room rehearsing with him, working on his voice, practising not moving her lips, thinking up jokes to perform with him.

Kris kept insisting the whole thing was really stupid. "I can't believe you're being such a nerd," she told her sister. She refused to be an audience for Lindy's routines.

But when Lindy brought Slappy into school on Friday, Kris's attitude began to change. A group of kids had gathered around Lindy outside her locker.

As Lindy made Slappy talk for them, Kris watched from down the hall. She's going to make a total fool of herself, Kris thought.

But to her surprise, the kids hooted and howled. They thought Slappy was a riot. Even Robby Martin, the boy Kris had had a crush on for two years, thought Lindy was terrific.

Watching Robby laugh along with the other kids made Kris think hard. Becoming a ventriloquist might be fun.

And profitable. Lindy was going to earn twenty dollars at the Marshalls' birthday party. And when word got round, she'd probably perform at a lot of parties and earn even more money.

After dinner that evening, Lindy and Kris washed and dried the dishes. Then Lindy asked her parents if she could practise her new comedy routine on them. She hurried up to her room to get Slappy.

Mr and Mrs Powell took a seat on the living room sofa. "Maybe Lindy will be a TV star," Mrs Powell said.

"Maybe," Mr Powell agreed, sitting back on the sofa, a pleased smile on his face. Barky yapped and climbed between Mr and Mrs Powell, his tiny stub of a tail wagging furiously.

"You know you're not allowed on the sofa," Mrs Powell said, sighing. But she made no move to push Barky off.

Kris sat down away from the others, on the floor by the stairs, cradling her chin in her hands.

"You're looking very glum this evening," her father remarked.

"Can I get a dummy, too?" Kris asked. She hadn't really planned to say it. The question just popped out of her mouth.

Lindy came back into the room, carrying Slappy around the waist. "Ready?" she asked. She pulled a dining room chair into the centre of the living room and sat down on it.

"Well, can I?" Kris repeated.

"You really want one, too?" Mrs Powell asked, surprised.

"Want *what*?" Lindy asked, confused.

"Kris says she wants a dummy, too," Mrs Powell reported.

"No way," Lindy said heatedly. "Why do you always have to be such a copycat?"

"It looks like fun," Kris replied, her cheeks turning bright pink. "If you can do it, I can do it, too," she added shrilly.

"You always copy everything I do," Lindy protested angrily. "Why don't you find something of your own for once? Go upstairs and work on your junk jewellery collection. That's *your* hobby. Let *me* be the ventriloquist."

"Girls—" Mr Powell started, raising a hand for quiet—"please, don't argue over a dummy."

"I really think I'd be better at it," Kris said. "I mean, Lindy isn't very funny."

"Everyone thinks I'm funny," Lindy insisted.

"That's not very nice, Kris," Mrs Powell scolded.

"Well, I just think if Lindy has one, I should be able to have one, too," Kris said to her parents.

"Copycat," Lindy repeated, shaking her head. "You've been putting me down all week. You said it was nerdy. But I know why you've changed your mind. You're upset because I'm going to earn some money and you're not."

"I really wish you two wouldn't argue about *everything*," Mr Powell said disgustedly.

"Well, can I have a dummy?" Kris asked him.

"They're expensive," Mr Powell replied, glancing at his wife. "A good one will cost more than a hundred dollars. I really don't think we can afford to buy one now."

"Why don't you both share Slappy?" Mrs Powell suggested.

"Huh?" Lindy's mouth dropped open in protest.

"You two always share everything," Mrs Powell continued. "So why don't you share Slappy?"

"But, Mum—" Lindy whined unhappily.

"Excellent idea," Mr Powell interrupted. He motioned to Kris. "Try it out. After you share him for a while, I'm sure one of you will lose interest in him. Maybe even both of you."

Kris climbed to her feet and walked over to Lindy. She reached out for the dummy. "I don't mind sharing," she said quietly, searching her sister's eyes for approval of the idea. "Can I hold him for just a second?"

Lindy held onto Slappy tightly.

Suddenly the dummy's head tilted back and his mouth opened wide. "*Beat it, Kris!*" he snarled in a harsh raspy voice. "*Get lost, you stupid moron!*"

Before Kris could back away, Slappy's wooden hand shot up, and he slapped her hard across the face.

"Ow!"

Kris screamed and raised her hand to her cheek, which was bright pink. She stepped back. "Stop it, Lindy! That *hurt!*"

"Me?" Lindy cried. "I didn't do it! Slappy did!"

"Don't be stupid," Kris protested, rubbing her cheek. "You really hurt me."

"But I didn't do it!" Lindy cried. She turned Slappy's face towards her. "Why were you so rude to Kris?"

Mr Powell jumped up from the sofa. "Stop being silly and apologize to your sister," he ordered.

Lindy bowed Slappy's head. "I'm sorry," she made the dummy say.

"No. In your own voice," Mr Powell insisted, crossing his arms in front of his chest. "Slappy didn't hurt Kris. You did."

"Okay, okay," Lindy muttered, blushing. She avoided Kris's angry stare. "I'm sorry. Here."

She dumped Slappy into Kris's arms.

Kris was so surprised, she nearly dropped the dummy. Slappy was heavier than she'd imagined.

"Now what am I supposed to do with him?" Kris asked Lindy.

Lindy shrugged and crossed the room to the sofa, where she dropped down beside her mother.

"Why'd you make such a fuss?" Mrs Powell whispered, leaning close to Lindy. "That was so childish."

Lindy blushed. "Slappy is *mine*! Why can't something be mine for once?"

"Sometimes you girls are so nice to each other, and sometimes . . ." Mrs Powell's voice trailed off.

Mr Powell sat down on the padded arm of the chair across the room.

"How do I make his mouth work?" Kris asked, tilting the dummy upside down to examine its back.

"There's a string in his back, inside the slit in his jacket," Lindy told her grudgingly. "You just pull it."

I don't want Kris to work Slappy, Lindy thought unhappily.

I don't want to share Slappy.

Why can't I have something that just belongs to me? Why do I have to share everything with her?

Why does Kris always want to copy me?

She gritted her teeth and waited for her anger to fade.

Later that night, Kris sat straight up in bed. She'd had a bad dream.

I was being chased, she remembered, her heart still pounding. Chased by what? By whom?

She couldn't remember.

She glanced round the shadowy room, waiting for her heartbeat to return to normal. The room felt hot and stuffy, even though the window was open and the curtains were fluttering.

Lindy lay sound asleep on her side in the twin bed next to Kris's. She was snoring softly, her lips slightly parted, her long hair falling loose about her face.

Kris glanced at the clock-radio on the bedside table between the two twin beds. It was nearly three in the morning.

Even though she was now wide awake, the nightmare wouldn't completely fade away. She still felt uncomfortable, a little frightened, as if she were still being chased by someone or something. The back of her neck felt hot and prickly.

She turned and fluffed up her pillow, propping it higher on the headboard. As she lay back on it, something caught her eye.

Someone sitting in the chair in front of the bedroom window. Someone staring at her.

After a sharp intake of breath, she realized it was Slappy.

Yellow moonlight poured over him, making his staring eyes glow. He was sitting up in the chair, tilted to the right at a slight angle, one arm resting on the slender arm of the chair.

His mouth locked in a wide, mocking grin, his eyes seemed to be staring right at Kris.

Kris stared back, studying the dummy's expression in the eerie yellow moonlight. Then, without thinking, without even realizing what she was doing, she climbed silently out of bed.

Her foot got tangled up in the sheet and she nearly tripped. Kicking the sheet away, she made her way quickly across the room to the window.

Slappy stared up at her as her shadow fell over him. His grin seemed to grow wider as Kris leaned closer.

A gust of wind made the soft curtains flutter against her face. Kris pushed them away and peered down at the dummy's painted head.

She reached a hand out and rubbed his wooden hair, shining in the moonlight. His head felt warm, warmer than she'd imagined.

Kris quickly jerked her hand away.

What was that sound?

Had Slappy sniggered? Had he laughed at her?

No. Of course not.

Kris realised she was breathing hard.

Why am I so freaked out by this stupid dummy? she thought.

In the bed behind her, Lindy made a gurgling sound and rolled onto her back.

Kris stared hard into Slappy's big eyes, gleaming in the light from the window. She waited for him to blink or to roll his eyes from side to side.

She suddenly felt foolish.

He's just a stupid wooden dummy, she told herself.

She reached out and pushed him over.

The stiff body swung to the side. The hard head made a soft *clonk* as it hit the wooden arm of the chair.

Kris stared down at him, feeling strangely satisfied, as if she'd somehow taught him a lesson.

The curtains rustled against her face again. She pushed them away.

Feeling sleepy, she started back to bed.

She had only gone one step when Slappy reached up and grabbed her wrist.

311

"Oh!" As the hand tightened round her wrist, Kris cried out and spun round.

To her surprise, Lindy was crouched beside her. Lindy had a tight grip on Kris's wrist.

Kris jerked her hand from Lindy's grasp.

Moonlight through the window lit up Lindy's devilish grin. "Gotcha again!" she declared.

"You didn't scare me!" Kris insisted. But her voice came out as a trembling whisper.

"You jumped a mile!" Lindy exclaimed gleefully. "You really thought the dummy grabbed you."

"Did not!" Kris replied. She hurried to her bed.

"What were you doing up, anyway?" Lindy demanded. "Were you messing around with Slappy?"

"No. I . . . uh . . . had a bad dream," Kris told her. "I just went to look out of the window."

Lindy sniggered. "You should've seen the look on your face."

"I'm going back to sleep. Leave me alone," Kris snapped. She pulled the covers up to her chin.

Lindy pushed the dummy back to a sitting position. Then she returned to her bed, still chuckling over the scare she'd given her sister.

Kris rearranged her pillows, then glanced across the room to the window. The dummy's face was half covered in shadow now. But the eyes glowed as if he were alive. And they stared into hers as if they were trying to tell her something.

Why does he have to grin like that? Kris asked herself, trying to rub away the prickly feeling on the back of her neck.

She pulled up the sheet, settled into the bed, and turned on her side, away from the wide, staring eyes.

But even with her back turned, she could feel them gazing at her. Even with her eyes closed and the covers pulled up to her head, she could picture the shadowy, distorted grin, the unblinking eyes. Staring at her. Staring. Staring.

She drifted into an uncomfortable sleep, drifted into another dark nightmare. Someone was chasing her. Someone very evil was chasing her.

But who?

On Monday afternoon, Lindy and Kris both

stayed after school to rehearse for the spring concert. It was nearly five when they arrived home, and they were surprised to see their dad's car in the drive.

"You're home so early!" Kris exclaimed, finding him in the kitchen helping their mother prepare dinner.

"I'm leaving tomorrow for a sales conference in Portland," Mr Powell explained, peeling an onion over the sink with a small kitchen knife. "So I only worked half a day today."

"What's for dinner?" Lindy asked.

"Meat loaf," Mrs Powell replied, "if your father ever gets the onion peeled."

"There's a trick to not crying when you peel an onion," Mr Powell said, tears rolling down his cheeks. "Wish I knew it."

"How was chorus rehearsal?" Mrs Powell asked, kneading a big ball of red ground beef in her hands.

"Boring," Lindy complained, opening the fridge door and taking out a can of Coke.

"Yeah. We're doing all these Russian and Yugoslavian songs," Kris said. "They're so sad. They're all about sheep or something. We don't really know what they're about. There's no translation."

Mr Powell rushed to the sink and began splashing cold water on his red, runny eyes. "I can't take this!" he wailed. He tossed the half-

314

peeled onion back to his wife.

"Crybaby," she muttered, shaking her head.

Kris headed up the stairs to drop her rucksack in her room. She tossed it onto the desk she shared with Lindy, then turned to go back downstairs.

But something by the window caught her eye.

Spinning round, she gasped.

"Oh, no!" The startled cry escaped her lips.

Kris raised her hands to her cheeks and stared in disbelief.

Slappy was propped up in the chair in front of the window, grinning at her with his usual wide-eyed stare. And beside him was seated another dummy, also grinning at her.

And they were holding hands.

"What's going on here?" Kris cried aloud.

"Do you like him?"

At first, Kris thought that Slappy had asked the question.

She gaped in stunned disbelief.

"Well? What do you think of him?"

It took Kris a long moment to realize that the voice was coming from behind her. She turned to find her father standing in the doorway, still dabbing at his eyes with a wet dishcloth.

"The—the new dummy?" Kris stammered.

"He's for you," Mr Powell said, stepping into the room, the wet cloth pressed against both eyes.

"Really?" Kris hurried over to the chair and picked the new dummy up to examine him.

"There's a tiny pawnshop on the corner opposite my office," Mr Powell said, lowering the cloth. "I was walking past and, believe it or not, this guy was in the window. He was cheap,

316

and I think the pawnbroker was glad to get rid of him."

"He's . . . cute," Kris said, searching for the right word. "He looks just like Lindy's dummy, except his hair is bright red, not brown."

"Probably made by the same company," Mr Powell said.

"His clothes are better than Slappy's," Kris said, holding the dummy out at arm's length to get a good view. "I hate that stupid grey suit on Lindy's dummy."

The new dummy wore blue jeans and a red-and-green checked shirt. And instead of the formal-looking, shiny brown shoes, he had white high-top trainers on his feet.

"So you like him?" Mr Powell asked, smiling.

"I *love* him!" Kris cried happily. She crossed the room and gave her dad a hug.

Then she picked up the dummy and ran out of the room, down the stairs, and into the kitchen. "Hey, everybody! Meet Mr Wood!" she declared happily, holding the grinning dummy up in front of her.

Barky yapped excitedly, leaping up to nip at the dummy's trainers. Kris pulled her dummy away.

"Hey!" Lindy cried in surprise. "Where'd you get that?"

"From Daddy," Kris said, her grin wider than the dummy's. "I'm going to start practising with him after dinner, and I'm going to be a better ventriloquist than you."

"Kris!" scolded Mrs Powell. "Not everything is a competition, you know!"

"I already have a job with Slappy," Lindy said with a superior sneer. "And you're just getting started. You're just a beginner."

"Mr Wood is much better looking than Slappy," Kris said, mirroring her twin's sneer. "Mr Wood is cool-looking. That grey suit on your dummy is the pits."

"You think that ratty old shirt is cool-looking?" Lindy scoffed, making a disgusted face. "Yuck. That old dummy probably has worms!"

"*You* have worms!" Kris exclaimed.

"Your dummy won't be funny," Lindy said nastily, "because you haven't got a sense of humour."

"Oh, yeah?" Kris replied, tossing Mr Wood over her shoulder. "I *must* have a sense of humour. I put up with *you*, don't I?"

"Copycat! Copycat!" Lindy cried angrily.

"Out of the kitchen!" Mrs Powell ordered with an impatient shriek. "Out! Get out! You two are impossible! The dummies have better personalities than either of you!"

"Thanks, Mum," Kris said sarcastically.

"Call me for dinner," Lindy called back. "I'm going upstairs to practise my act with

Slappy for the birthday party on Saturday."

It was the next afternoon, and Kris was sitting
at the dressing table she shared with Lindy. Kris
rummaged in the jewellery box and pulled out
another string of brightly coloured beads. She
slipped them over her head and untangled them
from the other three strands of beads she was
wearing. Then she gazed at herself in the mirror,
shaking her head to see the long, dangly earrings better.

I love my junk jewellery collection, she
thought, digging into the depths of the wooden
jewellery box to see what other treasures she
could pull out.

Lindy had no interest in the stuff. But Kris
could spend hours trying on the beads, fingering
the dozens of little charms, running her fingers
over the plastic bracelets, jangling the earrings.
Her jewellery collection always cheered her up.

She shook her head again, making the long
earrings jangle. A knock on the bedroom door
made her spin round.

"Hey, Kris, how's it going?" Her friend Cody
Matthews walked into the room. He had straight,
white-blond hair, and pale grey eyes in a slender,
serious face. Cody always looked as if he were
deep in thought.

"Did you ride your bike over?" Kris asked,
removing several strands of beads at once and

tossing them into the jewellery box.

"No. Walked," Cody replied. "Why'd you call? You just want to hang out?"

"No." Kris jumped to her feet. She walked over to the chair by the window and grabbed up Mr Wood. "I want to practise my act."

Cody groaned. "I'm the guinea-pig?"

"No. The audience. Come on."

She led him out to the bent old maple tree in the middle of her back garden. The afternoon sun was just beginning to lower itself in the clear, spring-blue sky.

She raised one foot against the tree trunk and propped Mr Wood up on her knee. Cody sprawled on his back in the shade. "Tell me if this is funny," she instructed.

"Okay. Shoot," Cody replied, narrowing his eyes in concentration.

Kris turned Mr Wood to face her. "How are you today?" she asked him.

"Pretty good. Touch wood," she made the dummy say.

She waited for Cody to laugh, but he didn't. "Was that funny?" she asked.

"Kind of," he replied without enthusiasm. "Keep going."

"Okay." Kris lowered her head so that she was face-to-face with her dummy. "Mr Wood," she said, "why were you standing in front of the mirror with your eyes closed?"

"Well," answered the dummy in a high-pitched, squeaky voice, "I wanted to see what I look like when I'm asleep!"

Kris tilted the dummy's head back and made him look as if he were laughing. "How about that joke?" she asked Cody.

Cody shrugged. "Better, I suppose."

"Oh, you're no help!" Kris screamed angrily. She lowered her arms, and Mr Wood crumpled onto her lap. "You're supposed to tell me if it's funny or not."

"I suppose *not*," Cody said thoughtfully.

Kris groaned. "I need some good joke books," she said. "That's all. Some good joke books with some really funny jokes. Then I'd be ready to perform. Because I'm a pretty good ventriloquist, right?"

"I suppose so," Cody replied, pulling up a handful of grass and letting the moist, green blades sift through his fingers.

"Well, I don't move my lips very much, *do* I?" Kris demanded.

"Not too much," Cody allowed. "But you don't really throw your voice."

"No one can throw their voice," Kris told him. "It's just an illusion. You make people *think* you're throwing your voice. You don't *really* throw it."

"Oh," Cody said, pulling up another handful of grass.

Kris tried out several more jokes. "What do you think?" she asked Cody.

"I think I have to go home," Cody said. He tossed a handful of grass at her.

Kris brushed the green blades off Mr Wood's wooden head. She rubbed her hand gently over the dummy's painted red hair. "You're hurting Mr Wood's feelings," she told Cody.

Cody got to his feet. "Why do you want to mess about with that thing, anyway?" he asked, pushing his white-blond hair back off his forehead.

"Because it's fun," Kris replied.

"Is that the real reason?" Cody demanded.

"Well . . . I suppose I want to show Lindy that I'm better at it than she is."

"You two are *weird*!" Cody declared. "See you at school." He gave her a little wave, then turned and headed for his home down the road.

Kris pulled down the blankets and climbed into bed. Pale moonlight filtered in through the bedroom window.

Yawning, she glanced at the clock-radio. Nearly ten. She could hear Lindy brushing her teeth in the bathroom across the landing.

Why does Lindy always hum when she brushes her teeth? Kris wondered. How can one twin sister do so many annoying things?

She gave Mr Wood one last glance. He was

propped in the chair in front of the window, his hands carefully placed in his lap, his white trainers hanging over the chair edge.

He looks like a real person, Kris thought sleepily.

Tomorrow I'm going to check out some good joke books from the library at school. I can be funnier than Lindy. I *know* I can.

She settled back sleepily on her pillow. I'll be asleep as soon as we turn off the lights, she thought.

A few seconds later, Lindy came into the room, wearing her nightshirt and carrying Slappy under one arm. "You asleep?" she asked Kris.

"Almost," Kris replied, yawning loudly. "I've been studying for the maths exam all evening. Where've you been?"

"Over at Alice's," Lindy told her, setting Slappy down in the chair beside Mr Wood. "Some kids were round there, and I practised my act for them. They laughed so hard, I thought they'd bust a gut. When Slappy and I did our rap routine, Alice spat her chocolate milk out of her nose. What a riot!"

"That's nice," Kris said without enthusiasm. "I suppose you and Slappy are ready for Amy's birthday party on Saturday."

"Yeah," Lindy replied. She placed Slappy's arm around Mr Wood's shoulder. "They look so cute together," she said. Then she noticed the clothing neatly draped over the desk chair. "What's that?" she asked Kris.

Kris raised her head from the pillow to see what her sister was pointing at. "My outfit for tomorrow," she told her. "We're having a formal party in Miss Finch's class. It's a farewell party. For Margot. You know. The student teacher."

Lindy stared at the clothes. "Your best skirt? Your silk blouse?"

"We're supposed to get really dressed up," Kris said, yawning. "Can we go to sleep now?"

"Yeah. Okay." Lindy made her way to her bed, sat down, and clicked off the bedside table lamp. "Are you getting any better with Mr Wood?" she asked, climbing between the sheets.

Kris was stung by the question. It was such an obvious put-down. "Yeah. I'm getting really good. I did some stuff for Cody. Out in the back garden. Cody laughed so hard, he couldn't breathe. Really. He was holding his sides. He said Mr Wood and I should be on TV."

"Really?" Lindy replied after a long moment's hesitation. "That's weird. I never thought Cody had much of a sense of humour. He's always so grim. I don't think I've ever seen him laugh."

"Well, he was laughing at Mr Wood and me," Kris insisted, wishing she were a better liar.

"Awesome," Lindy muttered. "I can't wait to see your act."

Neither can I, Kris thought glumly.

A few seconds later, they were both asleep.

Their mother's voice, calling from downstairs, awoke them at seven the next morning. Bright, morning-orange sunlight poured in through the window. Kris could hear birds chirping happily in the old maple tree.

"Rise and shine! Rise and shine!" Every morning, Mrs Powell shouted up the same thing.

Kris rubbed the sleep from her eyes, then stretched her arms high above her head. She glanced across the room, then uttered a quiet gasp. "Hey—what's going on?" She reached across to Lindy's bed and shook Lindy by the shoulder. "What's going on?"

"Huh?" Lindy, startled, sat straight up.

"What's the joke? Where is he?" Kris demanded.

"Huh?"

Kris pointed to the chair across the room.

Sitting straight up in the chair, Slappy grinned back at them, bathed in morning sunlight.

But Mr Wood had gone.

Kris blinked several times and pushed herself up in bed with both hands. Her left hand tingled. She must have been sleeping on it, she realized.

"What? What's wrong?" Lindy asked, her voice fogged with sleep.

"Where's Mr Wood?" Kris demanded impatiently. "Where'd you put him?"

"Huh? Put him?" Lindy struggled to focus her eyes. She saw Slappy sitting stiffly on the chair across the room. By himself.

"It's not funny," Kris snapped. She climbed out of bed, pulled down the hem of her nightshirt, and made her way quickly to the chair in front of the window. "Don't you ever get tired of playing stupid jokes?"

"Jokes? Huh?" Lindy lowered her feet to the floor.

Kris bent down to search the floor under the chair. Then she moved to the foot of the bed and got down on her knees to search under both twin beds.

"Where *is* he, Lindy?" she asked angrily, on her knees at the foot of the bed. "I don't think this is funny. I really don't."

"Well, neither do I," Lindy insisted, standing up and stretching.

Kris climbed to her feet. Her eyes went wide as she spotted the missing dummy.

"Oh!"

Lindy followed her sister's startled gaze.

Mr Wood grinned at them from the doorway. He appeared to be standing, his skinny legs bent at an awkward angle.

He was wearing Kris's smart clothes, the skirt and the silk blouse.

Her mouth wide open in surprise, Kris made her way quickly to the doorway. She immediately saw that the dummy wasn't really standing on his own. He had been propped up, the doorknob shoved into the opening in his back.

She grabbed the dummy by the waist and pulled him away from the door. "My blouse. It's all wrinkled," she cried, holding it so Lindy could see. She narrowed her eyes angrily at her sister. "This was so obnoxious of you, Lindy."

"Me?" Lindy shrieked. "I swear, Kris, I didn't do it. I slept like a log last night. I didn't move.

327

I didn't get up till you woke me. I didn't do it. Really!"

Kris stared hard at her sister, then lowered her eyes to the dummy.

In her blouse and skirt, Mr Wood grinned up at her, as if enjoying her bewilderment.

"Well, Mr Wood," Kris said aloud, "I suppose you put on my clothes and walked to the door all by yourself!"

Lindy started to say something. But their mother's voice interrupted from downstairs. "Are you girls going to school today? Where *are* you? You're late!"

"Coming!" Kris called down, casting an angry glance at Lindy. She carefully put Mr Wood down on his back on her bed and pulled her skirt and blouse off him. She looked up to see Lindy making a mad dash across the landing to be first in the bathroom.

Sighing, Kris stared down at Mr Wood. The dummy grinned up at her, a mischievious grin.

"Well? What's going on?" she asked the dummy. "I didn't dress you up and move you. And Lindy swears *she* didn't do it."

But if we didn't do it, she thought, *who did*?

"Tilt his head forward," Lindy instructed. "That's it. If you bounce him up and down a little, it'll make it look as if he's laughing."

Kris obediently bounced Mr Wood on her lap, making him laugh.

"Don't move his mouth so much," Lindy told her.

"I think you're both crazy," Lindy's friend Alice said.

"So what else is new?" Cody joked.

All four of them were sitting in a small patch of shade under the bent old maple tree in the Powells' back garden. It was a hot Saturday afternoon, the sun high in a pale blue sky, streaks of yellow light filtering down through the shifting leaves above their heads.

Barky sniffed busily around the garden, his little tail wagging nonstop.

Kris sat on a folding chair, which leaned back

against the gnarled tree trunk. She had Mr Wood on her lap.

Lindy and Alice stood at the edge of the shade, their hands crossed over their chests, watching Kris's performance with frowns of concentration on their faces.

Alice was a tall, skinny girl, with straight black hair down to her shoulders, a snub nose, and a pretty, heart-shaped mouth. She was wearing white shorts and a bright blue midriff top.

Cody was sprawled on his back in the grass, his hands behind his head, a long blade of grass between his teeth.

Kris was trying to show off her ventriloquist skills. But Lindy kept interrupting with "helpful" suggestions. When she wasn't making suggestions, Lindy was nervously glancing at her watch. She didn't want to be late for her job at Amy's birthday party at two o'clock.

"I think you're really weird," Alice told Lindy.

"Hey, no way," Lindy replied. "Slappy is a lot of fun. And I'm going to make a lot of money with him. And maybe I'll be a comedy star or something when I'm older." She glanced at her watch again.

"Well, everyone at school thinks that both of you are weird," Alice said, swatting a fly off her bare arm.

"Who cares?" Lindy replied sharply. "They're all weird, too."

"And so are you," Kris made Mr Wood say.

"I saw your lips move," Lindy told Kris.

Kris rolled her eyes. "Give me a break. You've been giving me a hard time all morning."

"Just trying to help," Lindy said. "You don't have to be so defensive, do you?"

Kris uttered an angry growl.

"Was that your stomach?" she made Mr Wood say.

Cody laughed.

"At least *one* person thinks you're funny," Lindy said dryly. "But if you want to do parties, you really should get some better jokes."

Kris let the dummy slump to her lap. "I can't find any good joke books," she said dejectedly. "Where do you find your jokes?"

A superior sneer formed on Lindy's face. She tossed her long hair behind her shoulder. "I make up my own jokes," she replied snootily.

"You *are* a joke!" Cody said.

"Ha-ha. Remind me to laugh later," Lindy said sarcastically.

"I can't believe you haven't got *your* dummy out here," Alice told Lindy. "I mean, don't you want to rehearse for the party?"

"No need," Lindy replied. "I've got my act pretty much sorted out. I don't want to over-rehearse."

Kris groaned loudly.

"Some of the other parents are staying at the birthday party to watch Slappy and me," Lindy continued, ignoring Kris's sarcasm. "If the kids like me, their parents might hire me for *their* parties."

"Maybe you and Kris should do an act together," Alice suggested. "That could be really awesome."

"Yeah. What an act! Then there'd be *four* dummies!" Cody joked.

Alice was the only one to laugh.

Lindy made a face at Cody. "That might actually be fun," she said thoughtfully. And then she added, "When Kris is ready."

Kris drew in her breath and prepared to make an angry reply.

But before she could say anything, Lindy grabbed Mr Wood from her hands. "Let me give you a few tips," Lindy said, putting one foot on Kris's folding chair and arranging Mr Wood on her lap. "You have to hold him up straighter, like this."

"Hey—give him back," Kris demanded, reaching for the dummy.

As she reached up, Mr Wood suddenly lowered his head until he was staring down at her. "*You're a jerk!*" he rasped in Kris's face, speaking in a low, throaty growl.

"Huh?" Kris pulled back in surprise.

"*You're a stupid jerk!*" Mr Wood repeated nastily in the same harsh growl.

"Lindy—stop it!" Kris cried.

Cody and Alice both stared in open-mouthed surprise.

"*Stupid moron! Get lost! Get lost, stupid jerk!*" the dummy rasped in Kris's face.

"Whoa!" Cody exclaimed.

"Make him stop!" Kris screamed at her sister.

"I can't!" Lindy cried in a trembling voice. Her face became pale, her eyes wide with fear. "I can't make him stop, Kris! He—he's speaking for himself!"

The dummy glared at Kris, its grin ugly and evil.

"I—I can't make him stop. I'm not doing it," Lindy cried. Tugging with all her might, she pulled Mr Wood out of Kris's face.

Cody and Alice flashed each other bewildered glances.

Frightened, Kris raised herself from the folding chair and backed up against the tree trunk. "He—he's talking on his own?" She stared hard at the grinning dummy.

"I—I think so. I'm . . . all mixed up!" Lindy declared, her cheeks bright pink.

Barky yipped and jumped on Lindy's legs, trying to get her attention. But she kept her gaze on Kris's frightened face.

"This is a joke—right?" Cody asked hopefully.

"What's going on?" Alice demanded, her arms crossed in front of her chest.

Ignoring them, Lindy handed Mr Wood back

to Kris. "Here. Take him. He's yours. Maybe *you* can control him."

"But, Lindy—" Kris started to protest.

Lindy glared at her watch. "Oh, no! The party! I'm late!" Shaking her head, she took off towards the house. "Later!" she called without looking back.

"But Lindy—" Kris called.

The kitchen door slammed behind Lindy.

Holding Mr Wood by the shoulders, Kris lowered her eyes to his face. He grinned up at her, a devilish grin, his eyes staring intently into hers.

Kris swung easily, leaning back and raising her feet into the air. The chains squeaked with every swing. The old garden swingset, half covered with rust, hadn't been used much in recent years.

The early evening sun was lowering itself behind the house. The aroma of a roasting chicken floated out from the kitchen window. Kris could hear her mother busy in the kitchen preparing dinner.

Barky yapped beneath her. Kris dropped her feet to the ground and stopped the swing to avoid kicking him. "Silly dog. Don't you know you could get hurt?"

She looked up to see Lindy come running up the drive, holding Slappy under her arm. From the smile on Lindy's face, Kris knew at once that the birthday party had been a triumph. But she had to ask anyway. "How'd it go?"

"It was awesome!" Lindy exclaimed. "Slappy and I were *great*!"

Kris pulled herself off the swing and forced a smile to her face. "That's nice," she offered.

"The kids thought we were a riot!" Lindy continued. She pulled Slappy up. "Didn't they, Slappy?"

"They liked me. Hated you!" Slappy declared in Lindy's high-pitched voice.

Kris forced a laugh. "I'm glad it went okay," she said, trying hard to be a good sport.

"I did a sing-along with Slappy, and it went over really well. Then Slappy and I did our rap routine. What a hit!" Lindy gushed.

She's spreading it on a little thick, Kris thought bitterly. Kris couldn't help feeling jealous.

"The kids all lined up to talk to Slappy," Lindy continued. "Didn't they, Slappy?"

"Everyone loved me," she made the dummy say. "Where's my share of the loot?"

"So you got paid twenty dollars?" Kris asked, kicking at a clump of weeds.

"Twenty-five," Lindy replied. "Amy's mum said I was so good, she'd pay me extra. Oh. And guess what else? You know Mrs Evans? The woman who always wears the leopardskin trousers? You know—Anna's mum? She asked me to do Anna's party next Sunday. She's going to pay me *thirty* dollars! I'm going to be rich!"

"Wow. Thirty dollars," Kris muttered, shaking her head.

"I get twenty. You get ten," Lindy made Slappy say.

"I have to go and tell Mum the good news!" Lindy said. "What have you been doing all afternoon?"

"Well, after you left, I was pretty upset," Kris replied, following Lindy to the house. "You know. About Mr Wood. I—I put him upstairs. Alice and Cody went home. Then Mum and I went shopping."

His tail wagging furiously, Barky ran right over their feet, nearly tripping both of them. "Barky, look out!" Lindy yelled.

"Oh. I nearly forgot," Kris said, stopping on the back steps. "Something good happened."

Lindy stopped, too. "Something good?"

"Yeah. I ran into Mrs Berman at the shopping centre." Mrs Berman was their music teacher and organizer of the spring concert.

"Thrills," Lindy replied sarcastically.

"And Mrs Berman asked if Mr Wood and I wanted to be master of ceremonies for the spring concert." Kris smiled at her sister.

Lindy swallowed hard. "She asked *you* to host the concert?"

"Yeah. I get to perform with Mr Wood in front of everyone!" Kris gushed happily. She saw a flash of jealousy on Lindy's face, which made her even happier.

Lindy pulled open the screen door. "Well, good luck," she said dryly. "With that weird dummy of yours, you'll *need* it."

Dinner was spent talking about Lindy's performance at Amy Marshall's birthday party. Lindy and Mrs Powell chatted excitedly. Kris ate in silence.

"At first I thought the whole thing was pretty strange, I have to admit," Mrs Powell said, scooping ice cream into bowls for dessert. "I just couldn't believe you'd be interested in ventriloquism, Lindy. But I suppose you have got a flair for it. I suppose you have some talent."

Lindy beamed. Mrs Powell wasn't normally big on compliments.

"I found a book in the school library about ventriloquism," Lindy said. "It had some pretty good tips in it. It even had a comedy routine to perform." She glanced at Kris. "But I like making up my own jokes better."

"You should watch your sister's act," Mrs Powell told Kris, handing her a bowl of ice cream. "I mean, you could probably pick up some ideas for the concert at school."

"Maybe," Kris replied, trying to hide how annoyed she was.

After dinner, Mr Powell phoned from Portland, and they all talked to him. Lindy told him about her success with Slappy at the birthday party. Kris told him about being asked to host the concert with Mr Wood. Her father promised he wouldn't schedule any trips away so that he could attend the concert.

After watching a video their mother had got out, the two sisters went up to their room. It was just after eleven.

Kris clicked on the light. Lindy followed her in.

They both glanced across the room to the chair where they kept the two dummies—and gasped.

"Oh, no!" Lindy cried, raising one hand to her wide open mouth.

Earlier that night, the dummies had been placed side by side in a sitting position.

But now Slappy was upside down, falling out of the chair, his head on the floor. His brown shoes had been pulled off his feet and tossed against the wall. His suit jacket had been pulled halfway down his arms, trapping his hands behind his back.

"L-look!" Kris stammered, although her sister was already staring in horror at the scene. "Mr Wood—he's . . ." Kris's voice caught in her throat.

Mr Wood was sprawled on top of Slappy. His hands were trapped around Slappy's throat, as if he were strangling him.

"I—I don't believe this!" Kris managed to whisper. She turned and caught the frightened expression on Lindy's face.

"What's going *on*?" Lindy cried.

Both sisters hurried across the room. Kris grabbed Mr Wood by the back of the neck and pulled him off the other dummy. She felt as if she were separating two fighting boys.

She held Mr Wood up in front of her, examining him carefully, staring at his face as if half-expecting him to talk to her.

Then she lowered the dummy and tossed it face down onto her bed. Her face was pale and taut with fear.

Lindy stooped and picked up Slappy's brown shoes from the floor. She held them up and studied them, as if they would offer a clue as to what had happened.

"Kris—did you do this?" Lindy asked softly.

"Huh? Me?" Kris reacted with surprise.

340

"I mean, I *know* you're jealous of Slappy and me—" Lindy started.

"Whoa. Wait a minute," Kris replied angrily in a shrill, trembling voice. "I didn't do this, Lindy. Don't accuse me."

Lindy glared at her sister, studying her face. Then her expression softened and she sighed. "I don't get it. I just don't get it. Look at Slappy. He's nearly been torn apart."

She put the shoes down on the chair and picked the dummy up gently as if picking up a baby. Holding him in one hand, she struggled to pull his suit jacket up with the other.

Kris heard her sister mutter something. It sounded like "Your dummy is creepy."

"What did you say?" Kris demanded.

"Nothing," Lindy replied, still struggling with the jacket. "I'm . . . uh . . . I'm kind of scared about this," Lindy confessed, blushing, avoiding Kris's eyes.

"Me, too," Kris admitted. "Something weird is going on. I think we should tell Mum."

Lindy buttoned up the jacket. Then she sat down on the bed with Slappy on her lap and started to replace the dummy's shoes. "Yeah. I think we should," she replied. "It—it's just so weird."

Their mother was in bed, reading a Stephen King novel. Her bedroom was dark except for a tiny reading lamp on her headboard that threw down a narrow triangle of yellow light.

Mrs Powell uttered a short cry as her two daughters appeared out of the shadows. "Oh. You startled me. This is such a scary book, and I think I was just about to fall asleep."

"Can we talk to you?" Kris asked eagerly in a low whisper.

"Something weird is going on," Lindy added.

Mrs Powell yawned and closed her book. "What's wrong?"

"It's about Mr Wood," Kris said. "He's been doing a lot of strange things."

"Huh?" Mrs Powell's eyes opened wide. She looked pale and tired under the harsh light from the reading lamp.

"He was strangling Slappy," Lindy reported. "And this afternoon, he said some really gross things. And—"

"Stop!" Mrs Powell ordered, raising one hand. "Just stop."

"But, Mum—" Kris started.

"Give me a break, girls," their mother said wearily. "I'm tired of your silly competitions."

"You don't understand," Lindy interrupted.

"Yes, I *do* understand," Mrs Powell said sharply. "You two are even competing with those ventriloquist dummies."

"Mum, please!"

"I want it to stop right now," Mrs Powell insisted, tossing the book onto her bedside table.

"I mean it. I don't want to hear another word from either of you about those dummies. If you two have problems, settle them between yourselves."

"Mum, listen—"

"And if you can't settle them, I'll take the dummies away. Both of them. I'm serious." Mrs Powell reached above her head and clicked off the reading light, throwing the room into darkness. "Goodnight," she said.

The girls had no choice but to leave the room. They slunk down the hall in silence.

Kris hesitated at the doorway to their bedroom. She expected to find Mr Wood strangling Slappy again. She breathed a sigh of relief when she saw the two dummies on the bed where they had been left.

"Mum wasn't too helpful, was she," Lindy said dryly, rolling her eyes. She picked up Slappy and started to arrange him in the chair in front of the window.

"I think she was asleep and we woke her up," Kris replied.

She picked up Mr Wood and started towards the chair with him—then stopped. "You know what? I think I'm going to put him in the wardrobe tonight," she said thoughtfully.

"Good idea," Lindy said, climbing into bed.

Kris glanced down at the dummy, half-expecting him to react. To complain. To start calling her names.

But Mr Wood grinned up at her, his painted eyes dull and lifeless.

Kris felt a chill of fear.

I'm becoming afraid of a stupid ventriloquist's dummy, she thought.

I'm shutting him up in the wardrobe tonight because I'm afraid.

She carried Mr Wood to the wardrobe. Then, with a groan, she raised him high above her head and slid him onto the top shelf. Carefully closing the wardrobe door, listening for the click, she made her way to her bed.

She slept fitfully, tossing and turning, her sleep filled with disturbing dreams. She awoke to find her nightshirt completely twisted, cutting off the circulation to her right arm. She struggled to straighten it, then fell back to sleep.

She awoke early, drenched in sweat. The sky was still dawn-grey outside the window.

The room felt hot and stuffy. She sat up slowly, feeling weary, as if she hadn't slept at all.

Blinking away the sleep, her eyes focused on the chair in front of the window.

There sat Slappy, exactly where Lindy had placed him.

And beside him sat Mr Wood, his arm around Slappy's shoulder, grinning triumphantly at Kris as if he had just pulled off a wonderful joke.

"Now, Mr Wood, do you go to school?"

"Of course I do. Do you think I'm a dummy?"

"And what's your favourite lesson?"

"Woodwork, of course!"

"What project are you building in woodwork, Mr Wood?"

"I'm building a *girl* dummy! What else? Ha-ha! Think I want to spend the rest of my life on *your* lap?!"

Kris sat in front of the dressing table mirror with Mr Wood on her lap, studying herself as she practised her routine for the school concert.

Mr Wood had been well-behaved for two days. No frightening, mysterious incidents. Kris was beginning to feel better. Maybe everything would be okay from now on.

She leaned close to the mirror, watching her lips as she made the dummy talk.

The b's and the m's were impossible to pronounce without moving her lips. She'd just have to avoid those sounds as best she could.

I'm getting better at switching from Mr Wood's voice back to mine, she thought happily. But I've got to switch faster. The faster he and I talk, the funnier it is.

"Let's try it again, Mr Wood," she said, pulling her chair closer to the mirror.

"Work, work, work," she made the dummy grumble.

Before she could begin the routine, Lindy came rushing breathlessly into the room. Kris watched her sister in the mirror as she came up behind her, her long hair flying loosely over her shoulders, an excited smile on her face.

"Guess what?" Lindy asked.

Kris started to reply, but Lindy didn't give her a chance.

"Mrs Petrie was at Amy Marshall's birthday party," Lindy gushed excitedly. "She works for Channel Three. You know. The TV station. And she thinks I'm good enough to go on *Talent Search*, the show they have every week."

"Huh? Really?" was all Kris could manage in reply.

Lindy leapt excitedly in the air and cheered. "Slappy and I are going to be on TV!" she cried. "Isn't that *fabulous*?"

Staring at her sister's jubilant reflection in the mirror, Kris felt a stab of jealousy.

"I've got to tell Mum!" Lindy declared. "Hey,

Mum! Mum!" She ran from the room. Kris heard her shouting all the way down the stairs.

"Aaaaaargh!" Kris couldn't hold it in. She uttered an angry cry.

"Why does everything good happen to Lindy?" Kris screamed aloud. "I'm hosting a stupid concert for maybe a hundred parents—and she's going to be on TV! I'm just as good as she is. Maybe better!"

In a rage, she raised Mr Wood high above her head and slammed him to the floor.

The dummy's head made a loud *clonk* as it hit the hardwood floor. The wide mouth flew open as if about to scream.

"Oh." Kris struggled to regain her composure.

Mr Wood, crumpled at her feet, stared up at her accusingly.

Kris lifted him up and cradled the dummy against her. "There, there, Mr Wood," she whispered soothingly. "Did I hurt you? Did I? I'm so sorry. I didn't mean to."

The dummy continued to stare up at her. His painted grin hadn't changed, but his eyes seemed cold and unforgiving.

It was a still night. No breeze. The curtains in front of the open bedroom window didn't flutter or move. Pale silver moonlight filtered in, creating long, purple shadows that appeared to creep across the girls' bedroom.

Lindy had been sleeping fitfully, a light sleep filled with busy, colourful dreams. She was startled awake by a sound. A gentle *thud*.

"Huh?" she raised her head from the damp pillow and turned.

Someone was moving in the darkness.

The sounds she'd heard were footsteps.

"Hey!" she whispered, wide awake now. "Who is it?"

The figure turned in the doorway, a shadow against even blacker shadows. "It's only me," came a whispered reply.

"Kris?"

"Yeah. Something woke me up. My throat is sore," Kris whispered from the doorway. "I'm going down to the kitchen for a glass of water."

She disappeared into the shadows. Her head still raised off the pillow, Lindy listened to her footsteps padding down the stairs.

When the sounds faded, Lindy shut her eyes and lowered her head to the pillow.

A few seconds later, she heard Kris's scream of horror.

Her heart pounding, Lindy struggled out of bed. The sheet tangled around her legs, and she nearly fell.

Kris's bloodcurdling scream echoed in her ears.

She practically leapt down the dark staircase, her bare feet thudding hard on the thin carpet of the steps.

It was dark downstairs, except for a thin sliver of yellow light from the kitchen.

"Kris—Kris—are you okay?" Lindy called, her voice sounding small and frightened in the dark hallway.

"Kris?"

Lindy stopped at the kitchen doorway.

What was that eerie light?

It took her a while to focus. Then she realized she was staring at the dim yellow light from inside the fridge.

The fridge door was wide open.

And . . . the fridge was empty.

"What—what's going on here?"

She took a step into the kitchen. Then another. Something cold and wet surrounded her foot.

Lindy gasped and, looking down, saw that she had stepped into a wide puddle.

An overturned milk carton beside her foot revealed that the puddle was spilled milk.

She raised her eyes to Kris, who was standing in darkness across the room, her back against the wall, her hands raised to her face in horror.

"Kris, what on earth—"

The scene was coming into focus now. It was all so weird, so . . . *wrong*. It was taking Lindy a long time to see the whole picture.

But, now, following Kris's horrifed stare, Lindy saw the mess on the floor. And realized why the fridge was empty.

Everything inside it had been pulled out and dumped on the kitchen floor. An orange juice bottle lay on its side in a puddle of orange juice. Eggs were scattered everywhere. Fruits and vegetables were strewn over the floor.

"Ohh!" Lindy moaned in utter disbelief.

Everything seemed to sparkle and gleam.

What was all that shiny stuff among the food?

Kris's jewellery!

There were earrings and bracelets and strands of beads tossed everywhere, mixed with the spilled, strewn food like some kind of bizarre salad.

"Oh, no!" Lindy shrieked as her eyes came to rest on the figure on the floor.

Sitting upright in the middle of the mess was Mr Wood, grinning gleefully at her. He had several strands of beads around his neck, long, dangling earrings hanging from his ears, and a platter of leftover chicken on his lap.

13

"Kris, are you *okay*?" Lindy cried, turning her eyes away from the grinning, jewellery-covered dummy.

Kris didn't seem to hear her.

"Are you okay?" Lindy repeated the question.

"Wh-what's going on?" Kris stammered, her back pressed against the wall, her expression taut with terror. "Who—who *did* this? Did Mr Wood—?"

Lindy started to reply. But their mother's howl of surprise from the doorway cut off her words. "Mum—" Lindy cried, spinning round.

Mrs Powell clicked on the ceiling light. The kitchen seemed to flare up. All three of them blinked, struggling to adjust to the sudden brightness.

"What on earth!" Mrs Powell cried. She started to call to her husband, then rememberd he wasn't at home. "I—I don't believe this!"

Barky came bounding into the room, his tail

353

wagging. He lowered his head and started to lick up some spilled milk.

"Out you go," Mrs Powell said sternly. She picked up the dog, carried him out, and closed the kitchen door. Then she strode into the middle of the room, shaking her head, her bare feet narrowly missing the puddle of milk.

"I came down for a drink, and I—I found this mess," Kris said in a trembling voice. "The food. My jewellery. Everything . . ."

"Mr Wood did it," Lindy accused. "Look at him!"

"*Stop it! Stop it!*" Mrs Powell screamed. "I've had enough."

Mrs Powell surveyed the mess, frowning and tugging at a strand of blonde hair. Her eyes stopped on Mr Wood, and she uttered a groan of disgust.

"I knew it," she said in a low voice, raising her eyes accusingly to the two girls. "I knew this had something to do with those ventriloquist dummies."

"Mr Wood did it, Mum," Kris said heatedly, stepping away from the wall, her hands tensed into fists. "I know it sounds stupid, but—"

"Stop it," Mrs Powell ordered, narrowing her eyes. "This is just sick. Sick!" She stared hard at the jewel-bedecked dummy, who grinned up at her over the big platter of chicken.

"I'm going to take the dummies away from

you both," Mrs Powell said, turning back to Lindy and Kris. "This whole thing has just got totally out of hand."

"No!" Kris cried.

"That's not fair!" Lindy declared.

"I'm sorry. They have to be put away," Mrs Powell said firmly. She let her eyes move over the cluttered floor, and let out another weary sigh. "Look at my kitchen."

"But I didn't do anything!" Lindy screamed.

"I need Mr Wood for the spring concert!" Kris protested. "Everyone is counting on me, Mum."

Mrs Powell glanced from one to the other. Her eyes stayed on Kris. "That's *your* dummy on the floor, right?"

"Yeah," Kris told her. "But I didn't do this. I swear!"

"You both swear you didn't do it, right?" Mrs Powell said, suddenly looking very tired under the harsh ceiling light.

"Yes," Lindy answered quickly.

"Then you both lose your dummies. I'm sorry," Mrs Powell said. "One of you is lying. I—I really can't believe this."

A heavy silence blanketed the room as all three Powells stared down in dismay at the mess on the floor.

Kris was the first to speak. "Mum, what if Lindy and I clear everything up?"

Lindy caught on quickly. Her face brightened.

"Yeah. What if we put everything back. Right now. Make the kitchen just like normal. Make it spotless. Can we keep our dummies?"

Mrs Powell shook her head. "No. I don't think so. Look at this mess. All the vegetables are spoiled. And the milk."

"We'll replace it all," Kris said quickly. "With our pocket money. And we'll clear it up perfectly. Please. If we do that, give us one more chance?"

Mrs Powell twisted her face in concentration, debating with herself. She stared at her daughters' eager faces. "Okay," she finally replied. "I want the kitchen spotless when I come down in the morning. All the food, all the jewellery. Everything back in its place."

"Okay," both girls said in unison.

"And I don't want to see either of those dummies down here in my kitchen again," Mrs Powell demanded. "If you can do that, I'll give you one more chance."

"Great!" both girls cried at once.

"And I don't want to hear any more arguments about those dummies," Mrs Powell continued. "No more fights. No more competing. No more blaming everything on the dummies. I don't want to hear *anything* about them. Ever."

"You won't," Kris promised, glancing at her sister.

"Thanks, Mum," Lindy said. "You go to bed.

We'll clear up." She gave her mother a gentle shove towards the doorway.

"Not another word," Mrs Powell reminded them.

"Right, Mum," the twins agreed.

Their mother disappeared towards her room. They began to clear up. Kris pulled a large dustbin bag from the drawer and held it while Lindy tossed in empty boxes and spoiled food.

Kris carefully collected her jewellery and carried it upstairs.

Neither girl spoke. They worked in silence, picking up, cleaning, and mopping until the kitchen was clean. Lindy closed the fridge door. She yawned loudly.

Kris inspected the floor on her hands and knees, making sure it was spotless. Then she picked up Mr Wood. He grinned back at her as if it was all a big joke.

This dummy has been nothing but trouble, Kris thought.

Nothing but trouble.

She followed Lindy out of the kitchen, clicking off the light as she left. The two girls climbed the stairs silently. Neither of them had spoken a word.

Pale moonlight filtered into their room through the open window. The air felt hot and steamy.

Kris glanced at the clock. It was a little past three in the morning.

Slappy sat slumped in the chair in front of the window, moonlight shining on his grinning face. Lindy, yawning, climbed into bed, pushed down the blanket, and pulled up the sheet. She turned her face away from her sister.

Kris lowered Mr Wood from her shoulder. *You're nothing but trouble*, she thought angrily, holding him in front of her and staring at his grinning face.

Nothing but trouble.

Mr Wood's wide, leering grin seemed to mock her.

A chill of fear mixed with Kris's anger.

I'm beginning to hate this dummy, she thought.

Fear him and hate him.

Angrily, she pulled open the wardrobe door and tossed the dummy inside. It fell in a crumpled heap on the wardrobe floor.

Kris slammed the wardrobe door shut.

Her heart thudding, she climbed into bed and pulled up the covers. She suddenly felt very tired. Her whole body ached from weariness.

She buried her face in the pillow and shut her eyes.

She had just about fallen asleep when she heard the tiny voice.

"Let me out! Let me out of here!" it cried. A muffled voice, coming from inside the wardrobe.

"Let me out! Let me out!" the high-pitched voice called angrily.

Kris sat up with a jolt. Her entire body convulsed in a shudder of fear.

Her eyes darted to the other bed. Lindy hadn't moved.

"Did—did you hear it?" Kris stammered.

"Hear what?" Lindy asked sleepily.

"The voice," Kris whispered. "In the wardrobe."

"Huh?" Lindy asked sleepily. "What are you talking about? It's three in the morning. Can't we get some sleep?"

"But, Lindy—" Kris lowered her feet to the floor. Her heart was thudding in her chest. "Wake up. Listen to me! Mr Wood was calling to me. He was *talking*!"

Lindy raised her head and listened.

Silence.

"I don't hear anything, Kris. Really. Maybe

359

you were dreaming."

"No!" Kris shrieked, feeling herself lose control. "It wasn't a dream! I'm so scared, Lindy. I'm just so *scared!*"

Suddenly Kris was trembling all over, and hot tears were pouring down her cheeks.

Lindy stood up and moved to the edge of her sister's bed.

"Something h-horrible is going on here, Lindy," Kris stammered through her tears.

"And I know who's doing it," Lindy whispered, leaning over her twin, putting a comforting hand on her quivering shoulder.

"Huh?"

"Yes. I know who's been doing it all," Lindy whispered. "I know who it is."

"Who?" Kris asked breathlessly.

"Who?" Kris repeated, letting the tears run down her cheeks. "Who?"

"*I* have," Lindy said. Her smile spread into a grin almost as wide as Slappy's. She closed her eyes and laughed.

"Huh?" Kris didn't understand. "What did you say?"

"I said I have been doing it," Lindy repeated. "Me. Lindy. It was all a joke, Kris. I gotcha again." She nodded her head as if confirming her words.

Kris gaped at her twin in disbelief. "It was all a joke?"

Lindy kept nodding.

"You moved Mr Wood during the night? You dressed him in my clothes and made him say those gross things to me? You put him in the kitchen? You made that horrible mess?"

Lindy chuckled. "Yeah. I really scared you, didn't I?"

Kris balled her hands into angry fists. "But—but—" she spluttered. "*Why?*"

"For fun," Lindy replied, dropping back onto her bed, still grinning.

"Fun?"

"I wanted to see if I could scare you," Lindy explained. "It was just a joke. You know. I can't *believe* you fell for that voice in the wardrobe just now! I must be a really good ventriloquist!"

"But, Lindy—"

"You really believed Mr Wood was alive or something!" Lindy said, laughing, enjoying her victory. "You're such a nit!"

"Nit?"

"Half a nitwit!" Lindy burst into wild laughter.

"It isn't funny," Kris said softly.

"I know," Lindy replied. "It's a riot! You should've seen the look on your face when you saw Mr Wood downstairs in your precious beads and earrings!"

"How—how did you ever *think* of such a horrible joke?" Kris demanded.

"It just came to me," Lindy answered with some pride. "When you got your dummy."

"You didn't want me to get a dummy," Kris said thoughtfully.

"You're right," Lindy quickly agreed. "I wanted something that would be mine, for a change. I'm getting so tired of you being a copycat. So—"

"So you thought of this mean joke," Kris accused.

Lindy nodded.

Kris strode angrily to the window and pressed her forehead against the glass. "I—I can't believe I was so stupid," she muttered.

"Neither can I," Lindy agreed, grinning again.

"You really made me start thinking that Mr Wood was alive or something," Kris said, staring out of the window to the back garden below. "You really made me afraid of him."

"Aren't I brilliant!" Lindy proclaimed.

Kris turned to face her sister. "I'm never speaking to you again," she said angrily.

Lindy shrugged. "It was just a joke."

"No," Kris insisted. "It was too mean to be just a joke. I'm never speaking to you again. Never."

"Fine," Lindy replied curtly. "I thought you had a sense of humour. Fine." She slid into bed, her back to Kris, and pulled the covers up over her head.

I've got to find a way to pay her back for this, Kris thought. *But how?*

After school a few days later, Kris walked home with Cody. It was a hot, humid afternoon. The trees were still, and seemed to throw little shade on the pavement. The air above the pavement shimmered in the heat.

"Wish we had a swimming pool," Kris muttered, pulling her rucksack off her shoulder.

"I wish you had one, too," Cody said, wiping his forehead with the sleeve of his red T-shirt.

"I'd like to dive into an enormous pool of iced tea," Kris said, "like in the TV adverts. It always looks so cold and refreshing."

Cody made a face. "Swim in iced tea? With ice cubes and lemon?"

"Forget it," Kris muttered.

They crossed the street. A couple of kids they knew rode past on bikes. Two men in white uniforms were up on ladders, leaning against the corner house, painting the gutters.

"Bet they're hot," Cody remarked.

"Let's change the subject," Kris suggested.

"How are you doing with Mr Wood?" Cody asked.

"Not bad," Kris said. "I think I've got some pretty good jokes. I should be ready for the concert tomorrow night."

They stopped at the corner and let a large blue van rumble past.

"Are you talking to your sister?" Cody asked as they crossed the street. The bright sunlight made his white-blond hair glow.

"A little," Kris said, making a face. "I'm talking to her. But I haven't forgiven her."

"That was such a nasty stunt she pulled," Cody said sympathetically. He wiped the sweat off his forehead with the sleeve of his T-shirt.

"It just made me feel like such a dork," Kris admitted. "I mean, I was so stupid. She really had me believing that Mr Wood was doing all that stuff." Kris shook her head. Thinking about it made her feel embarrassed all over again.

Her house came into view. She unzipped the back compartment of her rucksack and searched for the keys.

"Did you tell your mum about Lindy's practical joke?" Cody asked.

Kris shook her head. "Mum is totally disgusted. We're not allowed to mention the dummies to her. Dad got home from Portland last night, and Mum told him what was going

365

on. So we're not allowed to mention the dummies to him, either!" She found the keys and started up the drive. "Thanks for walking home with me."

"Yeah. Sure." Cody gave her a little wave and continued on towards his house up the street.

Kris pushed the key into the front door lock. She could hear Barky jumping and yipping excitedly on the other side of the door. "I'm coming, Barky," she called in. "Hold your horses."

She pushed open the door. Barky began leaping on her, whimpering as if she'd been away for months. "Okay, okay!" she cried, laughing.

It took several minutes to calm the dog down. Then Kris got a snack from the kitchen and headed up to her room to practise with Mr Wood.

She hoisted the dummy up from the chair where it had spent the day beside Lindy's dummy. A can of Coke in one hand, the dummy over her shoulder, she headed for the dressing table and sat down in front of the mirror.

This was the best time of day to rehearse, Kris thought. No one was at home. Her parents were at work. Lindy was at some after-school activity.

She arranged Mr Wood on her lap. "Time to go to work," she made him say, reaching into his back to move his lips. She made his eyes slide back and forth.

A button on his plaid shirt had come un-buttoned. Kris leaned him down against the dressing table and started to fasten it.

Something caught her eye. Something yellow inside the pocket.

"Weird," Kris said aloud. "I've never noticed anything in there before."

Slipping two fingers into the slender pocket, she pulled out a yellowed sheet of paper, folded up.

Probably just the receipt for him, Kris thought.

She unfolded the sheet of paper and held it up to read it.

It wasn't a receipt. The paper contained a single sentence handwritten very cleanly in bold black ink. It was in a language Kris didn't recognise.

"Did someone send you a love note, Mr Wood?" she asked the dummy.

It stared up at her lifelessly.

Kris lowered her eyes to the paper and read the strange sentence out loud:

"Karru marri odonna loma molonu karrano."

What language is *that*? Kris wondered.

She glanced down at the dummy and uttered a low cry of surprise.

Mr Wood appeared to blink.

But that wasn't possible—*was* it?

Kris took a deep breath, then let it out slowly.

The dummy stared up at her, his painted eyes as dull and wide open as ever.

Let's not get paranoid, Kris scolded herself.

"Time to work, Mr Wood," she told him. She folded up the piece of yellow paper and slipped it back into his shirt pocket. Then she raised him to a sitting position, searching for the eye and mouth controls with her hand.

"How are things around *your* house, Mr Wood?"

"Not good, Kris. I've got termites. I need termites like I need another hole in my head! Ha-ha!"

"Lindy! Kris! Could you come downstairs, please!" Mr Powell called from the foot of the stairs.

It was after dinner, and the twins were up in their room. Lindy was sprawled on her stomach on the bed, reading a book for school. Kris was in front of the dressing table mirror, rehearsing quietly with Mr Wood for tomorrow night's concert.

"What do you want, Dad?" Lindy shouted down, rolling her eyes.

"We're kind of busy," Kris shouted, shifting the dummy on her lap.

"The Millers are here, and they're dying to see your ventriloquist acts," their father shouted up.

Lindy and Kris both groaned. The Millers

368

were the elderly couple who lived next door. They were very nice people, but very boring.

The twins heard Mr Powell's footsteps on the stairs. A few seconds later, he poked his head into their room. "Come on, girls. Just put on a short show for the Millers. They came over for coffee, and we told them about your dummies."

"But I have to rehearse for tomorrow night," Kris insisted.

"Rehearse on them," her father suggested. "Come on. Just do five minutes. They'll get a real kick out of it."

Sighing loudly, the girls agreed. Carrying their dummies over their shoulders, they followed their father down to the living room.

Mr and Mrs Miller were side by side on the sofa, coffee mugs in front of them on the low coffee table. They smiled and called out cheerful greetings as the girls appeared.

Kris was always struck by how much the Millers looked alike. They both had slender, pink faces topped with spongy white hair. They both wore silver-framed bifocals, which slipped down on nearly identical, pointy noses. They both had the same smile. Mr Miller had a small, grey moustache. Lindy always joked that he grew it so the Millers could tell each other apart.

Is *that* what happens to you when you've been married a long time? Kris found herself thinking. You start to look exactly alike?

The Millers were even dressed alike, in loose-fitting Bermuda shorts and white cotton sports shirts.

"Lindy and Kris took up ventriloquism a few weeks ago," Mrs Powell was explaining, twisting herself forward to see the girls from the armchair. She motioned them to the centre of the room. "And they both seem to have some talent for it."

"Have you girls ever heard of Bergen and McCarthy?" Mrs Miller asked, smiling.

"Who?" Lindy and Kris asked in unison.

"Before your time," Mr Miller said, chuckling. "They were a ventriloquist act."

"Can you do something for us?" Mrs Miller asked, picking up her coffee mug and setting it in her lap.

Mr Powell pulled a dining room chair into the centre of the room. "Here. Lindy, why don't you go first?" He turned to the Millers. "They're very good. You'll see," he said.

Lindy sat down and arranged Slappy on her lap. The Millers applauded. Mrs Miller nearly spilled her coffee, but she caught the mug just in time.

"Don't applaud—just throw money!" Lindy made Slappy say. Everyone laughed as if they'd never heard that before.

Kris watched from the stairs as Lindy did a short routine. Lindy was really good, she had to admit. Very smooth. The Millers were laughing so hard, their faces were bright red. An identical shade of red. Mrs Miller kept squeezing her husband's knee when she laughed.

Lindy finished to big applause. The Millers gushed about how wonderful she was. Lindy told them about the TV show she might be on, and they promised they wouldn't miss it. "We'll tape it," Mr Miller said.

Kris took her place on the chair and sat Mr Wood on her lap. "This is Mr Wood," she told the Millers. "We're going to be the hosts of the spring concert at school tomorrow night. So I'll give you a preview of what we're going to say."

"That's a nice-looking dummy," Mrs Miller said quietly.

"*You're a nice-looking dummy, too!*" Mr Wood declared in a harsh, raspy growl of a voice.

Kris's mother gasped. The Millers' smiles faded.

Mr Wood leaned forward on Kris's lap and stared at Mr Miller. "*Is that a moustache, or are you eating a rat?*" he asked nastily.

Mr Miller glanced uncomfortably at his wife, then forced a laugh. They both laughed.

"*Don't laugh so hard. You might drop your false teeth!*" Mr Wood shouted. "*And how do you get your teeth that disgusting shade of yellow? Does your bad breath do that?*"

"Kris!" Mrs Powell shouted. "That's enough!"

371

The Millers' faces were bright red now, their expressions bewildered.

"That's not funny. Apologize to the Millers," Mr Powell insisted, crossing the room and standing over Kris.

"I—I didn't say any of it!" Kris stammered. "Really, I—"

"Kris—apologize!" her father demanded angrily.

Mr Wood turned to the Millers. "*I'm sorry*," he rasped. "*I'm sorry you're so ugly! I'm sorry you're so old and stupid, too!*"

The Millers stared at each other unhappily. "I don't understand her humour," Mrs Miller said.

"It's just crude insults," Mr Miller replied quietly.

"Kris—what is *wrong* with you!" Mrs Powell demanded. She had crossed the room to stand beside her husband. "Apologize to the Millers right now! I don't *believe* you!"

"I—I—" Gripping Mr Wood tightly around the waist, Kris rose to her feet. "I—I—" She tried to utter an apology, but no words would come out.

"Sorry!" she finally managed to scream. Then, with an embarrassed cry, she turned and fled up the stairs, tears streaming down her face.

"You *have* to believe me!" Kris cried in a trembling voice. "I really didn't say any of those things. Mr Wood was talking by himself!"

Lindy rolled her eyes. "Tell me another one," she muttered sarcastically.

Lindy had followed Kris upstairs. Down in the living room, her parents were still apologizing to the Millers. Now, Kris sat on the edge of her bed, wiping tears off her cheeks. Lindy stood with her arms crossed in front of the dressing table.

"I don't make insulting jokes like that," Kris said, glancing at Mr Wood, who lay crumpled in the middle of the floor where Kris had tossed him. "You know that isn't my sense of humour."

"So why'd you do it?" Lindy demanded. "Why'd you want to make everyone angry?"

"But I *didn't*!" Kris shrieked, tugging at the sides of her hair. "Mr Wood said those things! I didn't!"

"How can you be such a copycat?" Lindy

asked disgustedly. "I've already *done* that joke, Kris. Can't you think of something original?"

"It's not a joke," Kris insisted. "Why don't you believe me?"

"No way," Lindy replied, shaking her head, her arms still crossed in front of her chest. "No way am I going to fall for the same gag."

"Lindy, please!" Kris pleaded. "I'm frightened. I'm really frightened."

"Yeah. Sure," Lindy said sarcastically. "I'm shaking all over, too. Wow. You really fooled me, Kris. Guess you showed me you can play funny tricks, too."

"Shut up!" Kris snapped. More tears formed in the corners of her eyes.

"Very good crying," Lindy said. "But it doesn't fool me, either. And it won't fool Mum and Dad." She turned and picked up Slappy. "Maybe Slappy and I should practise some jokes. After your performance tonight, Mum and Dad might not let you do the concert tomorrow night."

She slung Slappy over her shoulder and, stepping over the crumpled form of Mr Wood, hurried from the room.

It was hot and noisy backstage in the main hall. Kris's throat was dry, and she kept walking over to the water fountain and slurping mouthfuls of the warm water.

374

The voices of the audience on the other side of the curtain seemed to echo off all four walls and the ceiling. The noise became louder, and as the hall filled, the more nervous Kris felt.

How am I ever going to do my act in front of all those people? she asked herself, pulling the edge of the curtain back a few centimetres and peering out. Her parents were off to the side, in the third row.

Seeing them brought memories of the night before flooding back to Kris. Her parents had grounded her for two weeks as punishment for insulting the Millers. They almost hadn't let her come to the concert.

Kris stared at the kids and adults filing into the large hall, recognizing a lot of faces. She realized her hands were ice cold. Her throat was dry again.

Don't think of it as an audience, she told herself. Think of it as a bunch of kids and parents, most of whom you know.

Somehow that made it worse.

She let go of the curtain, hurried to get one last drink from the fountain, then retrieved Mr Wood from the table where she'd left him.

It suddenly grew quiet on the other side of the curtain. The concert was about to begin.

"Break a leg!" Lindy called across to her as she hurried to join the other chorus members.

"Thanks," Kris replied weakly. She pulled up

Mr Wood and straightened his shirt. "Your hands are clammy!" she made him say.

"No insults tonight," Kris told him sternly.

To her shock, the dummy blinked.

"Hey!" she cried. She hadn't touched his eye controls.

She had a stab of fear that went beyond stage fright. Maybe I shouldn't go on with this, she thought, staring intently at Mr Wood, watching for him to blink again.

Maybe I should say I'm ill and not perform with him.

"Are you nervous?" a voice whispered.

"Huh?" At first, she thought it was Mr Wood. But then she quickly realized that it was Mrs Berman, the music teacher.

"Yeah. A little," Kris admitted, feeling her face grow hot.

"You'll be terrific," Mrs Berman gushed, squeezing Kris's shoulder with a sweaty hand. She was a large, stocky woman with several chins, a red lipsticked mouth, and flowing black hair. She was wearing a long, loose-fitting dress of red-and-blue flower patterns. "Here goes," she said, giving Kris's shoulder one more squeeze.

Then she stepped onstage, blinking against the harsh white light of the spotlight, to introduce Kris and Mr Wood.

Am I really doing this? Kris asked herself.

Can I do this?

Her heart was pounding so hard, she couldn't hear Mrs Berman's introduction. Then, suddenly, the audience was applauding, and Kris found herself walking across the stage to the microphone, carrying Mr Wood in both hands.

Mrs Berman, her flowery dress flowing around her, was heading offstage. She smiled at Kris and gave her an encouraging wink as they passed each other.

Squinting against the bright spotlight, Kris walked to the middle of the stage. Her mouth felt as dry as cotton wool. She wondered if she could make a sound.

A folding chair had been set up for her. She sat down, arranging Mr Wood on her lap, then realized that the microphone was much too high.

This drew titters of soft laughter from the audience.

Embarrassed, Kris stood up and, holding Mr Wood under one arm, struggled to lower the microphone.

"Are you having trouble?" Mrs Berman called from the side of the stage. She hurried over to help Kris.

But before the music teacher got halfway across the stage, Mr Wood leaned into the microphone. *"What time does the tent go up?"* he rasped nastily, staring at Mrs Berman's dress.

"What?" She stopped in surprise.

"*Your face reminds me of a wart I had removed!*" Mr Wood growled at the startled woman.

Her mouth dropped open in horror. "Kris!"

"*If we count your chins, will it tell us your age?*"

There was laughter floating up from the audience. But it was mixed with gasps of horror.

"Kris—that's enough!" Mrs Berman cried, the microphone picking up her angry protest.

"*You're more than enough! You're enough for two!*" Mr Wood declared nastily. "*If you got any bigger, you'd need your own postal code!*"

"Kris—really! I'm going to ask you to apologize," Mrs Berman said, her face bright red.

"Mrs Berman, I—I'm not doing it!" Kris stammered. "I'm not saying these things!"

"Please apologize. To me and to the audience," Mrs Berman demanded.

Mr Wood leaned into the microphone. "*Apologize for THIS!*" he screamed.

The dummy's head tilted back. His jaw dropped. His mouth opened wide.

And a thick green liquid came spewing out.

"Yuck!" someone screamed.

It looked like pea soup. It spurted out of Mr Wood's open mouth like water rushing from a fire hose.

Voices screamed and cried out their surprise as the thick, green liquid showered over the people in the front rows.

"Stop it!"

"Help!"

"Somebody—turn it off!"

"It stinks!"

Kris froze in horror, staring as more and more of the disgusting substance poured from her dummy's gaping mouth.

A putrid stench—the smell of sour milk, of rotten eggs, of burning rubber, of decayed meat—rose up from the liquid. It puddled over the stage and showered over the front seats.

Blinded by the spotlight, Kris couldn't see the audience in front of her. But she could hear the choking and the gagging, the frantic cries for help.

"Clear the hall! Clear the hall!" Mrs Berman was shouting.

Kris heard the rumble and scrape of people shoving their way up the aisles out of the doors.

"It stinks!"

"I'm ill!"

"Somebody—help!"

Kris tried to clamp her hand over the dummy's mouth. But the force of the putrid green liquid frothing and spewing out was too strong. It pushed her hand away.

Suddenly she realized she was being shoved

from behind. Off the stage. Away from the shouting people fleeing the hall. Out of the glaring spotlight.

She was backstage before she realized that it was Mrs Berman who was pushing her.

"I—I don't know how you did that. Or why!" Mrs Berman shouted angrily, frantically wiping splotches of the disgusting green liquid off the front of her dress with both hands. "But I'm going to see that you're suspended from school, Kris! And if I have my way," she spluttered, "you'll be suspended for *life*!"

"That's right. Close the door," Mr Powell said sternly, glaring with narrowed eyes at Kris.

He stood a few centimetres behind her, arms crossed in front of him, making sure she followed his instructions. She had carefully folded Mr Wood in half and shoved him to the back of her cupboard shelf. Now she closed the cupboard, making sure it was completely shut, as he ordered.

Lindy watched silently from her bed, her expression troubled.

"Does the cupboard door lock?" Mr Powell asked.

"No. Not really," Kris told him, lowering her head.

"Well, that will have to do," he said. "On Monday, I'm taking him back to the pawn shop. Do not take him out until then."

"But, Dad—"

He raised a hand to silence her.

"We have to talk about this," Kris pleaded. "You have to listen to me. What happened tonight—it wasn't a practical joke. I—"

Her father turned away from her, a scowl on his face. "Kris, I'm sorry. We'll talk tomorrow. Your mother and I—we're both too angry and too upset to talk now."

"But, Dad—"

Ignoring her, he stormed out of the room. She listened to his footsteps, hard and hurried, down the stairs. Then Kris slowly turned to Lindy. "Now do you believe me?"

"I—I don't know what to believe," Lindy replied. "It was just so . . . unbelievably gross."

"Lindy, I—I—"

"Daddy's right. Let's talk tomorrow," Lindy said. "I'm sure everything will be clearer and calmer tomorrow."

But Kris couldn't sleep. She shifted from side to side, uncomfortable, wide awake. She pulled the pillow over her face, held it there for a while, welcoming the soft darkness, then tossed it to the floor.

I'm never going to sleep again, she thought.

Every time she closed her eyes, she saw the hideous scene in the main hall once again. She heard the astonished cries of the audience, the kids and their parents. And she heard the cries of shock turn to groans of disgust as the putrid gunk poured out over everyone.

Sickening. So totally sickening.

And everyone blamed her.

My life is ruined, Kris thought. I can never go back there again. I can never go to school. I can never show my face *anywhere*.

Ruined. My whole life. Ruined by that stupid dummy.

In the next bed, Lindy snored softly, in a slow, steady rhythm.

Kris turned her eyes to the bedroom window. The curtains hung down over the window, filtering the pale moonlight from outside. Slappy sat in his usual place in the chair in front of the window, bent in two, his head between his knees.

Stupid dummies, Kris thought bitterly. So stupid.

And now my life is ruined.

She glanced at the clock. One-twenty. Outside the window, she heard a low, rumbling sound. A soft whistle of brakes. Probably a large truck going by.

Kris yawned. She closed her eyes and saw the gross green gunk spewing out of Mr Wood's mouth.

Will I see that every time I close my eyes? she wondered.

What on earth *was* it? How could everyone

blame *me* for something so ... so ...

The rumbling of the truck faded into the distance.

But then Kris heard another sound. A rustling sound.

A soft footstep.

Someone was moving.

She sucked in her breath and held it, listening hard.

Silence now. Silence so heavy, she could hear the loud thudding of her heart.

Then another soft footstep.

A shadow moved.

The wardrobe door swung open.

Or was it just shadows shifting?

No. Someone was moving. Moving from the open wardrobe. Someone was creeping towards the bedroom door. Creeping so softly, so silently.

Her heart pounding, Kris pulled herself up, trying not to make a sound. Realizing that she'd been holding her breath, she let it out slowly, silently. She took another breath, then sat up.

The shadow moved slowly to the door.

Kris lowered her feet to the floor, staring hard into the darkness, her eyes staying with the silent, moving figure.

What's happening? she wondered.

The shadow moved again. She heard a scraping sound, the sound of a sleeve brushing the doorframe.

Kris pushed herself to her feet. Her legs felt shaky as she crept to the door, following the moving shadow.

Out into the hallway. Even darker out here because there were no windows.

Towards the stairs.

The shadow moved more quickly now.

Kris followed, her bare feet moving lightly over the thin carpet.

What's happening? What's happening?

She caught up to the shadowy figure on the landing. "Hey!" she called, her voice a tight whisper.

She grabbed the shoulder and turned the figure round.

And stared into the grinning face of Mr Wood.

Mr Wood blinked, then hissed at her, an ugly sound, a menacing sound. In the darkness of the staircase, his painted grin became a threatening leer.

In her fright, Kris squeezed the dummy's shoulder, wrapping her fingers around the harsh fabric of his shirt.

"This—this is impossible!" she whispered.

He blinked again. He giggled. His mouth opened, making his grin grow wider.

He tried to tug out of Kris's grasp, but she hung on without even realizing she was holding him.

"But—you're a *dummy*!" she squealed.

He giggled again. "So are you," he replied. His voice was a deep growl, like the angry snarl of a large dog.

"You can't walk!" Kris cried, her voice trembling.

The dummy giggled its ugly giggle again.

386

"You can't be alive!" Kris exclaimed.

"Let go of me—*now!*" the dummy growled.

Kris held on, tightening her grip. "I'm dreaming," Kris told herself aloud. "I have to be dreaming."

"I'm not a dream. I'm a nightmare!" the dummy exclaimed, and tossed back his wooden head, laughing.

Still gripping the shoulder of the shirt, Kris stared through the darkness at the grinning face. The air seemed to grow heavy and hot. She felt as if she couldn't breathe, as if she were suffocating.

What was that sound?

It took her a while to recognize the strained gasps of her own breathing.

"Let go of me," the dummy repeated. "Or I'll throw you down the stairs." He tried once again to tug out of her grasp.

"No!" Kris insisted, holding tight. "I—I'm putting you back in the wardrobe."

The dummy laughed, then pushed his painted face close to Kris's face. "You can't keep me there."

"I'm locking you in. I'm locking you in a box. In *something!*" Kris declared, panic clouding her thoughts.

The darkness seemed to descend over her, choking her, weighing her down.

"Let go of me." The dummy pulled hard.

Kris reached out her other hand and grabbed him around the waist.

"Let go of me," he snarled in his raspy, deep rumble of a voice. "I'm in charge now. You will listen to me. This is *my* house now."

He pulled hard.

Kris encircled his waist.

They both fell onto the stairs, rolling down a few steps.

"Let go!" the dummy ordered. He rolled on top of her, his wild eyes glaring into hers.

She pushed him off, tried to pin his arms behind his back.

He was surprisingly strong. He pulled back one arm, then shoved a fist hard into the pit of her stomach.

"Ohhh." Kris groaned, feeling the breath knocked out of her.

The dummy took advantage of her momentary weakness, and pulled free. Grasping the banister with one hand, he tried to pull himself past her and down the stairs.

But Kris shot out a foot and tripped him.

Still struggling to breathe, she pounced onto his back. Then she pulled him away from the banister and pushed him down hard onto a step.

"Oh!" Kris gasped loudly as the overhead hall light flashed on. She closed her eyes against the sudden harsh intrusion. The dummy struggled to pull out from under her, but she pushed down on his back with all her weight.

"Kris—what on earth—?!" Lindy's startled voice called down from the top step.

"It's Mr Wood!" Kris managed to cry up to her. "He's . . . *alive!*" She pushed down hard, sprawled over the dummy, keeping him pinned beneath her.

"Kris—what are you doing?" Lindy demanded. "Are you okay?"

"No!" Kris exclaimed. "I'm not okay! Please—Lindy! Go and get Mum and Dad! Mr Wood—he's alive!"

"It's just a dummy!" Lindy called down, taking a few reluctant steps towards her sister. "Get up, Kris! Have you lost your mind?"

"*Listen to me!*" Kris shrieked at the top of her lungs. "Get Mum and Dad! Before he escapes!"

But Lindy didn't move. She stared down at her sister, her long hair falling in tangles about her face, her features twisted in horror. "Get up, Kris," she urged. "Please—get up. Let's go back to bed."

"I'm *telling* you, he's *alive!*" Kris cried desperately. "You've got to believe me, Lindy. You've *got* to!"

The dummy lay lifeless beneath her, his face buried in the carpet, his arms and legs sprawled out to the sides.

"You had a nightmare," Lindy insisted,

climbing down step by step, holding her long nightshirt up above her ankles until she was standing right above Kris. "Come back to bed, Kris. It was just a nightmare. The horrible thing that happened at the concert—it gave you a nightmare, that's all."

Gasping for breath, Kris lifted herself up and twisted her head to face her sister. Grabbing the banister with one hand, she raised herself a little.

The instant she eased up on him, the dummy grabbed the edge of the stair with both hands and pulled himself out from under her. Half-falling, half-crawling, he scrambled down the rest of the stairs.

"No! No! I don't *believe* it!" Lindy shrieked, seeing the dummy move.

"Go and get Mum and Dad!" Kris said. "Hurry!"

Her mouth wide open in shocked disbelief, Lindy turned and headed back up the stairs, screaming for her parents.

Kris dived off the step, thrusting her arms in front of her.

She tackled Mr Wood from behind, wrapping her arms around his waist.

His head hit the carpet hard as they both crumpled to the floor.

He uttered a low, throaty cry of pain. His eyes closed. He didn't move.

Dazed, her chest heaving, her entire body trembling, Kris slowly climbed to her feet. She quickly pressed a foot on the dummy's back to hold him in place.

"Mum and Dad—where *are* you?" she cried aloud. "Hurry."

The dummy raised its head. He let out an angry growl and started to thrash his arms and legs wildly.

Kris pressed her foot hard against his back.

"Let go!" he growled viciously.

Kris heard voices upstairs.

"Mum? Dad? Down here!" she called up to them.

Both of her parents appeared at the upstairs landing, their faces filled with worry.

"Look!" Kris cried, frantically pointing down to the dummy beneath her foot.

"Look at *what*?" Mr Powell cried, adjusting his pyjama top.

Kris pointed down to the dummy under her foot. "He—he's trying to get away," she stammered.

But Mr Wood lay lifeless on his stomach.

"Is this supposed to be a joke?" Mrs Powell demanded angrily, hands at the waist of her cotton nightgown.

"I don't get it," Mr Powell said, shaking his head.

"Mr Wood—he ran down the stairs," Kris said frantically. "He's been doing everything. He—"

"This isn't funny," Mrs Powell said wearily, running a hand back through her blonde hair. "It isn't funny at all, Kris. Waking everyone up in the middle of the night."

"I really think you've lost your mind. I'm very worried about you," Mr Powell added. "I mean, after what happened at school tonight—"

"Listen to me!" Kris shrieked. She bent down and pulled Mr Wood up from the floor. Holding him by the shoulders, she shook him hard. "He moves! He runs! He talks! He—he's *alive!*"

She stopped shaking the dummy and let go. He slumped lifelessly to the floor, falling in an unmoving heap at her feet.

"I think maybe you need to see a doctor," Mr Powell said, his face tightening with concern.

"No. *I* saw him, too!" Lindy said, coming to Kris's aid. "Kris is right. The dummy *did* move." But then she added, "I mean, I *think* it moved!"

You're a big help, Lindy, Kris thought, suddenly feeling weak, drained.

"Is this just another stupid prank?" Mrs Powell asked angrily. "After what happened at school tonight, I'd think that would be enough."

"But, Mum—" Kris started, staring down at the lifeless heap at her feet.

"Back to bed," Mrs Powell ordered. "There's no school tomorrow. We'll have plenty of time to discuss punishments for you two."

"*Me*?" Lindy cried, outraged. "What did *I* do?"

"Mum, we're telling the truth!" Kris insisted.

"I still don't get the joke," Mr Powell said, shaking his head. He turned to his wife. "Were we supposed to believe her or something?"

"Get to bed. Both of you. Now!" their mother snapped. She and their father disappeared from the upstairs landing, heading angrily back down the hallway to their room.

Lindy remained, one hand on the top of the banister, staring down regretfully at Kris.

"You believe me, don't you?" Kris called up to her.

"Yeah. I suppose so," Lindy replied doubtfully, lowering her eyes to the dummy at Kris's feet.

Kris looked down, too. She saw Mr Wood blink. He started to straighten up.

"Whoa!" She uttered an alarmed cry and grabbed him by the neck. "Lindy—hurry!" she called. "He's moving again!"

"Wh-what should we do?" Lindy stammered, making her way hesitantly down the stairs.

"I don't know," Kris replied as the dummy thrashed his arms and legs against the carpet, trying desperately to free himself from her two-handed grip on his neck. "We've got to—"

"There's *nothing* you can do," Mr Wood snarled. "You will be my slaves now. I'm alive once again! Alive!"

"But—how?" Kris demanded, staring at him in disbelief. "I mean, you're a dummy. How—?"

The dummy sniggered. "*You* brought me back to life," he told her in his raspy voice. "You read the ancient words."

The ancient words? What was he talking about?

394

And then Kris remembered. She had read the strange-sounding words from the sheet of paper in the dummy's shirt pocket.

"I am back, thanks to you," the dummy growled. "And now you and your sister will serve me."

As she stared in horror at the grinning dummy, an idea popped into Kris's mind.

The paper. She had tucked it back into his pocket.

If I read the words again, Kris thought, it will put him back to sleep.

She reached out and grabbed him. He tried to jerk away, but she was too quick.

The folded sheet of yellow paper was in her hand.

"Give me that!" he cried. He swiped at it, but Kris swung it out of his reach.

She unfolded it quickly. And before the dummy could grab the paper out of her hands, she read the strange words aloud:

"Karru marri odonna loma molonu karrano."

Both sisters stared at the dummy, waiting for him to collapse.

But he gripped the banister and tossed his head back in an amused, scornful laugh. "Those are the words of the ancient sorcerer to bring me to life!" he proclaimed. "Those aren't the words to kill me!"

Kill him?

Yes, Kris thought frantically. She tossed down the yellow paper disgustedly.

We have no choice.

"We have to kill him, Lindy."

"Huh?" Her sister's face filled with surprise.

Kris grabbed the dummy by the shoulders and held on tightly. "I'll hold him. You pull his head off."

Lindy was beside her now. She had to duck away from Mr Wood's thrashing feet.

"I'll hold him still," Kris repeated. "Grab his head. Pull it off."

"You—you're sure?" Lindy hesitated, her features tight with fear.

"*Just do it!*" Kris screamed.

She let her hands slide down around Mr Wood's waist.

Lindy grabbed his head in both hands.

"*Let go of me!*" the dummy rasped.

"Pull!" Kris cried to her terrified sister.

Holding the dummy tightly around the waist, she leaned back, pulling him away from her sister.

Lindy's hands were wrapped tightly around the dummy's head. With a loud groan, she pulled hard.

The head didn't come off.

Mr Wood uttered a high-pitched giggle. "Stop. You're tickling me!" he rasped.

"Pull harder!" Kris ordered her sister.

Lindy's face was bright red. She tightened her grip on the head and pulled again, tugging with all her strength.

The dummy giggled his shrill, unpleasant giggle.

"It—it won't come off," Lindy said, sighing in defeat.

"Twist it off!" Kris suggested frantically.

The dummy thrashed out with his feet, kicking Kris in the stomach. But she held on. "Twist the head off!" she cried.

Lindy tried to turn the head.

The dummy giggled.

"It won't twist!" Lindy cried in frustration. She let go of the head and took a step back.

Mr Wood raised his head, stared up at Lindy, and grinned. "You can't kill me. I have powers."

"What do we do?" Lindy cried, raising her eyes to Kris.

"This is my house now," the dummy rasped, grinning at Lindy as it struggled to wriggle out of Kris's arms. "You will do as I say now. Put me down."

"What do we *do*?" Lindy repeated.

"Take him upstairs. We'll *cut* his head off," Kris replied.

Mr Wood swung his head around, his eyes stretched open in an evil glare.

"Ow!" Kris cried out in surprise as the dummy snapped his jaws over her arm, biting her. She pulled her arm away and, without thinking, slapped the dummy's wooden head with the palm of her hand.

The dummy giggled in response. "Violence! Violence!" he said in a mock scolding tone.

"Get those sharp scissors. In your drawer," Kris instructed her sister. "I'll carry him up to our room."

Her arm throbbed where he had bitten her. But she held onto him tightly and carried him up to their bedroom.

Lindy had already pulled the long metal

scissors from the drawer. Her hand trembled as she opened and closed the blades.

"Below the neck," Kris said, holding Mr Wood tightly by the shoulders.

He hissed furiously at her. She dodged as he tried to kick her with both feet.

Holding the scissors with two hands, Lindy tried cutting the head off the neck. The scissors didn't cut, so she tried a sawing motion.

Mr Wood giggled. "I told you. You can't kill me."

"It isn't going to work," Lindy cried, tears of frustration running down her cheeks. "Now what?"

"We'll put him in the wardrobe. Then we can think," Kris replied.

"You have no need to think. You are my slaves," the dummy rasped. "You will do whatever I ask. I will be in charge from now on."

"No way," Kris muttered, shaking her head.

"What if we *won't* help you?" Lindy demanded.

The dummy turned to her, casting her a hard, angry stare. "Then I'll start hurting the ones you love," he said casually. "Your parents. Your friends. Or maybe that disgusting dog that's always yapping at me." He tossed back his head and a dry, evil laugh escaped from his wooden lips.

"Lock him in the wardrobe," Lindy suggested. "Till we work out how to get rid of him."

"You *can't* get rid of me," Mr Wood insisted. "Don't make me angry. I have powers. I'm warning you. I'm starting to get tired of your stupid attempts to harm me."

"The wardrobe doesn't lock—remember?" Kris cried, struggling to hold onto the wriggling dummy.

"Oh. Wait. How about this?" Lindy hurried to the wardrobe. She pulled out an old suitcase from the back.

"Perfect," Kris said.

"I'm warning you—" Mr Wood threatened. "You are becoming very tiresome."

With a hard tug, he pulled himself free of Kris.

She dived to tackle him, but he darted out from under her. She fell face down onto her bed.

The dummy ran to the centre of the room, then turned his eyes to the doorway, as if trying to decide where to go. "You must do as I tell you," he said darkly, raising a wooden hand towards Lindy. "I will not run from you two. You are to be my slaves."

"No!" Kris cried, pushing herself up.

She and her sister both dived for the dummy. Lindy grabbed his arms. Kris ducked to grab his ankles.

Working together, they stuffed him into the open suitcase.

"You will regret this," he threatened, kicking his legs, struggling to hit them. "You will pay dearly for this. Now someone will die!"

He continued screaming after Kris latched the suitcase and shoved it into the wardrobe. She quickly closed the wardrobe door, then leaned her back against it, sighing wearily.

"Now what?" she asked Lindy.

"We'll bury him," Kris said.

"Huh?" Lindy stifled a yawn.

They had been whispering together for what seemed like hours. As they tried to come up with a plan, they could hear the dummy's muffled cries from inside the wardrobe.

"We'll bury him. Under that huge mound of soil," Kris explained, her eyes going to the window. "You know. Next door, at the side of the new house."

"Yeah. Okay. I don't know," Lindy replied. "I'm so tired, I can't think straight." She glanced at the bedside table clock. It was nearly three-thirty in the morning. "I still think we should wake up Mum and Dad," Lindy said, fear reflected in her eyes.

"We can't," Kris told her. "We've been over that a hundred times. They won't believe us. If we wake them up, we'll be in even bigger trouble."

"How could we be in *bigger* trouble?" Lindy demanded, gesturing with her head to the wardrobe where Mr Wood's angry cries could still be heard.

"Get dressed," Kris said with renewed energy. "We'll bury him under all that earth. Then we'll never have to think about him again."

Lindy shuddered and turned her eyes to her dummy, folded up in the chair. "I can't bear to look at Slappy any more. I'm so sorry I got us interested in dummies."

"Ssshhh. Just get dressed," Kris said impatiently.

A few minutes later, the two girls crept down the stairs in the darkness. Kris carried the suitcase in both arms, trying to muffle the sound of Mr Wood's angry protests.

They stopped at the bottom of the stairs and listened for any sign that they had awakened their parents.

Silence.

Lindy pulled open the front door and they slipped outside.

The air was surprisingly cool and wet. A heavy dew had begun to fall, making the front lawn glisten under the light of a half-moon. Blades of wet grass clung to their trainers as they made their way to the garage.

As Kris held onto the suitcase, Lindy slowly,

quietly, pulled open the garage door. When it was halfway up, she ducked and slipped inside.

A few seconds later she emerged, carrying a large snow shovel. "This should do it," she said, whispering even though no one was around.

Kris glanced down the street as they headed across the garden to the plot next door. The heavy morning dew misted the glow of the streetlamps, making the pale light appear to bend and flicker like candles. Everything seemed to shimmer under the dark purple sky.

Kris set the suitcase down beside the tall mound of soil. "We'll dig right down here," she said, pointing towards the bottom of the mound. "We'll shove him in and cover him."

"I'm warning you," Mr Wood threatened, listening inside the suitcase. "Your plan won't work. I have powers!"

"You dig first," Kris told her sister, ignoring the dummy's threat. "Then I'll have a go."

Lindy dug into the pile and heaved up a shovelful of soil. Kris shivered. The heavy dew felt cold and damp. A cloud floated over the moon, darkening the sky from purple to black.

"Let me out!" Mr Wood called. "Let me out now, and your punishment won't be too severe."

"Dig faster," Kris whispered impatiently.

"I'm going as fast as I can," Lindy replied. She had dug a pretty good-sized square-shaped hole at the base of the mound. "How much deeper, do you think?"

"Deeper," Kris said. "Here. Watch the suitcase. I'll have a go." She changed places with Lindy and started to dig.

Something scampered heavily near the low bushes that separated the gardens. Kris looked up, saw a moving shadow, and gasped.

"Raccoon, I think," Lindy said with a shudder. "Are we going to bury Mr Wood in the suitcase, or are we going to take him out?"

"Think Mum will notice the suitcase is gone?" Kris asked, tossing a shovelful of wet soil to the side.

Lindy shook her head. "We never use it."

"We'll bury him in the suitcase," Kris said. "It'll be easier."

"You'll be sorry," the dummy rasped. The suitcase shook and nearly toppled onto its side.

"I'm so sleepy," Lindy moaned, tossing her socks onto the floor, then sliding her feet under the covers.

"I'm wide awake," Kris replied, sitting on the edge of her bed. "I think it's because I'm so happy. So happy we got rid of that awful creature."

"It's all so weird," Lindy said, adjusting her pillow behind her head. "I don't blame Mum or

Dad for not believing it. I'm not sure I believe it, either."

"You put the shovel back where you found it?" Kris asked.

Lindy nodded. "Yeah," she said sleepily.

"And you closed the garage door?"

"Ssshhh. I'm asleep," Lindy said. "At least there's no school tomorrow. We can sleep late."

"I hope I can fall asleep," Kris said doubtfully. "I'm just so exhausted. It's all like some kind of hideously gross nightmare. I just think . . . Lindy? Lindy—are you still awake?"

No. Her sister had fallen asleep.

Kris stared up at the ceiling. She pulled the blankets up to her chin. She still felt chilled. She couldn't shake the cold dampness of the early morning air.

After a short while, with thoughts of everything that had happened that night whirring crazily in her head, Kris fell asleep, too.

The rumble of machines woke her up at eight-thirty the next morning. Stretching, trying to rub the sleep from her eyes, Kris stumbled to the window, leaned over the chair holding Slappy, and peered out.

It was a grey, cloudy day. Two enormous yellow steamrollers were rolling over the plot next door behind the newly constructed house, flattening the land.

I wonder if they're going to flatten that big

mound of earth, Kris thought, staring down at them. That would really be *excellent*.

Kris smiled. She hadn't slept very long, but she felt refreshed.

Lindy was still sound asleep. Kris tiptoed past her, pulled her robe on, and headed downstairs.

"Morning, Mum," she called brightly, tying the belt of her robe as she came into the kitchen.

Mrs Powell turned from the sink to face her. Kris was surprised to see an angry expression on her face.

She followed her mother's stare to the breakfast counter.

"Oh!" Kris gasped when she saw Mr Wood. He was sitting on the worktop, his hands in his lap. His hair was matted with red-brown dirt, and he had dirt smears on his cheeks and forehead.

Kris raised her hands to her face in horror.

"I thought you were told never to bring that thing down here!" Mrs Powell scolded. "What do I have to do, Kris?" She turned angrily back to the sink.

The dummy winked at Kris and flashed her a wide, evil grin.

As Kris stared in horror at the grinning dummy, Mr Powell suddenly appeared in the kitchen doorway. "Ready?" he asked his wife.

Mrs Powell hung the tea towel on the rack and turned round, brushing a lock of hair off her forehead. "Ready. I'll get my bag." She brushed past him into the front hallway.

"Where are you going?" Kris cried, her voice revealing her alarm. She kept her eyes on the dummy on the worktop.

"Just doing a little shopping at the garden centre," her father told her, stepping into the room, peering out of the kitchen window. "Looks like rain."

"Don't go!" Kris pleaded.

"Huh?" He turned towards her.

"Don't go—please!" Kris cried.

Her father's eyes landed on the dummy. He walked over to him. "Hey—what's the big idea?" her father asked angrily.

"I thought you wanted to take him back to the pawn shop," Kris replied, thinking quickly.

"Not till Monday," her father replied. "Today is Saturday, remember?"

The dummy blinked. Mr Powell didn't notice.

"Do you have to go shopping now?" Kris asked in a tiny voice.

Before her father could answer, Mrs Powell reappeared in the doorway. "Here. Catch," she called, and tossed the car keys to him. "Let's go before it pours."

Mr Powell started to the door. "Why don't you want us to go?" he asked.

"The dummy—" Kris started. But she knew it was hopeless. They'd never listen. They'd never believe her. "Never mind," she muttered.

A few seconds later, she heard their car back down the drive. They had gone.

And she was alone in the kitchen with the grinning dummy.

Mr Wood turned towards her slowly, swivelling on the worktop. His big eyes locked angrily on Kris's.

"I warned you," he rasped.

Barky came trotting into the kitchen, his toenails clicking loudly on the lino. He sniffed the floor as he ran, searching for breakfast scraps someone might have dropped.

"Barky, where've you been?" Kris asked, glad to have company.

The dog ignored her and sniffed under the stool Mr Wood sat on.

"He was upstairs, waking me up," Lindy said, rubbing her eyes as she walked into the kitchen. She was wearing white tennis shorts and a sleeveless magenta T-shirt. "Stupid dog."

Barky licked at a spot on the lino.

Lindy cried out as she spotted Mr Wood. "Oh, no!"

"I'm back," the dummy rasped. "And I'm very unhappy with you two slaves."

Lindy turned to Kris, her mouth open in surprise and terror.

Kris kept her eyes trained on the dummy. *What does he plan to do*? she wondered. *How can I stop him*?

Burying him under all that soil hadn't kept him from returning. Somehow he had freed himself from the suitcase and pulled himself out.

Wasn't there any way to defeat him? Any way at all?

Grinning his evil grin, Mr Wood dropped down to the floor, his trainers thudding hard on the floor. "I'm very unhappy with you two slaves," he repeated in his growly voice.

"What are you going to do?" Lindy cried in a shrill, frightened voice.

"I have to punish you," the dummy replied. "I have to prove to you that I am serious."

"Wait!" Kris cried.

410

But the dummy moved quickly. He reached down and grabbed Barky by the neck with both hands.

As the dummy tightened his grip, the frightened terrier began to howl in pain.

"I warned you," Mr Wood snarled over the howls of the little black terrier. "You will do as I say—or one by one, those you love will suffer!"

"No!" Kris cried.

Barky let out a high-pitched *whelp*, a bleat of pain that made Kris shudder.

"Let go of Barky!" Kris screamed.

The dummy giggled.

Barky uttered a hoarse gasp.

Kris couldn't stand it any longer. She and Lindy leapt at the dummy from two sides. Lindy tackled his legs. Kris grabbed Barky and tugged.

Lindy dragged the dummy to the floor. But his wooden hands held a tight grip on the dog's throat.

Barky's howls became a muffled whimper as he struggled to breathe.

"Let go! Let *go*!" Kris shrieked.

"I *warned* you!" the dummy snarled as Lindy

held his kicking legs tightly. "The dog must die now!"

"No!" Kris let go of the gasping dog. She slid her hands down to the dummy's wrists. Then with a fierce tug, she pulled the wooden hands apart.

Barky dropped to the floor, wheezing. He scampered to the corner, his paws sliding frantically over the smooth floor.

"You'll pay now!" Mr Wood growled. Jerking free from Kris, he swung his wooden hand up, landing a hard blow on Kris's forehead.

She cried out in pain and raised her hands to her head.

She heard Barky yelp loudly behind her.

"Let go of me!" Mr Wood demanded, turning back to Lindy, who still held onto his legs.

"No way!" Lindy cried. "Kris—grab his arms again."

Her head still throbbing, Kris lunged forward to grab the dummy's arms.

But he lowered his head as she approached and clamped his wooden jaws around her wrist.

"Owww!" Kris howled in pain and pulled back.

Lindy lifted the dummy up by the legs, then slammed his body hard against the floor. He uttered a furious growl and tried to kick free of her.

Kris lunged again, and this time grabbed one

arm, then the other. He lowered his head to bite once more, but she dodged away and pulled his arms tight behind his back.

"I'm warning you!" he bellowed. "I'm warning you!"

Barky yelped excitedly, hopping up on Kris.

"What do we *do* with him?" Lindy cried, shouting over the dummy's angry threats.

"Outside!" Kris yelled, pressing the arms more tightly behind Mr Wood's back.

She suddenly remembered the two steam-rollers she had seen moving over the garden next door, flattening the ground. "Come on," she urged her sister. "We'll crush him!"

"I'm warning you! I have powers!" the dummy screamed.

Ignoring him, Kris pulled open the kitchen door and they carried their wriggling captive outside.

The sky was charcoal-grey. A light rain had begun to fall. The grass was already wet.

Over the low hedge that separated the gardens, the girls could see the two enormous yellow steamrollers, one in the back, one at the side of the next-door plot. They looked like huge, lumbering animals, their giant black rollers flattening everything in their path.

"This way! Hurry!" Kris shouted to her sister, holding the dummy tightly as she ran. "Toss him under that one!"

"Let me go! Let me go, slaves!" the dummy screamed. "This is your last chance!" He swung his head hard, trying to bite Kris's arm.

Thunder rumbled, low in the distance.

The girls ran at full speed, slipping on the wet grass as they hurried towards the fast-moving steamroller.

They were just a few metres away from the enormous machine when they saw Barky. His tail wagging furiously, he scampered ahead of them.

"Oh, no! How'd he get out?" Lindy cried.

Gazing back at them, his tongue hanging out of his mouth, prancing happily in the wet grass, the dog was running right into the path of the rumbling steamroller.

"No, Barky!" Kris shrieked in horror. "No! Barky—no!"

Letting go of Mr Wood, both girls dived towards the dog. Hands outstretched, they slid on their stomachs on the wet grass.

Unaware of any problem, enjoying the game of tag, Barky scampered away.

Lindy and Kris rolled out of the path of the steamroller.

"Hey—get away from there!" the angry operator shouted through the high window of the steamroller. "Are you girls crazy?"

They leapt to their feet and turned back to Mr Wood.

The rain began to come down a little harder. A jagged streak of white lightning flashed high in the sky.

"I'm free!" the dummy cried, hands raised victoriously above his head. "Now you will pay!"

"Get him!" Kris shouted to her sister.

The rain pelted down on their hair and

shoulders. The two girls lowered their heads, leaned into the rain, and began to chase after the dummy.

Mr Wood turned and started to run.

He never saw the other steamroller.

The gigantic black wheel rolled right over him, pushing him onto his back, then crushing him with a loud *crunch*.

A loud *hiss* rose up from under the machine, like air escaping from a large balloon.

The steamroller appeared to rock back and forth.

A strange green gas spurted up from beneath the wheel, into the air, spreading out in an eerie, mushroom-shaped cloud.

Barky stopped scampering and stood frozen in place, his eyes following the green gas as it floated up against the nearly black sky.

Lindy and Kris stared in open-mouthed wonder.

Pushed by the wind and the rain, the green gas floated over them.

"Yuck! It stinks!" Lindy declared.

It smelled like rotten eggs.

Barky uttered a low whimper.

The steamroller reversed. The driver jumped out and came running towards them. He was a short, stocky man with big, muscular arms bulging out from the sleeves of his T-shirt. His face was bright red under a short, blond crewcut, his eyes wide with horror.

"A kid?" he cried. "I—I ran over a kid?"

"No. He was a dummy," Kris told him. "He wasn't alive."

He stopped. His face faded from red to flour-white. He uttered a loud, grateful sigh. "Oh, man," he moaned. "Oh, man. I thought it was a child."

He took a deep breath and let it out slowly. Then he bent to examine the area beneath his wheel. As the girls came near, they saw the remains of the dummy, crushed flat inside its jeans and flannel shirt.

"Hey, I'm really sorry," the man said, wiping his forehead with his T-shirt sleeve as he straightened up to face them. "I couldn't stop in time."

"That's okay," Kris said, a wide smile forming on her face.

"Yeah. Really. It's okay," Lindy quickly agreed.

Barky moved close to sniff the crushed dummy.

The man shook his head. "I'm so relieved. It looked as if it was running. I really thought it was a kid. I was so scared."

"No. Just a dummy," Kris told him.

"Whew!" The man exhaled slowly. "Close one." His expression changed. "What are you girls doing out in the rain, anyway?"

Lindy shrugged. Kris said, "Just walking the dog."

The man picked up the crushed dummy. The head crumbled to powder as he lifted it. "You want this thing?"

"You can throw it in the rubbish," Kris told him.

"Better get out of the rain," he told them. "And don't scare me like that again."

The girls apologized, then headed back to the house. Kris cast a happy grin at her sister. Lindy grinned back.

I may grin forever, Kris thought. I'm so happy. So relieved.

They wiped their wet trainers on the mat, then held the kitchen door open for Barky. "Wow. What a morning!" Lindy declared.

They followed the dog into the kitchen. Outside, a flash of bright lightning was followed by a roar of thunder.

"I'm drenched," Kris said. "I'm going up to get changed."

"Me, too." Lindy followed her up the stairs.

They entered their bedroom to find the window wide open, the curtains slapping wildly, rain pouring in. "Oh, no!" Kris hurried across the room to shut the window.

As she leaned over the chair to grab the window frame, Slappy reached up and grabbed her arm.

"Hey, slave—has that other guy gone?" the dummy asked in a throaty growl. "I thought he'd never leave!"

The Outfit Robert Swindells

**"Faithful, fearless, full of fun,
Winter, summer, rain or sun,
One for five, and five for one –
THE OUTFIT!"**

*Meet The Outfit – Jillo, Titch, Mickey and Shaz. Share in
their adventures as they fearlessly investigate any mystery,
and injustice, that comes their way . . .*

Move over, Famous Five, The Outfit are here!

The Secret of Weeping Wood

The Outfit are determined to discover the truth about the
eerie crying, coming from scary Weeping Wood. Is the
wood really haunted?

We Didn't Mean To, Honest!

The marriage of creepy Kenneth Kilchaffinch to snooty
Prunella could mean that Froglet Pond, and all its
wildlife, will be destroyed. So it's up to The Outfit to
make sure the marriage is off . . . But how?

Kidnap at Denton Farm

Farmer Denton's new wind turbine causes a protest
meeting in Lenton, and The Outfit find themselves in
the thick of it. But a *kidnap* is something they didn't
bargain for . . .

The Ghosts of Givenham Keep

What is going on at spooky Givenham Keep? It can't be
haunted, can it? The Outfit are just about to find out . . .

If you like animals, then you'll love
Hippo Animal Stories!

Look out for:

Animal Rescue by Bette Paul

Tessa finds life in the country *so* different from life in
the town. Will she ever be accepted? But everything
changes when she meets Nora and Ned who run the
village animal sanctuary, and becomes involved in a
struggle to save the badgers of Delves Wood
from destruction . . .

Thunderfoot by Deborah van der Beek

Mel Whitby has always loved horses, and when she
comes across an enormous but neglected horse in a
railway field, she desperately wants to take care of it.
But little does she know that taking care of
Thunderfoot will change her life forever . . .

A Foxcub Named Freedom
by Brenda Jobling

A vixen lies seriously injured in the undergrowth. Her
young son comes to her for comfort and warmth. The
cub wants to help his mother to safety, but it is
impossible. The vixen, sensing danger, nudges him
away, caring nothing for herself – only for
his freedom . . .

Hippo Fantasy

Lose yourself in a whole new world, a world where anything is possible – from wizards and dragons, to time travel and new civilizations ... Gripping, thrilling, scary and funny by turns, these Hippo Fantasy titles will hold you captivated to the very last page.

The Night of Wishes
Michael Ende (author of *The Neverending Story*)

Malcolm and the Cloud-Stealer
Douglas Hill

The Wednesday Wizard
Sherryl Jordan

Ratspell

Paddy Mounter

Rowan of Rin
Emily Rodda

The Practical Princess
Jay Williams

The Babysitters Club

Need a babysitter? Then call the Babysitters Club. Kristy Thomas and her friends are all experienced sitters. They can tackle any job from rampaging toddlers to a pandemonium of pets. To find out all about them, read on!